STRIKE BACK

A Jason Mulder Thriller

Robert Goluba

Evertouch Publishing

CONTENTS

Chapter 1

Page, Arizona

Jason Mulder stood over the churning steel and water raging hundreds of yards below his feet as a breeze cooled his neck, reddened by the afternoon sun. Every minute, 1.3 million gallons of Lake Powell water rushed through the Glen Canyon Dam in Page, Arizona, without a hint of the immense force on the surface.

Jason strode to the railing, leaned over, and stared at the turbulent white water churning seven hundred feet below. A frothy mist wafted into the air like thin smoke, signaling the beginning of a new journey down the Colorado River until the water rested again in Lake Mead. He raised his gaze slowly, examining the vast concrete dam until his eyes were rewarded with the grandeur of the second-largest reservoir in the United States stretching into the distance.

He pushed himself away from the railing to walk the perimeter of the Carl Hayden Visitor Center parking lot for the third time. This was no ordinary event. Members of the media, local constituents, and well-heeled VIPs sat on white chairs unfolded in the grass expanse behind the adobe building. They waited for Senator James Conrad, the junior senator from Arizona, to announce the much-anticipated bill he had co-sponsored with Congresswoman Duarte from Nevada.

After Jason completed his perimeter scan, he stood at the rear of the seating area and turned toward the empty podium. Nature displayed a majestic tapestry backdrop behind the eventual speakers that no human could duplicate. A masterpiece of towering rust-red sandstone walls carved by the relentless hands of time framed the shimmering azure waters under the boundless horizon.

Anticipation hung in the dry air on the unseasonably warm March afternoon. The setting was serene, but Jason's stomach was in knots, and he couldn't stop pacing. It wasn't his first event on the private security detail, or PSD, for Senator Conrad's reelection campaign, but the warning from the head of security that the senator's proposed bill could attract angry dissenters had him on edge. He was no longer double-checking exit doors, HVAC systems, and back stairwells at hotel conference centers or convention halls. The upcoming speech by the "common sense candidate for senator" came with the highest stakes in Jason Mulder's five-month career as a member of his campaign security detail.

Once every seat was filled, audience members fanned themselves as the late afternoon sun beat on their necks and arms. Jason's piercing hazel eyes methodically moved up and down each row like they'd taught him at PSD school, but he didn't detect any potential threats. That changed once he spotted a man with wide eyes anxiously scanning every person who walked near his aisle seat six rows from the podium. The man appeared to be in his early twenties, and his messy brown mop of hair bounced every time he turned his head. Jason noted the lanyard with a press pass around his neck as the man continually checked his camera and clutched the case like it would fly away like a frightened bird if he loosened his grip.

"On-site in two," came over Jason's wireless microphone in his ear. It was Clay Landry, and he was in the vehicle with Senator

Conrad and his entourage. Clay recruited Jason into the senator's security detail a half year earlier after Jason quit his job at the DEA. They had become close friends two years earlier after meeting during a training mission. Jason was an active Air Force pararescueman, and Clay was a special recognizance specialist. After Jason joined the same Air Force Reserve unit, Clay was by Jason's side while he endured some of his darkest days. Together, they hunted down cartel members responsible for the death of Jason's younger brother, Josh. After a judge sentenced the last cartel member to prison and Jason attempted to rebuild his life, Clay remained by his side. He helped Jason evade US Marshals after crooked DEA agents set him up to be arrested in a suspicious drug bust.

The tough times forged a bond of respect and trust that made Clay Landry and Jason Mulder a formidable force.

"Has everyone here been wanded for weapons?" Jason asked.

"Yeah, why?" Clay responded quickly. "Do you see a threat?"

"Not sure yet, but I have eyes on a young male acting suspiciously."

"Location and description?"

"Watch Shaggy in the white shirt on the west end of row six. He seems nervous," Jason said.

Two Arizona Department of Public Service motorcycle officers pulled into the parking lot with their emergency lights on. Three black full-size SUVs followed them with two additional motorcycle escorts in the rear. The back door of the middle vehicle opened, and Clay exited, scanned the area for threats, and nodded to the person inside the open door. Senator Conrad slid his six-foot athletic frame out of the vehicle and waved at cheering onlookers behind the cameras. At fifty-six years old, James Conrad III maintained the air of a battle-tested warrior with his salt-and-pepper hair cropped close to his head and steel blue eyes narrowing in focus. His square jaw was set firmly, with a few faint wrinkles below his eyes, testifying to his years of experience and leadership. He wore a navy-blue suit and crisp white dress shirt, with an American flag lapel pin and gold crossed rifles on either side, paying homage to his service as a captain in the US Army Infantry.

He strode to the podium with the self-confidence of an experienced leader and stood resolute, ready to take on any challenge standing in the way of his objective. After he pointed and waved at several supporters in the audience, he pulled the microphone closer to his mouth.

"Ladies and gentlemen, before I start, I want to acknowledge the real reason why we are all here this fine afternoon." He turned and raised his hand to draw attention to Lake Powell and the mountains behind him.

"All of this is here because of the Colorado River, which is why I'm co-sponsoring a new bill with Congresswoman Duarte from Nevada... to protect this invaluable asset."

The crowd responded with enthusiastic applause.

Jason turned his attention from his principal and back to the individual that had caught his attention earlier. Shaggy didn't clap and sat expressionless during the senator's speech.

Jason felt a familiar rush of adrenaline surge into his stomach. He was no stranger to the feeling of cortisol coursing through his veins and as a pararescueman in the Air Force and a special agent in the DEA, he was well acquainted with the tense moments before being thrust into action. His gut always knew before his brain did when danger stalked nearby, ready to pounce. Jason sensed Shaggy was up to something, and he never took his eyes off the suspicious man.

Jason radioed the team, "Watch Shaggy. He looks like a shaken soda can ready to explode."

He instinctively reached for the SIG Sauer P226 pistol in his shoulder holster under his navy blue blazer. His right hand fell back to his side after confirming his weapon would be ready in an instant if needed.

I hope this guy doesn't try something stupid.

"I know it's warm out here and that I'm the one thing standing between you and some delicious food and refreshing drinks in an air-conditioned building, so I'll close with this," the senator said to chuckles in the audience. "The new bill I'm co-sponsoring will not be popular with everyone, but it's the right thing to do, and I won't stop fighting for you and the forty million people who depend on this river until we have a bill to protect it."

Shaggy stood seconds before the rest of the audience as they gave the senator a standing ovation. Jason moved toward the young man as he unscrewed the zoom lens from his camera and dumped something into his right hand.

Jason had little time to warn the others. "He's going for the senator!"

Shaggy moved into the aisle, stepped toward the podium, and reared back with something in his hand.

The newest security detail member rushed halfway up the aisle, his fingers on the handle of his pistol and a million questions swirling through his mind that required immediate answers.

What's in his hand? Is that a weapon? Should I draw? Should I shoot?

Before Jason arrived at an answer, Shaggy's hair whipped around his face as he chucked an egg at Senator Conrad. The senator ducked and dodged the poultry projectile as Shaggy shouted. "Shame on you. Your bill will be the end of small farmers in this state!"

As Shaggy transferred another egg from his left hand to his right and cocked to throw it, he was slammed to the turf by Ruben Zambrano from the security team while Clay rushed the senator to safety. The crowd scattered away from the egg thrower like a school of fish avoiding a shark, and several people fell over the chairs during the commotion.

Jason stopped over Shaggy writhing in pain on the ground and scanned for additional threats when Clay's voice boomed with the senator's code name over the radio. "Duke is secure. Sit rep?"

Clay secured the senator safely inside a bulletproof SUV.

Ruben Zambrano, or Zee, spoke first. "Assailant has been detained, and the threat neutralized."

Jason and the fourth security team member, Ian Park, responded next.

"All clear."

"Mulder, I need you over here with your aid kit. The protester got a nasty gash on his forehead when he hit the ground, and it looks like a reporter twisted her ankle," Zee said.

Jason arrived next to the protester as he sat on a sun-bleached sidewalk with his hands secured behind his back with zip ties. Members of Arizona DPS, who did not look amused by his shenanigans, surrounded him on each side. The former Air Force PJ raised Shaggy's face up by his chin to examine the wound. He noted the pockmarked skin on his cheeks, and the two-inch thin gash near his hairline, but the hatred in his eyes caught Jason by surprise. Jason wondered what was behind the vitriol coursing through his veins as he cleaned the wound and applied adhesive surgical tape strips over the bandage in an X pattern on the gash. He couldn't resist asking Shaggy the question burning in his mind.

"Why'd you do it?" Jason asked.

Shaggy's expression changed from indifferent to a murderous look of disdain. "You elites from Washington just don't get it. My family has farmed the same land here since before Arizona was a state. Now, a politician wants to take all of that away. Over what? A low river after a few years of drought?"

The intensity of Shaggy's anger caught Jason by surprise, causing him to take a step back. The DPS officer noticed and secured the protester. "Okay, your booboo is all fixed. Let's go."

After Jason wrapped up a reporter's ankle, he drove over the steel arch Navajo Bridge into Page. Born from a land exchange with the Navajo Nation ten miles south of the Utah border, the town of 7,000 residents was formed in 1957 as a housing community for the construction of the Glen Canyon Dam. Jason parked at the hotel hosting the senator and found the sports bar with a half dozen college basketball games beaming across the TVs. He sat at a table in the bar and waited for Clay to arrive. Clay appeared ten minutes later, shaking his head as he sat down.

"What the hell happened back there?"

Jason leaned back and exhaled loudly. He reacted to the potential threat like he was trained to do when it was clear that Shaggy had bad intentions for the senator. Jason knew he was slow to process whether or not to engage the threat with deadly force, and a slew of worst-case scenarios crept into his thoughts like an unwanted guest.

Don't ever let that happen again. Trust your training and instincts. Make a decision and live with it.

"I don't know, man," Jason responded. "I asked the protester when I applied a bandage to his wound why he did it, and he seemed like he wanted to kill someone."

Clay nodded. "Sometimes we attract the crazies."

A server wearing faded blue jeans and a black-and-white striped referee's shirt appeared beside their table. The young lady took their orders for two tall draft beers, and they waited quietly until their drinks arrived. Jason took a long draw and lowered his mug. "So much for watching the senator shake hands and kiss babies on the campaign trail. How was the senator once you got him out of there?"

"It's like nothing ever happened. Senator Conrad is laser-focused on the bill, and nothing can get in his way when he's like that. He's like a professional athlete with the game on the line. He's in a zone, and nothing will detract him from the mission of passing his new bill."

"Does he realize his proposed bill has people really pissed off?" Jason asked.

"It's only going to get worse."

Jason's eyebrows pinched together over his nose. "What? How?"

"I got a text from his chief of staff on the way down that he will reveal all the details of his controversial new bill during one of those Sunday news programs. Crenshaw said it got heated because he won't compromise on any of his talking points, and she's concerned the backlash will be severe."

"Shit. What's in that bill?"

"Don't know," Clay whispered.

"You don't know what's in the bill?"

"Nope," Clay said with a shake of his head. "But I do know it's not going to be easy keeping the senator safe for the rest of the campaign."

Jason nodded. He agreed. It would be a challenge to get the senator safely to the election. Of that, he was certain.

"I don't know about you," Clay started, "But I plan to watch Senator Conrad live on Sunday. I want to know right away how many people are going to want him dead."

Chapter 2

Whispering Pines, Arizona

JJ teetered on the brink of a fall that could result in a concussion, broken bones, or worse. Jason curled his arms around his son and pulled him away from the edge of the couch before he rolled onto the hardwood floor in the family room of their home in Whispering Pines. At six-months old, Jason and Shanna's son, Jason Joshua, showed some of the same tendencies to push safety boundaries as his father.

Jason lay next to his son in his pajamas with "Future Hunting Buddy" printed across the front and watched him explore everything with his eyes, hands, and mouth on a lazy Saturday morning.

The back door opened, and Shanna entered with an armful of split logs for the wood-burning stove. She placed them in the black wrought iron rack, poured herself a cup of coffee, and sat at the old oak dining room table a few feet from Jason and JJ.

"When do you have to leave again?" Shanna asked.

"Not for a few days. The senator is giving another speech about the new bill in Yuma on Thursday, so I'll head down there on Tuesday as the advanced security detail."

"Are you worried about another protester showing up?"

"We always have to prepare for protests at a campaign, but now I'll have to be extra thorough when I scout the location and present my threat analysis to Clay and Crenshaw."

"Why are people so upset about a bill to protect the Colorado River?"

"I'm not sure. Clay said the senator will be on TV tomorrow morning, and he'll share more details about what's in the bill. I plan to watch it so I know what has so many people angry at the senator."

"Okay, JJ and I will watch with you."

Five months earlier and one year before the next general election, Jason joined Senator Conrad's protective security detail at the urging of Clay Landry. Shortly after Jason successfully proved his innocence in a drug charge pinned on him by two crooked DEA Special Agents, Clay presented an opportunity to Jason after he'd accepted the team's lead position for Senator Conrad's PSD. Clay swiftly hired two experienced veterans from the special forces. Ian Park, an Englewood Cliffs, New Jersey native and former Navy Seal known as "Central," was the first to be hired. Ruben Zambrano, or "Zee," from Chicago, Illinois, by way of Venezuela when his parents immigrated to the United States, was the third member of the PSD responsible for protecting Senator Conrad and his staff. Zee served as an Army Ranger in the 75th Ranger Regiment.

While Central and Zee were at their PSD training, Clay convinced Crenshaw to increase the budget enough to add one more member for the extra reconnaissance work required for the reelection campaign. Crenshaw initially resisted, but once she heard the rumors of Conrad's new bill, she found the funds to hire Jason Mulder.

Jason drove ninety minutes from his home at Whispering Pines to the senator's office in Scottsdale, Arizona, to meet with the chief of staff, Julia Crenshaw, and Clay, twenty-four hours after joining the team. They showed Jason around the modest 2,000-square-foot office and officially welcomed him to the senator's staff.

The next day, Jason circled over the dense emerald green forests, carpeting the rolling hills and serpentine lakes of The Ozarks as he landed at Northwest Arkansas National Airport. It was Jason's turn to spend two weeks with an organization specializing in training law enforcement and high-level security professionals.

After Jason checked in at the training facility, he found his room and tossed his gear onto the bed of the two-person room in the trainee quarters. He strutted down the hall to get the lay of the land of his new home for the next fourteen days. The former PJ looked forward to meeting the other trainees and even prepared answers to the questions he expected to get about his background and training regimen that allowed him to excel in the PSD training. Jason knew little about private security professionals or the training he was about to endure, so if he was honest, he expected that his background as an Air Force pararescueman and DEA special agent would put him at the head of the class.

He first questioned his assumptions when he learned his roommate was a former Army Airborne Ranger and a current Los Angeles County SWAT team sniper. The deflation of his ego continued the next morning as he walked past squared-away men in formation who looked like they might snap him in two if he crossed them. By 7:00 am, he had fully shed the chip on his shoulder as he met with the teams from the British Royal Marine Commandos, an Oil and Gas PSD in Nigeria, an FBI Hostage Recovery Team (HRT), Los Angeles County SWAT and Department of Defense (DOD) individuals from unknown branches. Jason slunk down in the back of the room when the training leaders announced they had one member of a political PSD in the crowd.

Jason's prospects did not improve when he received his schedule and found he'd spend his first three days in a classroom. Although Jason knew he was surrounded by stiff competition, the former PJ still wanted to test his mettle against the best and brightest military and security professionals in the world.

His attitude about spending days in a classroom turned positive when the former Delta Force instructor started with techniques to conduct threat assessments and site survey risks for a high-value asset. This would be a significant part of Jason's job, so he soaked up two days of information on risk analysis, building surveys, site reconnaissance, convoy route selection, and explosive search techniques with and without a K9 asset. His head was swimming with all the intricate details of securing a location and getting principals to and from an event.

After another week of security driving techniques and weapons handling, with an emphasis on firing positions and proper use of weapons among uninvolved civilians, Jason's live training sessions, which he had circled on his schedule, finally arrived.

One hour before sunrise, the instructors called all the trainees outside to stand in the cool November mist. They stood at attention in silence for thirty minutes until the head instructor appeared in front of the twenty-four men in the training session.

"I know all of you have been trained by some of the most elite military and security agencies on the planet, but starting today, you're all rookie scum. The close-quarters force-on-force exercise in our kill houses is the most realistic training you'll receive in the PSD field. I need you all to give the instructors your undivided attention, master the techniques they teach you, and take this final phase of training seriously. If you don't, I'll fail you, and you get to spend two weeks with me again in the winter, which will suck but not as bad as being on a PSD whose principal gets whacked. Don't be that guy," the instructor barked.

Jason felt the intensity rise within the group as they shuffled off to learn individual reaction drills. After the sun rose and moved overhead, they broke out into teams for close protection team counter-action techniques, anti-ambush drills, and team evacuation actions when all else failed. The number one aim for a PSD was to keep the principal alive, so retreating with a breathing high-value asset was a win in the private security business.

After lunch, he was paired up with two British Commandos and two members of FBI HRT for the close-quarters force-on-force exercises in the kill house. Instead of live rounds, they were all given 9MM and 5.56MM marker rounds to simulate live fire. It reminded Jason of his training with the Marine Raiders in Afghanistan, and his team of five saved their principal and emerged from the kill houses unscathed.

It was time for the most realistic and challenging exercise, which was a source of most of Jason's nightmares about losing Senator Conrad. A transfer of a principal through a group of hostile protesters was Jason's biggest concern. It was easier to shoot anyone not on your team in a kill house because they were all bad guys except for the principal. The situation was flipped with the protester exercise, and only a handful of bad guys mixed in with civilians exercising their First Amendment rights. The opportunities for mistakes increased one-hundredfold.

Jason checked his gear one final time as he looked over the rectangle of concrete the size of a basketball court that represented a mock town plaza. The other trainees mingled on the plaza, acting as protestors, with new instructors they'd never met mixed in with the group but with intentions to kill their principal. Jason and his four teammates had to transport their principal through the protestors to the safety of the armored limousine on the other side.

The head instructor climbed to a platform over the plaza and blew the air horn to start the exercise. Although it was only training, Jason's heart raced as he took the first steps into the protestors holding signs and chanting. Humans could sense a predator waiting for the right time to strike, and our bodies dump adrenaline into the bloodstream regardless of whether it was caused by a genuine threat or a simulation.

Jason was in the lead position in the triangle around the principal. He attempted to scan every face and read body language to identify and neutralize any threats. Everyone in the crowd looked crazed and whipped into a frenzy by the recent political speech, and like the real world, Jason couldn't rely on his weapon until a threat appeared. Ten yards from the end of the crowd, Jason took his eyes off their faces and focused on a black SUV reinforced with enough armor to stop small-arms fire.

We're going to make it on the first try.

Jason turned around to pull the principal forward when he saw one of the British Commandos' eyes widen through his goggles.

"Weapon!" he shouted.

Before Jason could remove his pistol with simulated rounds from the holster, several marker rounds dotted his chest, the principal, and the rest of his team. The impact of each marker round stung, but the physical pain didn't bother Jason. The three red circles over his heart were visible markers of his failure. If this were an actual mission with real bad guys and bullets, everyone, including Jason, would be dead.

"Weapons up and halt mission," the head instructor yelled from his perch. He descended from his catwalk and continued until he stood in front of Jason. The instructor leaned closer until his nose was twelve inches from Jason's.

"What's your name?"

"Mulder."

"Well, Mulder, your principal, and your entire team are dead. Now I have to inform your wife that she's a widow. What the hell happened out there?"

Jason looked around and sighed. "It all happened so fast. I didn't have time to react."

"Exactly! Terrorists and criminals will not telegraph their intentions to you. Read them and know what they plan to do before they do it. Watch their eyes and their hands. They'll tell you everything you need to know. Learn to spot the cues because you must process and act upon them in a fraction of a second. You have to be sharp through chaos, fear, confusion, and direct contact. All of you have been highly trained by other institutions, including some of the most elite military units in the world, but the only thing that prepares you to make the right decisions when real bullets start flying is force-on-force exercises. You need to train like those bullets are real."

Jason's gaze moved beyond his crooked nose, focusing on his eyes full of red streaks that looked like bloody bolts of lightning, highlighting the instructor's fierce intensity.

"Do you understand Mulder?"

"Yes, sir."

"Regroup and rerun it until your principal and all of you make it to the vehicle and the safe house alive."

The instructor climbed back to the catwalk. "Run it again."

It took three attempts, but Jason and his team safely transferred their principal without taking a casualty while killing all the armed protesters. Everything slowed down so that Jason could see the protesters' actions more clearly, as the instructor said he would.

Jason passed and returned home on a high note. His new skills would be put to the test sooner than expected after Senator Conrad revealed the details of his new bill.

Chapter 3

Four Days after the Page Arizona Incident

Jason pruned the trees in the back acre of his property in Whispering Pines as sunlight flooded the dormant lawn. He focused on the lower branches of the trees that provided essential summer shade to their back patio, trimming them before the spring buds appeared. Jason picked up more branches and swiped at a swarm of gnats as he tossed them into a pile on the side of the house he'd burn on another day.

Shanna pushed through the back door with a cup of coffee in one hand and JJ in her other arm. Jason noticed his wife's full hands and ran up the patio stairs with extended arms.

"I'll take him."

Shanna passed JJ to his father and then the cup. "I thought you might like coffee before the morning talk show starts."

"Thanks. What time is it?"

"It's 8:47, so it starts in about ten minutes."

"Okay, I'll be right in."

The Mulder family found their way inside and sat together on the couch. Since they did not own a TV, Jason opened up his laptop on the coffee table and found the website for the news program. JJ sat propped up in the corner with a bottle while Shanna leaned on Jason to watch with her husband.

The distinctive neoclassical white dome of the United States Capital building filled the screen as the camera pulled out until viewers saw the entire studio. Jessica Halstead, the network anchor of Sunday Showdown, sat on one side of the table while Senator Conrad and Congresswoman Eva Duarte huddled beside each other, opposite Ms. Halstead. All three individuals sat behind white coffee mugs bearing the three letters of the TV network.

Halstead sat erect in her chair, and her wavy, shoulder-length brown hair framed her angular, middle-aged face. She adjusted her black, thick-rimmed glasses and faced the camera. "Good morning, and welcome to Sunday Showdown, where we ask the people leading this country the tough questions to get you the answers you deserve. Today, we have a former Republican turned Independent senator from Arizona and a Democratic congresswoman from Nevada making waves over their proposed bill to protect the Colorado River. Today, for the first time, they'll share the details of the bill they co-sponsored right here on Sunday Showdown."

The anchor turned toward her guests and addressed the congresswoman first. "Congresswoman Duarte, you're in your fourth term and have a track record of collaborating solely with members from your own party within the Environmental Solutions Caucus to develop your progressive environmental policies. Why did you choose to co-sponsor an environmental bill with Senator Conrad and not a member of your party with less of a reputation as a conservative?"

Congresswoman Duarte wore an elegant but professional black-sleeved dress with a thin string of pearls highlighting her slender neck. Her white teeth glowed through her ruby-red lipstick when she smiled at the camera.

"Thanks for having us here today to discuss such an important topic. I reached out to Senator Conrad because this issue goes beyond party and politics. He's from another Lower Basin state of the Colorado River Pact, and we both want to bring real solutions to the American people through smart legislation that tackles a tough topic that both parties have ignored for far too long."

Halstead nodded and turned to Senator Conrad. "You teased the bill last week during your speech at Lake Powell, so can you give us the details of the bill you co-sponsored today?"

"I also want to thank you for having us on today to share the details of the bill, which I'm excited to co-sponsor with Congresswoman Duarte. We agreed to co-sponsor this bill because the battle in the West for Colorado River water has been heating up for generations, and it's time to lower the temperature with some common sense legislation. That's why Congresswoman Duarte and I have collaborated to bring you the POLAR Act. The Preservation of Land and Rivers Act."

"Interesting name, but can you tell the viewers what's in the bill and why you're proposing it heading into election season?"

Senator Conrad delivered a genuine smile. "Absolutely. Irrigated agriculture is the largest water user in the Lower Basin states of Arizona, California, Nevada, and Utah, consuming over 70% of the available water supply. This is unsustainable, even if we weren't in a drought, so we have to act with smart legislation now. Our bill includes money to transition to less water-intensive crops, local infrastructure to support those new crops, new technologies to reduce water use on edible crops, and regulations to prevent predatory land grabs and wasteful groundwater use."

"That's not all, Jessica," Congresswoman Duarte interjected. "We need to invest today in large-scale farming that can feed the planet in the future. The POLAR Act provides low-cost loans for the construction of hydroponic, indoor, and vertical farming infrastructure that uses far less water than traditional outdoor farms."

"Are you referring to the rooftop gardens that are popping up in cities across the country?" Halstead asked.

"That may be a tiny part of a larger plan," Conrad said. "In the coming weeks and months, I'll visit some pioneers using the most advanced farming technology at scale to show the American people how advances in farming technology can help address the water shortages in the Colorado River Basin."

Halstead took off her glasses and tilted her head. "That sounds like a very ambitious and expensive plan, especially considering Capitol Hill faces immense pressure to reduce government spending. How do you intend to pay for your plan?"

Senator Conrad steepled his index fingers and pressed them against his lips as if giving the question deep thought.

"First, the cost of doing nothing is the most expensive option. We've tried that for the last thirty years, and it only gets more expensive. We'll directly fund everything in the POLAR Act with an export duty on agricultural exports grown in the Upper and Lower Colorado Basin that are not for human consumption. Nearly a third of the crops grown in the affected states are for animal feed shipped out of the United States. These operations consume vast amounts of our dwindling water supplies, and few Americans see any benefit from this deliberate abuse of limited resources. The export duty will recoup a substantial amount of the revenue needed to fully fund the POLAR Act and start the healing process of the Colorado River."

The anchor put her glasses back on and leaned back in her seat. She flipped her hair back in her signature move before asking a tricky question.

"Senator Conrad, I'm surprised you co-sponsored a bill with land restrictions and new taxes after running for the senate five years ago on a fiscal conservative platform. Many people commented on the POLAR Act leaks earlier this week, and while states, municipal governments, and environmentalists seem supportive, groups representing farmers, land owners, and investors, like Sustainable Future Alliance, are concerned. SFA president Brock Eckhart had this to say on his social media feed:

> 'Can someone conduct a wellness check on Senator Conrad because if what I've heard about his new bill is true, he must have gone mad. He's choosing the elites in the cities over the hard-working family farmers, ranchers, and land owners in Arizona. What happened to the conservative senator I voted for five years ago?'"

"How do you respond to that stinging rebuke?"

Senator Conrad flashed the winning smile that helped him gain 61% of the vote in the last election. "I appreciate Mr. Eckhart's passion for all the small farmers and wealthy investors he represents impacted by the water shortage. I'm also thinking of them in our bill. The problem is that too many people think water is abundant because sometimes it falls from the sky. However, the forty million people impacted by dwindling water supplies are quickly learning firsthand how untrue that is. They not only see the reduction in available water, they feel it in their everyday lives."

Senator Conrad took a sip from his coffee cup and continued. "The people of Arizona elected me to make well-researched, thoughtful decisions, even if they are difficult. That's why Congresswoman Duarte and I crafted the POLAR Act, and we'll keep pushing it through committees and both chambers until it's passed and sent to the President for his signature. The cost of doing nothing is too great."

"Thank you both for coming on today and sharing more about your new bill."

Halstead turned back to the camera. "We have to take a short break, and when we get back, I'll talk to the Deputy Chair of Homeland Security about the proposed changes the next time you go through the TSA when you fly."

Jason closed his laptop and leaned into the cushions on the couch. He stared at the ceiling with both hands interlocked behind his head. Conrad's bill wasn't as antagonistic as he'd feared, but he knew the land restrictions and new taxes would rile up a portion of the populace.

Shanna turned toward her husband. "I can see why some people are upset. It sounds like Senator Conrad's bill may negatively impact many farmers. I doubt they'll be too happy if they're forced to change what they've grown and sold for years. I know I wouldn't be if I were them," Shanna said.

Jason nodded but said nothing.

"You and Clay have to be extra careful at your future campaign events with the senator. Your job just got a lot harder."

And a lot more dangerous.

CHAPTER 4

Yuma, Arizona

Jason shifted his weight and bit his lower lip as Conrad's words from the talk show played in his mind again during his three-hour drive to Yuma, Arizona. His political jargon and smooth delivery created juicy soundbites for the news media, but Jason knew his proposed policies could cause real pain for farmers and ranchers. Now they were headed into the heart of Arizona farm country, and Jason wondered how the locals would react to Senator Conrad's first public event after the details of the POLAR Act were revealed.

He pushed harder on the accelerator, and his truck emerged from the low mountain pass into a valley blanketed in a patchwork of green squares and rectangles spreading across his windshield. Jason continued on Interstate 8 into the Yuma Valley in the southwestern corner of Arizona, near the California and Mexico borders. Neatly planted rows of lettuce, Swiss chard, and arugula passed outside Jason's truck, ready to be plucked to supply much of the United States with their winter greens.

His GPS guided him to a field of workers who removed weeds ahead of the looming harvest. After he exited the vehicle, a short man with his shirt unbuttoned to his upper abdomen and a wide-brimmed hat approached Jason.

"Hello, sir. Are you security?" the man said in a thick Spanish accent.

"Yes, I'm with the security detail. Are you Arturo Ruiz?"

"Si."

Jason completed a full turn as he scanned the crops, stretching for miles in all directions. He was happy to see only limited areas where someone could mount a surprise ambush from the flat fields.

"Which field can we set up a small platform for the speaker?"

The field boss knew a politician from Washington, DC, was coming to deliver a speech, but Jason did not mention Senator Conrad for operational security.

The man waved his arm across acres of green. "You can set up anywhere between these four fields."

Jason looked up at the sun and noted that the senator would speak in twenty-six hours, 3:00 pm the next day. He did not want the senator or the security team facing the setting sun in the west. It was acceptable for the media and audience to face the bright orange ball descending in the sky, but Jason's team couldn't risk anything impeding a clear view of the principal.

"Are the workers going to be out here tomorrow?" Jason asked. He pointed to the forty to fifty workers inching across the romaine lettuce field.

"Yes, sir. The work out here doesn't stop until everything is out of the ground."

Jason nodded. It wasn't ideal from a security standpoint, so he'd bring it up to Crenshaw and Clay and let them decide if they wanted workers in the field during Conrad's speech.

After dinner, Jason met Clay and Chief of Staff Crenshaw in the hotel's lobby. They exchanged greetings, and Clay got straight to business after everyone found a seat.

"Site analysis?"

"Good. It's flat for miles, so I recommend placing one man on an SUV roof to give us the elevation advantage. There are no areas to mass a group ambush or for a sniper to set up. It's a great location, but I have one concern."

"What is it?" Clay asked.

"The workers will be in the field during the speech, and we don't have time to vet them all, so I think we should ask the owner to have them work elsewhere tomorrow."

Crenshaw snapped her head from her phone. "Absolutely not. I want the American people to see those workers and how the rotation to edible crops is helping with jobs and preserving the Colorado River."

In Jason's short time on the team, he'd heard Crenshaw overrule recommendations from the PSD. Technically, as chief of staff, Clay reported to Crenshaw, but as head of security, Clay could trump her decision if it put Senator Conrad at risk. Jason wanted to see if this was one of those rare occasions Clay would wield his power.

"I understand Jason's concern, but I don't think the risk warrants removing the workers. We'll deal with it."

"Thank you," Crenshaw replied. Her eyes returned to her phone screen.

"I want to sweep the entire area before the senator arrives, so Jason, you need to get back out there bright and early tomorrow."

Jason asked, "Are any K9s available for my perimeter walk or to check vehicles when they enter?"

"Not tomorrow. The ATF called the retired K9 officer we've been using for an event in Tucson. It will be a visual inspection only tomorrow for the Yuma County deputies."

Morning dew moistened Jason's pants below the knee as he walked through the romaine lettuce field behind the temporary platform built to host Senator Conrad's speech. The greens were less than twenty inches tall, but Jason knew a determined marksman could low crawl close enough to get a shot. Crenshaw chose to work with this farmer because he had converted his fields from alfalfa to romaine lettuce fifteen years earlier. Now, instead of feeding cattle, the land provided millions of Americans with fresh vegetables while using thirty percent less water. It was the ideal example for Senator Conrad to promote the key tenets of his POLAR Act.

After lunch, Jason returned from searching the perimeter, satisfied that no bad actors could get close enough to harm the senator through the fields. The workers were three-quarters of a mile away and showed no interest in the political theater at the other end of the lettuce rows.

I hope the speech is over before they return to this end of the field. That's a lot of additional people to monitor.

The Yuma County Sheriff stationed four deputies at the entrance of the dirt path to validate credentials and check vehicles for explosives. Central from Conrad's PSD team monitored the audience area roped off with red, white, and blue streamers waving in the light breeze. Inside the roped-in area, one hundred and twenty empty folding chairs glistened in the sun.

Jason couldn't stay in one place. He studied the audience, which included primarily media, dignitaries, and local citizens, entering from every angle. Clay assigned Zee to the overwatch position, where he lay frozen in the prone position under a tarp on the roof of their Chevy Tahoe. Jason watched him peer through a spotting scope with a Heckler & Koch MP5 rifle nestled perfectly in his shoulder. Zee continually scanned the area from his position above all the other vehicles and spectators.

Right on cue, a convoy of black SUVs sandwiched between two Yuma County Sheriff cruisers passed the long column of vehicles parked alongside the dirt path. Once the SUV stopped and the dust settled, Clay inconspicuously followed Conrad to the podium as the senator occasionally stopped to wave and shake hands with supporters. Jason drifted to the back of the audience and continued his threat evaluation of everyone in a seat facing the senator. He did not detect any threats on his first scan, but that did not ease his sense of dread. Jason felt a heightened risk of danger since the egg-throwing incident at Lake Powell and the senator's appearance on the talk show promoting the POLAR Act.

Senator Conrad arrived at the podium and adjusted the microphone. Fifteen minutes into his planned half-hour speech, one of the local attendees shuffled uncomfortably in his seat and shook his head wildly. Jason noticed the signs of agitation and called it in.

"Cowboy wearing the brown hat in the fourth row seems agitated."

The man with a sharp scowl under the brim of his cowboy hat appeared to be in his mid-sixties. He grew more animated throughout the speech, and each word uttered by the senator seemed to spark more agitation. He swayed and jerked his head furiously in response to many of the senator's statements.

"My bill will bring the resources and funds to transform the rest of the Colorado Basin into the twenty-first century with cutting-edge food production while reducing the amount of water we require from the river," Senator Conrad boomed.

The audience responded with applause, and Jason braced for the cowboy to jump out of his chair. He leaned forward, ready to snatch the SIG Sauer P226 pistol from its holster. Jason inched closer to the man, but the cowboy remained seated through the end of the speech.

Jason sighed and let his shoulders relax as Clay escorted Senator Conrad to the secure SUV. He turned his attention to the media, constituents, and staffers returning to their vehicles. The lead SUV in the convoy with the Yuma County Sheriff's Office emblem on the side rolled forward, and the senator's SUV followed close behind. Jason turned to locate Zee and Central as the last vehicle in the convoy passed him. He wanted to congratulate his team on a successful mission but never made it.

A blinding burst of light caught his eye a split second before a massive explosion rocked the ground and knocked Jason from his feet. The shock wave hurtled him through the air and across the dirt path like a rag doll. He tasted dirt and the coppery tang of blood in his mouth as he stopped rolling near the edge of the unpaved road.

The concussion from the blast overwhelmed all of his senses. A high-pitched ringing filled his ears, and everything appeared white like he'd looked at a flashbulb at night.

Jason shook his head and pushed himself up to identify the source of the blast. Flames licked at the edges of his vision as his unfocused eyes scanned the area for answers.

Moments later, as the ringing faded, Jason's ears were filled with car alarms, shrill cries of distress, and wails of pain. A cacophony of chaos, yellow smoke, and destruction replaced the once cloudless indigo sky. He blinked away the disorientation, forcing his eyes to focus on the smoldering wreckage that was once a pickup truck. Jason's chest and limbs protested the movement as he staggered to his feet. He closed his eyes to concentrate on any areas of intense pain from shrapnel or his hard tumble to the ground. Once his mind confirmed that he suffered no severe injuries, Jason located the spot where the truck had once sat.

The sight of the waist-deep crater in the chalky brown soil washed away the brain fog like a rogue wave, and Jason understood he had survived a car bomb.

Jason spun around so fast that he nearly lost his balance.

"Where's the senator?"

CHAPTER 5

Jason shuffled up the smoldering path, searching for a mangled black Chevy Tahoe among the wreckage, when he spotted a police cruiser overturned on its roof thirty yards away. He recognized the crumpled car as the rear vehicle in the convoy that passed him seconds earlier. Jason started toward the cruiser to see if the SUV was in front of it when he heard screeching tires. He turned to see the black SUV with Senator Conrad, Clay, and Crenshaw inside, speeding behind the lead police vehicle onto the paved road. The squealing echoed across the fields as they turned and accelerated rapidly toward the heart of Yuma.

Okay, the senator is safe.

The guttural moans and bone-penetrating cries coming from all directions told Jason that others were injured. Instincts took over, and he scanned the carnage for the most seriously hurt individuals. His initial gaze settled on the Yuma County Sheriff's vehicle that nearly took a direct hit from the blast. The cruiser's rear was crumpled like a smashed soda can, and all the windows were blown out. After moving toward the cruiser to investigate further, Jason stopped when he saw a bloody arm emerge. He rushed to help the deputy crawl out from the smoking wreckage. Jason assisted the deputy to a grassy area and gently laid him on his back.

"Are you hurt?" Jason asked.

The deputy licked his lips and winced. "I think it's just cuts and bruises."

"I'm going to do a quick blood sweep."

Jason ran his open palms around the deputy's arms, legs, and torso and found only a tiny amount of blood from scrapes on his neck, face, and arms. He also checked for broken bones and concluded that the deputy had narrowly avoided serious injury.

"I didn't find any serious bleeding or obvious broken bones, but we'll get you to the paramedics when they arrive so they can check you out."

Jason looked around to see if any flashing lights were on the way, and that's when he saw the person trapped in the vehicle parked behind the exploded truck.

"Hang tight. The EMTs will be here soon."

Seconds later, Jason arrived at the driver's side door of the charred sedan, which came to rest ten yards from the crater in the road. Thin wisps of white smoke rose under the crumpled hood, and a hissing noise drifted through its shattered windows. Through the smoke, Jason identified a person amid the twisted metal slumped awkwardly over the steering wheel. The smoke under the hood turned to flames, and Jason knew he had to act fast.

First, he tried the door handle, but the door wouldn't open, so Jason leaned the person back to unbuckle the seatbelt. Despite the copious amount of blood and disfigured face, Jason recognized the young man. He couldn't remember his name, but he knew the recent Political Science graduate from Penn State University was a staffer for the congressional committee. The man in his mid-twenties arrived two days earlier to study the Yuma farms as part of his task to help write the bill for committee review.

Jason put his index and middle finger over the carotid artery in the man's neck but felt nothing. A searing plume of smoke assaulted Jason's nose, mouth, and throat, so he raised his head from the vehicle to inhale several gulps of cool air and look around for help. Seeing none, he reached through the open window and twisted the man a quarter turn so his back was against the door. Jason attempted a fireman's carry as he slid his arms around the man's chest to pull him from the wreckage before it became fully engulfed. The man rose several inches and stopped. After the third attempt, Jason concluded the man's foot was caught on one of the pedals.

Come on, man. I'm not leaving here without you.

Jason held his breath and dove into the smoke-filled vehicle with zero visibility. It was like diving at night without a flashlight, so Jason felt around until he identified the man's left foot. It rested on the left side of the brake pedal, so Jason used his hands and fingers to look for the right foot. He found his right knee and followed it down until he reached the foot stuck under the brake pedal. It was twisted one hundred and eighty degrees in the wrong direction. The mutilated foot wrapped around the brake pedal, so Jason had to wrench the lower half of the leg back in a normal direction to release it.

"On three. One, two, three."

Jason was glad he didn't hear the pop of the leg rotating a half turn over the crackle of the flames raging on the other side of the dash. The heat inside the car grew unbearable, so Jason pulled his head out and backed away. Flames sprouted from under the hood and reached three to four feet high. Jason wiped the beads of sweat from his forehead with his sleeve and took a few deep breaths to clear the smoke from his lungs. His years as an Air Force PJ allowed him to hold his breath for up to two minutes, but he didn't have that much time. He had to get the staffer out in the next half minute before the entire cabin erupted into flames. The risk of the gas tank in the car exploding increased with each passing second.

Jason repositioned the man and pulled. He slid through the broken glass in the driver's side door amid super-heated black smoke. The vehicle snapped and sizzled as the cabin's interior melted under the immense heat. Jason dragged the man twenty yards from the car and began CPR. A small crowd arrived and watched Jason try to revive the man. After three minutes, Jason checked again for a pulse and stopped chest compressions. The young man likely died instantly from the blast, but Jason had to do everything possible to save him.

"He's gone," Jason said to the onlookers. "One of you, please stay here and let the EMTs know he was in the burning car. He didn't have a pulse when I arrived, and resuscitation efforts were unsuccessful." A frazzled young woman, who looked barely old enough to drink legally, nodded.

Jason stood and scanned the area. Most audience members scattered away from the blast's epicenter, but Jason noticed Central from the PSD team tending to someone on the ground. He rushed to his teammate's side and saw a female reporter with her arm missing from just above her elbow. It reminded Jason of the dozens of amputees he encountered in Afghanistan. He had more experience than he wished in treating missing limbs from IEDs, so he got right to work.

"Central, run to my SUV and grab my kit. It's on the passenger seat."

The reporter's eyes fluttered open and closed, showing she was going into shock. Jason ripped off a patch of the cotton t-shirt underneath his tactical attire, wet it with a water bottle, and dabbed it on her head and neck. It seemed to help as the reporter's eyes locked on Jason.

"Wha, what happened?"

Jason put his index fingers on her lips. "You're going to be okay."

She attempted to turn her head toward her missing left arm, but he secured her chin to prevent it. He leaned closer. "What's your name?"

"My name?"

"Yes. What's your name?" Jason repeated calmly.

"I'm a... I'm Veronica."

Central slid next to Jason with a black canvas bag. Jason opened the bag, dug around, and emerged with a needle seconds later.

"Veronica, this is going to help with the pain. An ambulance is on the way."

She nodded.

After the ketamine injection, Jason applied one of his new speed tourniquets to stop the bleeding and wrapped the stump of her left arm in bandages. Jason leaned toward Central and whispered so Veronica couldn't hear him.

"She needs medical attention ASAP. How far out are the ambulances?"

Central leaped to his feet and stood on his tiptoes to see over the vehicles.

"I see several ambulances and a ton of cops turning in now. How can I help?"

"Guide an ambulance over here and have them bring a gurney. We can help them load her up."

Ten minutes later, the ambulance departed for Yuma Regional Medical Center, a level three trauma facility, to stabilize Veronica before transporting her to a level one facility in Tucson or Phoenix. Jason noticed that at least twenty law enforcement officers from the City of Yuma, Arizona Department of Public Safety and Yuma County Sheriff's Office were setting up a perimeter around the crater in the earth.

Jason shuffled toward the epicenter of the blast and saw paramedics from another ambulance load a gurney into the back with a person covered in a white sheet. The EMTs were not working on the patient, so Jason assumed it was the young male staffer.

He felt a gentle push on his elbow and whipped around to identify the source. His nerves were still on high alert after the blast.

A DPS officer faced Jason. He looked down at the blood on Jason's shirt and then back to his face. "You need to back up behind the yellow tape."

"I'm with the senator's security detail."

"Everyone needs to move behind the yellow tape," the officer stated. Jason knew it wasn't the right time to escalate the debate, so he moved into the field to look at the damage before they pushed him entirely out of the area. He felt something unusually hard through his boot as he stepped over rows of lettuce. Jason bent down to investigate and found a circular piece of metal. The object was twice as large and heavy as any currency Jason had seen and had ornate figures on the front and back. He did not know what type of metal or how old it could have been but guessed it was not new. Jason put it in his pocket and continued through the field until he was even with the crater.

The new perspective allowed him to see the damage to all six vehicles in front of and behind the pickup truck for the first time. The condition of the cars and trucks showed the bomb's power that moved three-ton vehicles like a kid's toy. Jason was sure he'd later hear of more casualties than the two he assisted.

A wave of nausea slammed Jason's gut as he recalled the proximity of the senator's SUV that passed by the steaming crater seconds before the bomb went off. Two undeniable realizations grew clear to Jason. The first was that Senator Conrad was the intended target of the blast. The second was more challenging to accept.

It may be impossible to protect the senator from someone with an unwavering determination to end his life.

The thought itself wasn't new. Jason had known what a challenge protecting the senator would be. And he'd still signed on for the job because he was confident he'd be able to see it through with success.

Now, for the first time, he wasn't so sure.

CHAPTER 6

Jason sat up in bed and watched the sun rise, casting hues of pink and orange across the mountain range east of Yuma. He had woken hours earlier and wasn't sure if he had slept over thirty minutes in a stretch the entire night. Like many of his missions in Afghanistan, his mind relentlessly flashed scenes of the chaos he'd experienced during the day.

I need coffee. Lots of coffee.

Jason turned on the TV and used the coffee maker in his room. He took one sip of the brownish, translucent liquid and spit it out in the sink.

"Shit! That's awful!"

Coffee was necessary to start that morning, so Jason dressed and walked across the street to a gas station full of field workers purchasing drinks, meals, and snacks before another twelve-hour day. He scanned the tired-looking men and women standing in line.

I wonder if any of them know anything about the bombing.

After returning to the hotel and downing a quarter of the coffee, Jason moved to the couch and opened his laptop. He reviewed the agenda for the 9:00 meeting with Clay, Crenshaw, and the rest of the PSD team. While he reviewed his notes from the day before, the TV caught his attention. A headline said Arrest Made `in Yuma Bombing` while the reporter stood outside Fourth Avenue Jail in Phoenix. Jason turned up the volume.

"We're still waiting for confirmation from the Arizona DPS spokesperson, but sources within the department have shared that a man is in custody in connection with the bombing yesterday in Yuma that killed one and injured three others after Senator Conrad's speech. Those sources have not provided a name but said a local man who attended the speech is in the Fourth Avenue Jail. I'll share more as we get those details from DPS. Back to you, Chris."

The morning news anchor thanked the reporter, turned to the teleprompter, and started the next story about a hit-and-run.

Did they arrest the nervous man in the cowboy hat? Could I have prevented the bombing if I'd acted on my suspicion of the cowboy?

The news continued in the background while Jason was deep in thought until the morning anchor mentioned Sustainable Future Alliance. He recalled that the SFA president slammed Conrad during the senator's national TV appearance, so Jason looked up and saw the headline at the bottom of the screen: `Farm Group Frosty on POLAR Act.`

In the prerecorded interview, the field reporter and SFA president Brock Eckhart stood next to an irrigation canal and a field of alfalfa west of Phoenix. As they walked along the canal and talked, Eckhart continued to rail against the POLAR Act. He said much of the same things Jessica Halstead quoted on Sunday Showdown, but his rhetoric escalated when he spoke about Senator Conrad.

"I just don't understand. I thought Senator Conrad was different, but after five years in Washington, DC, he's like all the others. Their egos explode, and they all want to pick winners and losers. For some reason, Senator Conrad has decided that family farms and ranches in the Colorado River Basin are the losers in his new bill."

"Senator Conrad says the status quo is unsustainable. If you disagree with his bill, what do you think Congress should do about the current water situation in Arizona and the West?" the reporter asked.

"There are many other ways to achieve a sustainable water supply in the West that won't wreck family farms. We'll share some of our recommendations in the coming days, and I hope that Senator Conrad and Congresswoman Duarte will seriously consider them in their bill. I refuse to let farmers and ranchers take the brunt of this bill without a fight."

The last sentence hung with Jason, not because of what Eckhart said but because of how he said it. The disdain for Senator Conrad in his eyes was apparent even through the filter of a TV camera.

What's his problem with the senator? Is he somehow connected to the bombing?

Jason packed his laptop and took the elevator to the hotel's first floor. Once inside the windowless conference room, he noted the somber look of the staff members sitting behind long tables arranged in a horseshoe shape. The bright fluorescent lights highlighted the fear, confusion, and concern on their faces as Jason took the final open chair.

Per Clay's protocol for meetings in a public facility, Zee set up anti-listening devices around the room. The rest of the staff put their phones into a half dozen Faraday pouches to prevent anyone who might be tracking their phones from knowing they were all huddled together.

Clay rose after everyone found a seat. "Zee, are the anti-listening devices active?"

He gave his boss a thumbs up. "Yes, sir."

"Devon, please run your test to confirm the devices are working."

Devon Reynolds was the IT and Data Science specialist on Senator Conrad's staff. He stared at the screen on his laptop for ten seconds and then looked up. "Listening abatement is active."

"Thank you. Ms. Crenshaw, the floor is yours."

Crenshaw stood and moved to the middle of the U-shaped tables. Her brown eyes drifted slowly around the room.

"First, I want to share my heartfelt condolences to everyone in this room impacted by the horrible tragedy we experienced yesterday. My thoughts and prayers are with Evan Smith's friends and family as we grieve the loss of a bright young man tragically taken too soon."

Jason bowed his head at the name of the man he tried to save yesterday. He heard muted sobs and sniffing from all corners of the room.

"I know some of you got to know Evan while he helped write the POLAR Act, so I'll share funeral details once his family finalizes the service."

Crenshaw cleared her throat and took a sip of coffee from her mug.

"A reporter and two audience members were also injured, and I understand many of you are frightened and probably apprehensive about future events after the car bombing yesterday. Early this morning, I received word from the director of Arizona DPS that a suspect was in custody. Details are still coming in, but we can all exhale now that the person likely responsible for yesterday's car bomb is in custody."

"Who was it? Was he at the event?" Central asked from his seat in the far corner of the room.

Crenshaw sighed and crossed her arms. "As I said, details are still coming in, but I've been told that a rancher and member of the SFA attended the speech and may have left with someone else just before the bomb detonated. The FBI is here now to aid in the investigation, so we'll have more information later from them."

Zee spit into a styrofoam cup with the same logo on the side as Jason's coffee. "What type of explosives did he use?"

"I wish you wouldn't do that," Crenshaw snapped.

"Do what?"

"Spit that nasty chewing tobacco into a cup during our meetings. It's disgusting."

Zee pushed the cup to the side. "Sorry, ma'am. Do they know what explosives they used?"

Crenshaw sighed loudly. "We'll review all the security-related details during our PSD brief. I want to address concerns from yesterday's event and prepare for our meeting with the SFA in three days."

"What?" Devon asked incredulously. "Brock Eckhart has been bashing Senator Conrad about the POLAR Act before he even announced it. Who had the bright idea to meet with that snake?"

Jason felt the air pressure in the room change and knew somebody had entered the room. He didn't have to turn around to identify that the person with the booming voice behind him was Senator Conrad.

"I agreed to meet with him!"

Devon's face dropped while everyone else looked toward the senator with mouths agape. Clay stood and marched toward Senator Conrad. "I said I'd come up and escort you down here when you were ready."

"Clay, I don't need someone to hold my hand when I take an elevator down five floors."

"I understand, sir, but I wish you'd—"

Senator Conrad cut Clay off. "I know you're just doing your job, but I can still handle myself in these situations."

He strode to the front of the room and stopped next to his chief of staff.

"I came down here to extend my condolences to all of Evan Smith's friends and colleagues and to thank all of you for showing up today to continue our fight for what is right. However, I do want to address Mr. Reynold's question. We're meeting with Brock Eckhart because he contacted Ms. Crenshaw and requested a meeting. I'm not naive. I know he's only trying to protect his wealthy donors who own land and may be negatively impacted by the POLAR Act if they refuse to make any changes. I also know he's making statements on the new bill with limited information, so I hope a conversation like mature adults can lead to some common ground. Having the SFA on our side with the POLAR Act would be great, but I also have no problem moving forward without them."

Devon nodded. Central stood and moved closer to Senator Conrad standing near the opening of the horseshoe-shaped tables. "Arizona DPS has a man in custody associated with the SFA. Is now a good time to meet with the people that may have ties to yesterday's IED attack?"

Senator Conrad opened his mouth to speak, but Crenshaw put her hand on his forearm to stop him.

"It looks like we're going to have that PSD briefing now, so everyone that's not part of the PSD team, please return to your rooms, and I'll schedule another meeting for this afternoon to finish everything else on our agenda."

Once all non-security related staff left the room, Senator Conrad sat atop a table and turned to Crenshaw. "What do you think? Should we cancel the meeting with Eckhart?"

Crenshaw sat on the opposite side of the U and crossed her legs. She momentarily looked up at the ceiling as if searching for inspiration and responded. "I think we should meet with SFA while we're still in Arizona, but I recommend we hold off on further stumping for the POLAR Act until we return to Washington. It's much more secure than these remote, far-flung areas along the Colorado River, making us an easy target for any deranged person with a bomb or rifle. I don't think it's safe out here right now."

Jason's jaw tightened as his hands curled into fists under the table. He verified the Yuma site and was responsible for securing all the sites in Arizona, even without critical resources like K9s. The newest member of the PSD turned to see how Senator Conrad would respond.

Conrad tilted his head. "What about the campaign? I can't run for reelection in Arizona from over two thousand miles away."

Crenshaw smiled. "We can hit the major population centers like Phoenix and Tucson. We may consider Prescott, Flagstaff, and Lake Havasu with careful planning, but we have to stick to places with ample security resources. No more speeches in the sticks."

An eerie quiet enveloped the room. Jason waited for the Senator to respond, but Clay spoke first.

"Isn't that what the terrorists want?"

It was only six words, but they landed with the force of a roundhouse punch to the jaw. Clay's face flushed red, and the plastic straw was missing from its usual position between his lips. Jason knew the leader of the PSD was livid.

Crenshaw must have sensed the blow to her recommendation and rose to defend her position. "This isn't about giving in to terrorists. The man in custody may not have done this alone. This is about keeping Senator Conrad and his entire staff alive so we can implement his plans after he's reelected later this year."

Despite the apparent rage swirling inside Clay, he did not respond.

"He's right," Conrad whispered.

Five sets of eyes turned toward the Senator.

"He's right. Anyone that tries to blow up innocent Americans is a terrorist in my book, and I will not let terrorists dictate the bills I sponsor, the speeches I deliver, or the places we campaign." His voice dripped with resolve in each word.

"But senator—"

Senator Conrad put up his hand to stop Crenshaw from voicing her rebuttal.

"I'm meeting with Eckhart, and I want a dozen more events in Arizona lined up over the next month. They messed with the wrong senator!"

Jason's eyes flashed to Clay, and he returned with a quick nod. He understood the mission without a single spoken word. Jason had to ready the team for a trip into hostile territory with a real possibility of another attempt to take the senator's life.

CHAPTER 7

Yuma, Arizona

Jason stared out over the rows of lettuce as he stood next to the crater that marked the location of death and destruction twenty hours earlier. The sudden burst of light, followed by the taste of dirt and blood after tumbling across the unpaved road, reappeared in Jason's mind as if it had happened moments before. He bent down and touched the dirt at the crater's edge, but his thoughts were with the young man who died after Jason tried to save him.

Could I have done more? If I'd gotten to him sooner, would he still be alive?

The former Air Force pararescueman hated to lose anyone in his care, and this one still stung.

Jason returned to the scene of the truck bomb to meet the FBI special agent assigned to the case. The agent had already spoken with Crenshaw, Clay, Zee, Central, and Senator Conrad yesterday at the hotel, and now it was Jason's turn to share his version of the blast that could have killed him.

Unlike the others, the FBI agent asked Jason to meet him at the scene. Jason wasn't sure why but was happy to leave the stale hotel conference room for a few hours while the rest of the staff reviewed the plans for the senator's next DC fundraiser.

A plume of dust appeared behind a black SUV that turned off the paved street to the dirt farm road. Jason strode back to his vehicle to meet the FBI special agent when he arrived, but instead of pulling up to Jason's vehicle, the SUV parked fifty yards away. A lanky African American man slid out and strode toward the crater. He took slow, deliberate steps like he was walking barefoot across shards of broken glass. As he got closer, Jason saw the wrinkles around his eyes and the gray hair winning the battle on top of his head. Jason thought the old man was lost for a second but saw the yellow FBI logo emblazoned on the navy windbreaker and the holstered pistol.

This guy has to be retiring soon.

"You must be Jason Mulder," the man said. A toothy smile, minus his left incisor, followed the statement.

"Yes, sir. I'm Jason Mulder."

"Great. I'm Special Agent Autry Woods, but you can call me Archie."

"Nice to meet you, Mr. Woods. How can I help you?"

"You can start by calling me Archie. My father was Mr. Woods."

Jason's lips curled upward. "Okay, Archie. Is there specific information you want from me?"

"What should I call you?"

Jason did not recall anyone asking him that before, and it was tougher to answer than expected. After careful consideration, he replied. "I respond to Jason or Mulder. Most people I work with call me Mulder."

"Great. Now that we have our greetings out of the way, I'll examine the explosion site and surrounding area again. I'd like you to hang around in case I have questions. Does that work for you, Mulder?"

"Yes, Agen—. Yes, Archie, that works."

Jason watched Archie walk in and out of the crater for ten minutes. He'd count paces out loud from one side to the other, look up into the sky for several seconds, and then nod. Jason had no clue what Archie was doing or why he had to drive to the field to meet him.

Finally, Archie returned and leaned against the vehicle next to Jason. "Were you scared?"

Involuntary wrinkles formed on Jason's forehead. "Scared? Someone needed help, and I sprang into action. I didn't think much about it."

"Hmmm. You're braver than me because I would have been terrified. That was a powerful bomb in that truck."

"I'm wasting my time here," Jason whispered.

"Mulder, come here. I want to show you something."

Jason debated whether the staff meeting would be better than dealing with an FBI special agent who seemed out of his depth for this investigation.

Archie descended into the crater, and Jason joined him at the bottom.

"Did you see anyone approach the pickup truck that was parked here during the speech?"

"No, but my focus was on the audience near the senator during his speech, so I wasn't paying attention to the parked vehicles. I knew the Yuma County deputies screened all the vehicles. Why?"

Archie rubbed the stubble on his chin. "I ask because somebody placed a large amount of ammonium nitrate into the truck's bed during the speech. They detonated it remotely, probably with a cell phone."

"How do you know all this?"

"Decades of experience," Archie laughed. "Officially, the ATF is analyzing the residue and soil samples now, but they'll simply confirm what I already know. Look down here."

Archie pointed to a circle of flattened dirt near the middle of the crater. "This is where the ammonium nitrate exploded, and based on the truck's position and blast direction, it was at the rear of the bed. I suspect someone or multiple people walked out of that field, tossed the explosives into the bed, and walked right back into that lettuce field."

The breezy tone and folksy southern twang from Archie had vanished. His words were crisp while his eyes locked in and focused on the crime scene. His demeanor was all business.

"Now that you mention it, I saw the workers at the end of the other field during my preliminary perimeter search, but I think they were much closer to us when the senator's convoy departed."

"There's your culprit."

"You think a field worker planted the explosives?"

"No, I don't."

Jason's eyebrows pinched just above his nose. "You just said someone from the field must have carried the explosives and placed them in the truck."

"I did, but I doubt it was a field worker." Archie bent down and picked up a curved piece of metal smaller than a dime.

"See this?"

Jason nodded.

"If I was a gambling man, which I'm not," Archie chuckled. "I'm putting my money on this coming from a blasting cap. They're regulated as explosives and require a federal explosives license or permit. Obtaining a permit takes several months and involves background checks and thorough vetting. It's unlikely a disgruntled farmer had blasting caps lying around a barn or applied for a permit after your boss got everyone riled up about his new river bill."

Jason opened his mouth to defend Senator Conrad but instead focused on the fresh evidence of a blasting cap.

"Who could have a federal explosives permit and access to the materials to make a bomb in such short order?"

"Companies involved in mining and demolition are the most common holders of those permits. Road construction companies, especially in the West, often have permits. The black market is also an option."

Jason's head snapped up from the crater to Archie. "The black market?"

Archie shrugged. "Unfortunately, it's more common than most citizens would like to believe."

Jason turned back to the crater as Archie crawled out. He followed the FBI agent back to the farm road.

"You know a lot about explosives," Jason noted.

"I better. I spent thirty years in the Critical Incident Response Group of the FBI Counter-IED Section. My team provided all the training and technical support to prevent and respond to criminal use of hazardous devices and explosives."

"Have you always been in the FBI?" Jason asked.

"Yeah, I started right out of college with the CIRG and worked in that section for three decades until I was fifty-three. Some stuff happened in my life, and I needed a change, so two years ago, due to my knowledge of explosives, I joined the Counterterrorism Unit in the National Security Branch, so that's who I'm with today."

Jason's jaw dropped open before he could stop it. He was sure Archie was in his mid to upper sixties.

Archie must have read Jason's expression because his infectious grin vanished.

"I know what you're thinking," Archie said. "It happens all the time."

"You do?" Jason asked.

"You're probably wondering how I'm fifty-five years old when you assumed I was in my upper thirties or lower forties when you first met me. Am I right?"

Jason's voice caught in his throat as he searched for the proper response, but Archie saved him when he burst into a high-pitched cackle.

"I'm just messing with you, Mulder. Everybody thinks I already have one foot in the grave, but I'm still kicking."

Jason's shoulders relaxed, and he let out a sigh of relief. The tension and fear on his face melted away. He liked Archie and hoped that they could collaborate on the case.

"Do you have questions for me?" Archie asked.

"Yeah. If your name is Autry, why do people call you Archie?"

Archie put his hands in his pockets, and his eyes narrowed. "That goes back to when I was a young boy outside Huntsville, Alabama. My little brother couldn't pronounce Autry when he was three or four years old, so he called me Archie, and it stuck. My family and friends have been calling me Archie since grammar school. I hope that's not your only question for me."

"It's not. I was just curious," Jason replied. "Based on what you've seen here, do you think Arizona DPS caught the right guy?"

Archie looked to the sky for a beat and then back to Jason. "I know little about the man they have in custody. Did he own a ranch and a construction company? I'll need more details on the man, but I wouldn't bet this farm right here that Arizona DPS got it right that fast," Archie said as he gestured to the lettuce field beside them. "What interests me more are the blasting caps. The lab can ID the manufacturer, which could lead us to the buyer. It will be a relatively small list, and then we can verify if DPS got the right guy or generate a new list of suspects."

"What if the blasting caps came from the black market?" Jason asked.

Archie focused on the dusty ground for several seconds and then locked eyes with Jason. "If they're from the black market, our jobs just got a lot harder."

Jason's face fell. It was the second reminder in less than a week that his task of protecting the senator had grown far more challenging.

Chapter 8

Tempe, Arizona

Jason veered into the right lane of the seven available lanes with bumper-to-bumper traffic surrounding his truck, all racing over 70 MPH on Interstate 10 through the Phoenix Metro area. He exited the freeway as his sunglasses reflected the undulating skyline of mid and high-rise buildings in Tempe, Arizona. Jason drove across the bridge over Tempe Town Lake and entered the parking garage of a building perched alongside the 225-acre man-made lake carved out of the Sonoran Desert. The lake's shimmering surface projected onto the building's twelve stories of glass, making the structure look like a ship set at sea. The advance scout for Senator Conrad's PSD team arrived long before the rest of the senator's staff to ensure all security protocols were in place before the senator arrived at the location.

The Sustainable Future Alliance aligned more closely with traditional lobbyists than the environmental activist group its name implied. Founder and president Brock Eckhart was born and raised in Stamford, Connecticut, attended Yale University, and moved to Wall Street after accepting an analyst position at a respected investment bank. During his years of researching commodities trading and agricultural real estate, Eckhart felt he could increase his net worth if he made direct investments in farms and ranches throughout the western United States. Months after his thirtieth birthday, Eckhart purchased his first ranch outside St. George, Utah. Over the years, he learned more about investing in farms and ranches in the arid southwest while adding more properties to his portfolio and entrenching himself deeper into the community. Fifteen years after he purchased his first property, Eckhart's investment firm owned eighteen properties totaling 27,000 acres in the Colorado River watershed. His holdings ranged from the Imperial Valley in south central California through Arizona, Utah, and Nevada up to the Colorado border with Wyoming on the western slope of Colorado.

Eckhart's growing scale brought new challenges, so he founded Sustainable Future Alliance as an advocacy organization for fellow ranchers, farmers, landowners, and investors to protect their collective interests and his investments. The alliance also created another income stream for Eckhart, with the dues and donations he received to lobby politicians to curb regulations and pass laws that benefit himself and his stakeholders.

Jason's first stop was the commercial property manager's office. He met with the senior manager, and they reviewed the blueprints of the four-building complex and recent building inspections. The buildings were less than ten years old and constructed with the latest technology for tenant comfort, productivity, and safety. This made Jason's scouting report faster and easier to complete.

Next, Jason visited the security team working at the front desk on the ground floor. He watched every person entering the building scan their badge or check in with the security staff before they could proceed to the elevators. After twenty minutes of observation, Jason met with the director of security to review their security protocols and emergency response plan. He left confident that Conrad's PSD team and building security could keep the senator and his staff safe during the meeting at the SFA office. Jason received a temporary badge and rode the elevator to the tenth floor. He exited when the doors opened, scanned the reception area, and turned back to the elevator as the doors shut.

Shit. I got off on the wrong floor.

"Can I help you?" a young lady asked. She stood behind a desk cut from a slab of Italian marble that made her look tiny.

Jason couldn't answer while his mind tried to absorb the opulence surrounding him. Two massive fish tanks larger than sedans framed the room on the right and left. Each tank contained colorful saltwater sea life, and Jason even noted multiple sharks swimming around the coral inside each tank. His eyes moved from the fish tanks to a Tuscan-style fountain bisecting the reception area, with water cascading over a ring of natural gas-fueled flames on each of the four levels. The SFA entrance felt yanked out of Florence, Italy, and the entire floor reeked of money. The furniture, lighting, and art on the walls conveyed that no expense was spared to make the grandest of first impressions on visitors to the Sustainable Future Alliance.

"Excuse me, can I help you?" the receptionist asked again. Her head tilted to her left, and annoyance replaced the previous pleasantness in her question this time.

"Is this the office for the Sustainable Future Alliance?"

"Yes, sir." She must have also noticed Jason's open mouth and furrowed brow because she expanded her response.

"This is also the office of Eckhart Investments. Brock likes to keep all of his interests under one roof."

Jason nodded at the explanation. He thought it was unusual for a receptionist to call the president of an organization by his first name but acknowledged that not every place was as formal as the staff of a US Senator.

"I'm with Senator Conrad's security detail. We have a meeting with Mr. Eckhart in a couple of hours, and I'm here to pre-screen the office and conference room before the senator and his staff arrive.

"Of course," the receptionist replied. "We have the entire tenth floor, and everything past me requires a key card to enter." She pointed to the doors on both sides of her desk.

"Give me one minute, and I'll show you around."

Jason did a full rotation of the reception area to take it all in while he waited.

"Follow me," the receptionist said with a wave.

Once they were through the door, Jason extended his hand. "I'm Jason Mulder. I'm responsible for advance security and scouting."

The receptionist returned a soft handshake. "I'm Madison, but everyone calls me Maddie. I'm Director of First Impressions, but I get paid like the entry-level job it is."

Jason mustered a fake smile. Now that he was closer, Jason realized Maddie was likely only twenty-three or twenty-four years old.

She led Jason to a conference room with floor-to-ceiling windows overlooking Tempe Town Lake and the northeast quadrant of the Phoenix Metropolitan Area.

"This is where Brock requested the meeting with the senator."

Maddie waved her hand toward the windows as if Jason may not have noticed. "The views from up here are amazing."

Jason nodded. "Mind if I look around?"

"Sure."

Jason circled the mahogany wood table surrounded by genuine leather chairs and peered out the window while Maddie waited in the hallway. Jason was happy to confirm that nobody with a sniper rifle could see into the conference room from the lower buildings next door. On his way out, he stopped at a picture of a man who looked like Eckhart kneeling beside a dead male lion.

"Is this Mr. Eckhart?" Jason asked, pointing to the picture.

Maddie stepped back into the room and smiled. "Oh yes, that is number five for Brock's African Big Five. He bagged the elephant, leopard, rhino, and Cape buffalo with little trouble on previous trips, but Brock said he had to track the lion for six days before taking the kill shot."

"He told you all of this?"

"Oh yes. He was so proud of his accomplishment that he set up a meeting to share all the details of his African trip with all employees. It looked like an amazing trip."

This guy's ego is off the charts.

She turned and exited the conference room, with Jason following close behind. He already disliked Brock Eckhart for his smug attitude and disparaging remarks of Senator Conrad, but the more he learned about the SFA president, the more he expected to meet a total douchebag in a couple of hours.

When Jason arrived in the hallway, his phone buzzed. He saw it was Clay and answered.

"We're ninety minutes out. Is everything ready for the senator?"

"Yes, it's a very secure building and meeting site. I'll meet you by the front door and watch your six when you bring in the senator."

"Roger."

An hour and a half later, Senator Conrad and his staff of five waited in the room for Brock Eckhart to arrive. Another young lady who introduced herself as Brock's assistant leaned into the conference room.

"I apologize for Brock's tardiness. He'll be in when he finishes a crucial phone call."

"Excuse me. I'm sorry I missed your name," Crenshaw chirped.

"It's Brittany," the assistant responded. She flipped her blond hair from one side to the other as if offended Crenshaw didn't recall her name.

"Brittany, please tell Mr. Eckhart that a sitting US Senator is in his conference room, and he is also extremely busy. Perhaps he can call back whomever he's on the phone with now after we leave."

Jason glanced at Clay, and they both flashed nearly imperceptible grins. They were usually on the receiving end of Crenshaw's verbal daggers, and it was enjoyable to see it aimed elsewhere this time. The two members of Conrad's PSD sat at the far end of the conference room table, so nobody saw their silent exchange.

"Yes, ma'am. I'll let him know."

Brittany almost bumped into a man entering the room behind her.

"Oh, here he is."

Brock Eckhart entered the room with a broad but seemingly forced smile.

"I'm sorry to keep you waiting. I was on a call with one of my largest donors, and I'm sure you know all about keeping donors happy," Eckhart's smile widened further. Jason noted that Senator Conrad and Crenshaw did not return the gesture.

"Thank you for inviting us to your lavish office, Mr. Eckhart. My staff said you'd like to discuss some areas where we could find common ground, so pardon my directness, but I'd like to hear what you have in mind," Conrad said.

Eckhart was about the same height as Jason, with a thin but athletic body that made him look taller. He pulled out a chair and sat down. Jason guessed the SFA president was on Yale's lacrosse or rowing team. His New England accent wasn't as strong as it probably used to be, but it was still noticeable. Eckhart exuded an air of privilege and old-money wealth.

"Could we introduce everyone else in the room first? I wasn't expecting such a large team from your side today."

Crenshaw introduced herself and then moved to deputy chief of staff, Jasmine Mitchell, policy adviser Ryan Kimpton, and then Jason and Clay as security team members.

"Two members of your security detail for this meeting? I'm feeling a bit—"

Eckhart paused as if searching for the right word. "Overmatched."

"Well, Mr. Eckhart," Crenshaw interjected. "A sick individual tried to take the Senator's life three days ago, and as you know, not everyone is pleased with his proposed legislation. I hope you'll understand the reason for our heightened diligence."

"Yes, of course. I heard about it on the news. Such a tragedy."

Jason's forearms tightened on the armrest, and his knuckles flashed white with irritation simmering inside him. Eckhart was even more detestable than he'd expected, and Jason's contempt grew at his casual attitude about the car bomb that took the life of a committee staff member.

"Mr. Eckhart, your proposal?" Conrad asked.

Eckhart folded his hands and lowered them onto the slick mahogany table. "Well, if I may be so blunt, your POLAR Act is a disaster. It will hurt family farms in Arizona and all around the country. I represent over two thousand farmers and ranchers that are very influential in their communities, especially on matters at the ballot box."

"I hope I'm not wasting my time here. You've said as much anytime a camera or microphone was in your face the last week asking for a comment on the POLAR Act. What are you proposing?" Conrad barked.

Eckhart shifted his weight in his chair. "You need to eliminate the export tax on high water use forage crops like alfalfa, grant exceptions on the limits to resell our water rights, and remove industries like mining from the water usage limits."

Jason's attention shot to the SFA president at the word he did not expect to hear during the meeting.

Why is an agriculture lobbyist concerned about mining?

Senator Conrad stared back at Eckhart for several seconds before shaking his head. "I can't do that. It's the crux of my bill and the only way to fund the POLAR Act and impose the changes needed to save the Colorado River."

Conrad turned to his staff around the table and then back to Eckhart. "We must make tough choices to guarantee that water is available for agriculture and ranching in the Colorado Basin for the coming generations. My bill is firm but fair because that's the only way to solve a problem that has been neglected for far too many years."

Jason turned his body to get a better look at Eckhart's face. The SFA president's eyes narrowed, and his body stiffened as his demeanor changed. He stood, leaned forward, and placed his palms on the table.

Eckhart set his jaw. "In that case, senator, you've left us no choice. Farmers and ranchers won't take these devastating blows to their way of life sitting down. You and your team better prepare to have one hell of a fight on your hands."

The SFA president stormed out of the conference room, leaving Conrad's staff in stunned silence. Jason leaned closer to Clay and whispered.

"I don't trust this guy. He's definitely up to something."

"I agree. What are you thinking?"

"I will ask the FBI agent on the case to look into him further."

Clay nodded. "Sounds good."

Everyone stood to leave when Eckhart's assistant returned to escort everyone out of the building, but Jason lingered next to the window overlooking the lake.

"I'll be back when the FBI comes to nail your ass to the wall," Jason said to the empty room.

CHAPTER 9

Jason eased off the gas of the SUV and turned sharply into a parking lot when the first gunshots rang out around them. Central and Zee accompanied Jason in the SUV while he selected a parking spot at a shooting range in Prescott, Arizona. The rapid pops of gunfire echoed throughout the barren expanse as Jason opened the insulated door of his SUV, unleashing a flood of thunderous reports from various pistols and rifles. The range nestled in a saddle between towering granite mountains, with proud flags fluttering in the breeze and rows of targets set up in the sprawling desert landscape. It was a popular spot for civilian gun enthusiasts, as well as military and law enforcement members.

Conrad's PSD team took a break from protecting the senator when he met with FBI investigators at the Phoenix field office before returning to Washington. Clay suggested they take advantage of Senator Conrad's six hours in a highly secure building. He drove south to Tucson to collect a past-due payment from his old drone business, while Central, Zee, and Jason headed north to Central Arizona.

Two long metal shade coverings, each two school bus lengths, covered the men and women sending full metal jacket rounds into targets. Jason, Central, and Zee approached a shed-like building bisecting the ranges when a man burst from a side door and marched toward the PSD team. Four strides later, the burly cowboy was within striking distance of Jason, with his arms outstretched.

"Jason Mulder, it's about damn time you came out here to see me," Former Air Force Technical Sergeant Jeff Bentley bellowed. He placed one paw on Jason's left shoulder and secured his right hand in one swift motion.

"Great to see you again, Bentley. I brought a few coworkers from Conrad's security detail to use this fine range."

Jason introduced Zee and Central to Bentley as the range owner guided them to the pistol bays. They found two open lanes and unpacked their weapons. Jason finished loading the 9MM rounds into his second magazine when Bentley asked the question that Jason expected to hear the moment he arrived on the property.

"What the hell is the senator doing with that arctic bill?" Bentley asked.

"You mean the POLAR Act?"

"Yeah, that water bill has ranchers, farmers, and good conservatives all over the area worried they will lose their land. What's next? Our guns?"

Jason shot a glance at Central and Zee. They understood the look and moved out of earshot.

"Look, I'm just part of the security detail, so I don't get involved with the politics, but I can tell you it's not like that. Senator Conrad wants ranchers, farmers, and everyone in the Southwest to have a reliable water supply for the next ten generations. Politicians have kicked the can for too long, and now somebody has to fix problems that should have been addressed decades ago. He's willing to take a few arrows to make the tough decisions that are long overdue."

"Taking arrows is right. No wonder you guys are out here today. I hear a lot of people are pissed off at your senator."

"You've heard that on your range?"

"The guy got elected by conservatives, and now he's turning on us. That's not the playbook I'd recommend if you want to get reelected in Arizona."

A political debate with Bentley was pointless, so Jason swallowed his rebuttal and nodded.

"Central and Zee have to get back to the Valley soon to catch a flight, so we better get started here. I appreciate you opening a few lanes for us on such short notice."

Bentley spit onto the dusty earth beside the concrete platform under the metal shade structure. "Anytime, Mulder."

Jason rejoined Central and Zee at the end of the bay. He removed the SIG Sauer P226 from the case and moved the slide back and forth several times.

"What's that all about? Another disgruntled voter?" Central asked.

"He speaks for a lot more citizens than you'd think. Bentley has a pulse on the people that use this range. Conrad has ruffled a lot of feathers, and we can't underestimate what a disgruntled person may do. We need to prepare for the worst."

The range fell silent as shooters in the other bay checked their targets, so Jason's last sentence sounded like he was shouting. The two other members of Conrad's PSD stared at Jason for several beats until Zee spoke.

"Thanks for ruining my range day, Mulder," Zee joked. "Let's put some lead in those targets."

Central stepped forward in the open lane, raised his pistol, and put 17 rounds center mass in the target fifteen yards down range. The former Navy Seal and combat diver was the PSD team's best shot with a pistol. He could draw his Glock 17 and fire off the entire magazine with deadly precision.

Wisecracks ensued after Zee and Jason discharged their pistols until the slides were locked back.

"Did you mean to shoot both ears?" Central asked Zee.

"At least you prevented him from having any kids in the future," Zee chided Jason.

"It was a gut shot," Jason replied with a wry smile. "In case we need to take someone alive."

They each took turns practicing with different targets and distances to hone their close-range weapons skills. Despite the friendly ribbing and sarcasm among the PSD team, no bad guy would be alive if their targets were real.

The trio moved to the rifle range, each shouldering a Heckler & Koch HK 416. This is where Zee rose to the best shot of the bunch, with Jason a close second. Zee's eight years of experience in the esteemed 75th Ranger Regiment, with thousands of hours on the range in the unrelenting Georgia sun, gave him the edge.

Zee lowered himself into the prone position and put a tight cluster center mass on the target, one hundred and fifty yards down range. The grouping was tight enough to cover with a baseball.

Jason replaced Zee in the open lane. He loaded thirty 5.56 mm rounds into the magazine and fed it into the magazine well. The former pararescueman assumed the prone position and peered through the reflex sight on the HK 416 rifle. The weapon felt like an extension of his body, the weight perfectly balanced in his hands and pressed against his cheek. Jason lined up the center of the target, exhaled slowly, and squeezed the trigger before taking his next breath. After the report, Jason saw the target wiggle and knew he'd hit close to center mass. Jason repeated the process twenty-nine more times until his cluster looked like Zee's, except for two errant bullets striking a shoulder and throat. A softball could cover Jason's cluster.

The trio continued taking turns at the rifle range until the growing shadows alerted Jason to check his watch.

"That was the last round. We need to head back to Phoenix, so you two can catch your flight."

Central packed up, but Zee reloaded. He returned to the prone position and fired a three-round burst down range.

"What are you doing?" Central asked.

"We have time for each of us to shoot one more full magazine."

"If we hit traffic, you may miss your flight," Jason added.

"I'd rather miss my flight than miss a shooter when Senator Conrad needs us to cover him on the worst day of his life."

Central and Jason looked at each other and joined Zee for one more round on the range.

As they pulled out from the parking lot, Jason opened the center console to locate the cord to charge his phone during the drive to Phoenix. He noticed the medallion-like metal object that he had found in Yuma and retrieved it. He flipped it over in his right hand several times and handed it to Central in the front passenger seat.

"What do you make of this?"

Central turned it over and stared at the round silver metal object. He ran his fingers over the raised markings, pressed his fingernail into the depressions, and tried to bend it.

"I'm not sure. Where's it from?"

"I found it in the field in Yuma the day after the bombing. It was about twenty-five feet from the pickup truck that exploded, just outside the area they taped off for evidence. I can't tell if it's related to the bomber."

"It's like an emblem. Maybe it fell off a tractor or something."

"Let me see," Zee said. His open palm appeared from the back seat to take the circular object.

The former Army Ranger was quiet for a half minute and then started talking to himself.

"It's not a contemporary piece and probably not domestic."

Zee flipped the object over and leaned closer to it.

"Is that a flower or the sun? Are those stars or something else?"

Central smacked the console. "You got anything yet, Indiana Jones, or are you stumped too?"

Zee looked up, and his eyes met Jason's through the rearview mirror.

"It's some kind of artifact. It looks like a medallion I saw at the Mayan Museum in Merida, Mexico. Maybe one of the field workers dropped it."

"Maybe," Jason replied. He didn't know what it was, but he didn't think Central or Zee were right. His gut told him it was related to the bomber, but he didn't know how.

He placed the round metal object back in the SUV's center console. Jason drove to Phoenix without talking. His mind was spinning a million possibilities about the Yuma bomber, and none of them led to the current cowboy in custody.

I'll share this with Archie the next time I see him. It may provide us with clues to the real bomber.

CHAPTER 10

La Paz County, Arizona

The hose choked and hissed until a stream of water surged into the parched field fourteen miles northwest of Vicksburg, Arizona. Jassim Al-Rashidi switched on the massive water pump and transferred seven thousand gallons a minute from the irrigation ditch into the thirsty alfalfa field. As the general manager of the 8,400-acre family farm covering a dozen square miles in rural southwest Arizona, he could have someone else perform the tedious task, but he understood the importance of water. After Saudi Arabia banned growing alfalfa in the Kingdom several years earlier due to the excessive amount of water required, Jassim and his younger brother, Amir, relocated to Arizona. Their father and president of the family dairy and horse breeding business purchased the working farm in Arizona and sent his sons to manage it. Jassim vowed to make the farm in unincorporated La Paz County in Arizona a growing and successful business. This was not just because his father spent over ten million dollars on the property but also because the shipment of alfalfa hay back to Saudi Arabia was critical to the survival of the business that had been in the family for six generations. The acquisition, distribution, and management of water for their precious crops were incredibly challenging in a desert during a drought, so Jassim couldn't leave the most critical job on the farm up to anyone.

After verifying the water flow into the property's northeast quarter, Jassim checked in with the maintenance crew. He walked up and down the aisle of mowers, balers, and collection trailers that converted forage in the field into a commercial product suitable to sell locally or ship back to Saudi Arabia.

"Ibrahim, why is that mower still down?" Jassim asked the maintenance manager. Al-Rashidi Farms hired dozens of local workers, but Jassim preferred his managers to originate from his home country.

"The blade broke, and I'm still waiting for a new one to be delivered."

"Didn't you order it last week?"

"Yes, but the manufacturer is backed up with production, so they couldn't ship it until this week."

Jassim took a long, steady breath and released it slowly as if gradually releasing the tension building inside him. "Ibrahim, we have a limited window to cut the alfalfa. Do you think their poor planning is something that should negatively impact our operation?"

Ibrahim wagged his head.

"Then be sure it doesn't. I want to see that mower in the fields again in two days."

Jassim left the building, knowing it would happen. Due to equal parts respect and fear, every staff member on the farm did exactly what Jassim commanded.

Six hours after he started his day, Jassim arrived at the main building in the center of the farm. As usual, Amir was at his desk in the air-conditioned office, his nose inches from the computer monitor and his lunch within reach.

"Amir, how are things looking?"

His younger brother, by four years, looked up. "Another analyst on Wall Street just increased the forecast demand for alfalfa hay by three percent for next year."

Amir looked up at his brother standing beside him with a widening grin and continued. "Prices have already spiked up six percent today."

"Great news, brother. Did you get the shipment cleared and unloaded at the Port of Nagoya in Japan?"

Amir's smile vanished, and his narrow face dropped. "No, it's still hung up with the Port Authority."

Jassim stepped forward until he towered over his brother, nearly half his size. His shadow seemed to weigh heavily on Amir as his body sank deeper into his chair. Their father didn't place Jassim in charge of the Arizona farm due to birth order or his age but rather because he had the experience and the will to deliver results. When he turned eighteen, Jassim joined the Saudi Arabian National Guard, or SANG, the military wing assigned to protect the Royal Saudi Family. Because of his family ties and Najd lineage, he entered as a 2nd lieutenant stationed at SANG headquarters in Riyadh. He spent his first year as a military policeman at the King Khalid Military Academy, two years working in Logistics Command, and his final three years as a liaison to the Fowj tribal battalions. His time with the tribal militia component of the national guard in the eastern region hardened Jassim and taught him the guerrilla warfare skills for which the militia was famous.

Amir served three years in the Royal Saudi Navy as a diver in the Western Fleet operating from the King Faisal Naval Base at Jeddah. They assigned Amir to the Abdul-Aziz patrol boat in the Red Sea as a gunner and maintenance diver. The military had less of an impact on Amir. He exited with the same analytical skills and ideological views as he entered.

"Fix it!" Jassim barked.

Amir looked up and met Jassim's eyes. His younger brother was unafraid to challenge the general manager of Al-Rashidi Farms but also knew his place in the business and pecking order within the family.

"I will," Amir said through gritted teeth.

Jassim turned to leave the office but stopped. "Did the wire transfer from father come through from the last shipment home?"

"Yes, it arrived yesterday. We could use it to buy more horses for Malham," Amir stated. Malham was the location of their family dairy and Arabian horse compound twenty kilometers northwest of the Saudi capital, Riyadh.

"I found a seller with six stallions. They are Egyptian with Al Khamsa bloodlines. They don't come up for sale often, so I want to meet with the seller as soon as possible."

"We don't need more horses. Plus, if they are as pure as you say, they will be very expensive."

"They will not be cheap," Amir agreed. "However, we can get a fair price if we take all six."

"It doesn't matter. The money from the shipment has already been spent," Jassim stated.

Amir jumped to his feet. "What do you mean, spent?"

Jassim's eyes challenged Amir's angry gaze. "Sit down, brother, and I'll tell you."

He knew Amir was upset, but instead of arguing, Jassim moved to his desk next to Amir's workstation and leaned against the edge.

"While you carefully track the price of alfalfa hay, I've been watching the price of farmland around us increase since we moved here five years ago. It's still affordable compared to other areas but is rising fast. I heard on the news that an investment firm out of New York City was buying up large swaths of land along the Colorado River, so I purchased another eight hundred acres of farmland eight miles west of here. The deal closes in three weeks."

"Why more farmland? Did Father buy more horses or cattle that we need to feed?"

"No. I have no intentions of planting a single seed of alfalfa hay on that land," Jassim replied.

"Then why did you spend our entire payment on more farmland?"

"Water."

"Water? We have plenty of groundwater, plus even more available with our rights to the Colorado River that Father secured when he purchased the farm. Why do we need more water?"

A sinister grin melted up on Jassim's face. "We don't, but because of the drought, more farms, ranches, and cities in Arizona and California are looking to secure water or water rights. The river is already low and getting lower, so the farmers and city people will pay a premium for access to water. We can sell our rights to them for three to four times more than we paid and never turn the soil a day in our life."

"Are you sure?" Amir asked.

"Yes, I've been researching this for a long time."

Amir's lips remained straight for several beats and then turned skyward. "That is brilliant, Jassim. Can we buy even more land with water rights?"

"Perhaps, but there is one potential problem. Politicians in Washington, DC, don't like that foreigners like us can legally purchase land with water rights. They are working on laws to prevent this and maybe even levy crushing export taxes on the alfalfa hay we export home and elsewhere."

Amir tilted his head. "That doesn't sound good."

"It's not!" Jassim replied. He stood, and his voice grew louder with each word. "I am not happy that inept politicians want to take away the opportunity to grow our business. We have followed all their rules for the last five years and paid our taxes. Now they want to take it all away from us."

Jassim turned quiet and stared at the blank wall.

"What are we going to do about it, Jassim?"

Fury raged in Jassim's eyes when he turned back to his brother.

"If this farm fails, the family business back home will not survive. Al-Rashidi Farms will never fail on my watch."

CHAPTER 11

Whispering Pines, Arizona

It was late morning when Jason strode through the back door with a bundle of kindling under his arm. He'd spent the better part of the last hour splitting wood and felt good after the intense workout. His mind was clear, and the smell of fresh coffee made him smile.

The simple things, he thought.

When he entered, he saw Shanna sitting next to JJ's highchair. He added two logs to the red embers twinkling in the stove that kept their family room and kitchen at a comfortable seventy degrees. "That should last us a while."

"When do you have to travel again?" Shanna asked.

Jason wiped his brow with the back of his long-sleeve shirt and exhaled loudly. "I'll be home for the next ten days while both chambers are in session in Washington. After that, the campaign will heat up again when they head back to Arizona for the Easter break and remain hot until the elections. We have primary elections, town halls, debates, and you name it in the coming months."

Shanna nodded and turned back to JJ. She placed cut-up pieces of banana and sweet potato on the tray for their six-month-old child.

Jason moved into the kitchen to join his wife and son. "How's your mom doing?"

Shanna stiffened and turned to face Jason. "Okay, I guess. She's still on those dating apps, which makes me nervous. Yesterday, I found out she's been going out with the same guy she met on an app for a few weeks now," Shanna said. A frown replaced her usual positive demeanor. "She told me about some of their dates, and I don't like him. He's very possessive for someone that's only been on four or five dates."

"That's not good. She should cut him loose now before he becomes a bigger problem."

"I agree, but my mom thinks she has everything under control. I wish she'd meet a nice guy for once."

Jason bent over and kissed Shanna on the lips. "Let me know if there is any way I can help."

He turned to his young son and planted a kiss on his forehead. JJ quickly wiped it off with a scowl and shot his father a disapproving stare. His parents laughed in unison, and Jason kissed him again on top of his head.

"I'll kiss you whenever I please," Jason told his son.

JJ seemed to accept defeat and returned his attention to the food before him. Jason straightened and loosened his back. He moved to the window overlooking the backyard.

"I'm going to finish the shed today," Jason said.

"You mean your man cave?"

"I don't need a man cave. I need a place to store my fishing gear and do the woodworking I've been talking about for months."

"Okay, go build your man cave," Shanna said sheepishly.

"Can I take JJ with me?"

"It's still pretty cold outside. You can take him as long as you keep him warm."

Jason secured JJ in his car seat and carried him twenty yards from the back patio to the partially built shed. He gently set his young son onto the far end of the 10 × 12-foot foundation, which was already surrounded by a wood frame and metal roof. The unfinished building looked like a skeleton wearing a top hat.

A stack of precut pine planks was neatly stacked in the middle of the floor, so Jason snagged several and began enclosing his new shed. Ninety minutes later, he finished and stepped back to admire his handiwork. With the light breeze blocked by the new walls, it immediately felt warmer inside, and JJ pulled at his straps.

Jason unzipped his coat and removed his stocking hat. "I can loosen you up, but if your mom sees you crawling around, this will turn into my final resting place instead of our man cave."

Next, Jason installed a door and two windows and built a hasty workbench. "We've been out here awhile, buddy. I think we're done out here today."

JJ's chocolate eyes darted around the room as he took in the new structure where Jason hoped they'd fix and build things together in the future. His son appeared utterly content, and Jason couldn't help but gaze at him as if he were a work of art in a museum.

What are you thinking, JJ?

Jason's love for his son was stronger than he imagined possible when Shanna first announced she was pregnant. The brooding young father pictured deep conversations about important things and not-so-important topics around the workbench or the fire pit in their backyard, just like he had done with his parents.

"Okay, JJ, you talked me into it. We'll stay a little longer while I finish my first woodworking project."

Jason secured his cordless saw and drill along with more wood planks.

"Plug your ears, buddy," Jason warned his son.

He cut all the necessary pieces and saw JJ watching him intently. Jason loved holding his tiny son in his arms but also longed for the future when JJ was big enough to go hiking, hunting, and fishing. He couldn't wait until he could talk to JJ, teach him everything he knew, and learn about what was going on in his son's life.

Why wait? I can have those conversations now.

Jason cleared his throat and shared something weighing heavily on his mind.

"JJ, I don't think the police have the right guy in the Yuma bombing. My concern is that every minute Arizona DPS and the FBI question the farmer in custody, the real bomber is still running loose and may strike again."

Jason stopped to focus on gluing the wood planks and pressing them together with bar clamps. He wiped his hands on an old rag and continued.

"I'm also not sure I should stick with the PSD team for Conrad's campaign or look for a new job closer to home. Protecting the senator is more dangerous now after he announced his new bill. It wouldn't bother me if I were alone, but now I have you and Mom to protect. Plus, I'm away from home more than I thought I would be. Would you like me to be home more often, JJ?"

JJ's alert eyes moved from the woodworking project to his father at the sound of his name. At the sight of his father, a toothless grin formed under the dimples on his cheeks.

Jason screwed in hinges on the pine box and opened the top for JJ to see.

"This is for you to keep, son. It's our Mulder Legacy Box. Once it's done, I will put small but important things into this box that I want to pass on to you."

After dinner, Jason read more articles about the bombing on his laptop while Shanna put JJ to bed. She returned to the family room, sat beside Jason on the couch, and opened a book. She closed the book and placed it on her lap a minute later.

"How is everything at work after the bombing?" Shanna asked.

Jason looked up from his screen and closed his laptop. "It's fine. It's more stressful now, but we have a great team, so it's not too bad."

"I was worried sick about you when I heard about the bombing on the news, but I feel better now knowing that they caught the guy."

Jason opened his mouth to talk but thought better of it.

"What?" Shanna asked.

"Nothing."

"You can tell me. What is it?"

"Really. It's nothing."

Shanna tilted her head until Jason's eyes caught with hers. "You can tell me anything. Come on."

Jason drew a deep breath, holding it for a moment before exhaling. "I don't think they got the right guy."

Her eyebrows pinched together. "You don't?"

"No. Something about the arrest has felt off from the beginning. I met the FBI special agent assigned to the case when I was in Yuma, and he shared some evidence that convinced me it was someone else."

"Does he have another suspect?"

Jason shook his head. "I don't think so. It's just a gut feeling, and right now, his supervisors in Washington are pushing him to get a confession from the guy they have in custody. I'm not sure what to do at this point."

Shanna nodded.

"I was—" Jason started.

"There's something I want to—" Shanna interrupted. "Sorry, I cut you off. What were you going to say?"

"I've been blabbing all night. Tell me what you were going to say."

Shanna moved closer to Jason. "What do you think about me quitting my job so I can spend more time with JJ?"

"Quitting? I thought you liked your job."

"I do, but I hate that JJ spends so much time in daycare. Usually, I drop him off in Payson when they open and pick him up right before they close. That's much more time in daycare than I'd like for JJ. Plus, I'd like to spend more time with him."

Jason rubbed the back of his neck. "What about your income? I'm not sure we can afford everything on what I make."

"Most of my paycheck goes to daycare and gas driving to Show Low, so there's not much left of my check each month after those expenses. I'm basically working to put our kid in daycare, and you're making almost double now than you did at the DEA."

Jason knew Shanna was right, but the timing was terrible. He'd have to take less money to find a full-time job near his home in Whispering Pines, and then money would be tight if Shanna stopped working. He turned to Shanna and bit his lower lip.

"I love the idea of JJ spending less time in daycare and more time with you. I also hate that you commute so far, but I'm concerned that money could get tight. My PSD gig for the senator is only good through the election in seven months."

"Could you stay on Conrad's PSD team after the election?" Shanna asked. Jason could see the longing in her eyes to stay home with their son.

"Maybe. It depends on whether he gets reelected, so I won't know anything until after the election."

Jason leaned back into the couch cushions and stared at the beams on the ceiling.

Shanna kissed Jason and then stood. "I'm heading to bed now. Will you at least consider it?"

Jason nodded. "Yeah, I'll consider it."

He knew it was the best thing for Shanna and JJ, but he wasn't ready to fully commit. The prospect of spending more nights in hotels away from his family while protecting a politician with a target on his back wasn't appealing, but at least the current threat was temporary. Or was it?

CHAPTER 12

Jason slid his elbow out of the open window of his truck as he drove down the sun-bleached highway, descending through the rocky canyon towards the state line between Nevada and Arizona. When he crossed the bridge over the Colorado River, Jason slowed and craned his neck to admire the iconic Hoover Dam taming a sliver of the largest reservoir in the country. The massive sand-colored concrete structure stood in stark contrast to the blue-gray body of water shimmering in the morning sun, waiting behind the dam to resume its journey down the Colorado River to the Sea of Cortez. Jason noticed the white, calcium carbonate bathtub ring around the lake that looked to be over 100 feet below its high water mark in 1985. Each inch of the bright ring emphasized the need for the POLAR Act that Senator Conrad and Congresswoman Duarte pushed passionately at every opportunity and why Jason was en route to Henderson, Nevada.

The Yuma bombing stole the focus from the POLAR Act that Senator Conrad hoped to generate during his speech amid the lettuce and spinach fields. After Yuma, the national conversation turned to border crimes and security and away from protecting the river that had sustained life for tens of millions in the Southwest for centuries. Both bill sponsors agreed to host a joint Conrad and

Duarte fundraising rally in Nevada to get the POLAR Act back in the media's spotlight.

Jason arrived in a parking garage surrounded by a stately line of palm trees outside the Green Valley Ranch Resort Spa and Casino in Henderson. As with all of Senator Conrad's events in Arizona, Jason was the first to arrive to ensure sufficient security measures for the senator and his staff. Unlike the Arizona events, this was Congresswoman Duarte's home turf, so her PSD team took the primary role in securing the event site.

The dramatic contrast from the bright sunlight to the cavernous casino caused Jason to pause and let his eyes adjust. Once his pupils fully expanded, he noted the rich crimson, gold, and black hues accented by classic, modern Mediterranean décor. Jason found Duarte's PSD in the casino security office with a wall of monitors displaying every public inch of the resort property. A stout man with a midnight black beard and a closely cropped haircut extended his hand to Jason. His look and stance screamed ex-special forces.

"I'm Marco Florenzi, head of security for Congresswoman Duarte."

"Jason Mulder with Senator Conrad's security detail."

The two men shook hands and turned in unison to the wall of screens.

"Everything a go for tonight?" Jason asked.

"Yeah," Florenzi replied. "Henderson PD has the perimeter. They'll use their dogs for all loading docks and points of entry. I'll be the eyes in the sky with the cameras all night, and I'll have another guy on the roof for the cocktail hour outside. He'll transition inside when the event moves to the ballroom for the speeches. I want your team to stay close to the principals throughout the night."

"Done," Jason replied. "We'll have our mics on the same frequency as your team to communicate anything we see."

"Perfecto."

The advance security audit went faster than expected, so Jason strolled across the street to an outdoor mall and found a 24-hour sports bar. He chose a seat with a superb view of one of the baseball games between two East Coast rival teams and ordered a plate of beer-battered fish tacos. Jason appeared to watch the game as restaurant patrons arrived and departed the tables around him, but his mind was elsewhere.

Did a simple alfalfa farmer acquire highly regulated blasting caps for the bomb in Yuma? If not him, who then?

Questions streamed through Jason's mind like a ticker on the bottom of a television screen. He couldn't accept that the Arizona State Police had the bomber just because a suspect was in custody. His gut told him they were wrong, and if they had the wrong guy, the real bomber was still out there.

Jason finished his lunch and met Clay, Zee, and Central at the resort to review the security plan. Together, the PSD quartet reviewed the extraction exit from the ballroom, ingress, and egress to the outdoor patio for the cocktail hour and the secure back entrance to the resort for the senator and staff. Jason introduced the team to Florenzi and the rest of Congresswoman Duarte's PSD.

Once the sun dropped behind the Spring Mountains west of the Las Vegas Strip, the first guests arrived in ball gowns and tuxedos for the black-tie event. Clay rented tuxedos for his team to assimilate them with the high-net-worth guests better and not stand out as the security detail. Jason had only worn a tux two other times in his life and appreciated the unique, high-end uniform for the night. He wished his wife Shanna could also be there with him in a ball gown that was too expensive for them to afford. It reminded Jason they hadn't had many special dates since they got married, and he made a mental note to schedule one when he returned home.

Not everyone was as enamored with the tuxedo uniform as Jason. Zee regularly bitched about his attire over their discreet wireless headsets.

"I hate this bow tie. It's choking me. This sucks," Zee complained as guests poured onto the outdoor patio.

Clay met Senator Conrad and his convoy at the back entrance and escorted him to the outdoor patio next to the ballroom. String lights cast a golden glow over the sea of round tables draped in crisp white linens, with grand centerpieces highlighted by flameless three-wick candles flickering like fireflies in the desert. Herds of supporters and donors stood near the fiery-red patio heaters with drinks in their hands as the night air cooled. Jason stood at his post near the ballroom entrance and maintained visual contact with the senator as he made the rounds to shake hands and take pictures with the guests.

The cocktail hour ended, and Jason was happy to move indoors. The early April temps dipped into the low fifties, and he couldn't steal any warmth from the patio heaters. Once inside, Jason took a position in the corner to observe the crowd moving orderly, like cattle, into the ballroom. Once everyone was seated, he radioed Florenzi.

"Mulder, for Florenzi, everything looks good in the ballroom. How's everything else look?"

"Back entrance and hallways are clear. I have two men in the ballroom with you if needed."

"Roger."

Conrad spoke first, covering many of the same talking points Jason had already heard in Yuma. While Jason scanned the crowd for unusual behavior, the senator touched on protecting critical resources like the Colorado River and Lake Mead. Everything looked good until — "Clay, I see Eckhart at the middle table three rows back. He looks ready for the fight he warned us about, so I'll reposition myself closer to him."

"He's on a short leash tonight, so don't take any chances. If he makes one wrong move, take action."

"Who is Eckhart?" Florenzi asked.

"He's an activist who is pissed about the POLAR Act and speaks out regularly against it on TV or to anyone else who will listen," Clay responded.

Conrad's speech ended, and Jason exhaled and let his shoulders relax. He'd kept his eyes locked on Eckhart like a predator tracking prey, and it was physically and mentally taxing. Jason expected Eckhart to act out and was relieved when he didn't have to intervene.

Congresswoman Duarte replaced Conrad on the podium. She waved and pointed to supporters in the audience and started her speech once the applause ended. Jason was less attentive than when Conrad spoke but still maintained a watchful eye on the crowd.

Hopefully, the worst of the storm has passed.

Five minutes into the speech, a loud male voice filled the room.

"You're a liar, and you're killing farming as we know it all over the Southwest!"

Jason turned to the source and saw the SFA president, Brock Eckhart, standing behind his table with his finger pointed at the congresswoman. Eckhart's narrow eyes and fierce intensity were such a departure from what Jason experienced at the SFA office in Tempe that the outburst caught him off guard.

Before Jason took his first step toward Eckhart, an enormous man pushed him aside and marched toward the protestor. The red-haired mammoth member of Duarte's PSD moved with surprising grace toward Eckhart. The man looked six and a half feet tall, with his tux barely containing the muscles in his chest, neck, and shoulders. His square jaw and chiseled face displayed a determined contempt as he closed in on Eckhart. Central approached from the other side of the room, and Jason hoped he'd get there first before Duarte's security guy murdered Eckhart in front of the entire audience.

"Eckhart is yelling at Duarte. Central and one of her guys will have him in a second," Jason relayed to the rest of the team.

Central arrived first, but the ginger giant yanked Eckhart by the arm so hard that he almost pulled him off his feet.

"I'm sorry for the interruption, ladies and gentlemen, but we are going to escort this gentleman to another part of the resort where he'll be a little more comfortable," Congresswoman Duarte said to the audience. A low murmur and a few laughs came from the audience as Eckhart left the ballroom with a member of security on each arm.

"Take him to room 11B next to security. I'll meet you there," Florenzi said.

Jason remained at his post until Duarte's speech ended, and both members of Congress left the ballroom for their vehicles. Per the plan, Jason joined the convoy in the last SUV to the Las Vegas strip.

Ninety minutes after Eckhart's outburst during the fundraiser, the principals were safely in their suites on the top floor of the Paris Hotel, and Jason was out of his tuxedo. He replaced his formal attire with jeans, a long-sleeve T-shirt, and a worn khaki hat with the rescue angel adorned in black ink. Jason's phone chirped with a text message from Clay.

Are you up for a couple of drinks on the strip? Zee and Central are in.

Who's on duty with Conrad?

Duarte's PSD team is on the same floor. Florenzi said he'd cover for us for a few hours.

I'm in.

Meet at Beer Park in 20 minutes.

Beer Park?

It's part of the Paris hotel, right on the strip. It closes in 90 minutes, so let's go.

See you there.

Jason arrived at Beer Park and sat between Clay and Zee at the bar as the crew recounted the Eckhart drama earlier that night. He nodded often, but Jason wasn't paying close attention. He drained his beer until he saw the dancing Bellagio fountain across the street through the bottom of his empty glass. He couldn't get the indignation in Eckhart's face out of his head. Linking the president of the SFA to the bombing seemed more likely after every snide remark, nasty comment, and public outburst.

Was everything we experienced with Eckhart and his staff at the SFA office in Tempe just an act? Was the real Yuma bomber under our noses in the ballroom tonight?

CHAPTER 13

Henderson, Nevada

Natalie Bennett sat up in bed one hour before sunrise and swallowed hard to soothe the sandpaper feeling in her throat. She rose from the bed and tripped over the crumpled sheets and pillows on the carpeted floor that were nearly invisible in the dark bedroom. Natalie stumbled into the bathroom and bumped into the wall, the effects of a third glass of wine from the previous evening still coursing through her veins. The field representative on Congresswoman Duarte's staff celebrated a successful event late into the evening with her fellow staffers from the US Capitol in town.

Natalie, known as "Nat" among her colleagues, was a driven, single woman in her late twenties. Born and raised in Carson City, Nevada, Nat developed an early interest in politics and social issues. After excelling as a student-athlete in high school, Nat earned a bachelor's degree in political science from the University of Nevada in Reno, thirty miles north of her hometown. Her intelligence and hard work led her to the bustling corridors of Capitol Hill in Washington, D.C., as an intern for a congressman from Idaho. She assumed her first full-time position as a legislative assistant during Congresswoman Duarte's second term. During her third term, Nat jumped at the opportunity to take the field representative position back in Henderson, Nevada. It was a lateral move, but Nat missed the eternal sun of the West and the holidays with her family less than an hour away by plane. The self-proclaimed extrovert also loved her new focus on building relationships with constituents in Southern Nevada, attending local events, and gathering feedback on the Representative's performance.

As Nat settled back into bed, hoping to snooze through breakfast and wake up for lunch, a sound from the first floor of her modest townhome shattered the silence. It wasn't the usual settling of the house or the ice maker in the freezer. It was a distinct thud like someone had bumped into a wall, just as she'd done on the way to the bathroom. Her first instinct was to ignore it, but her father's voice, a former Marine, echoed in her mind, urging her to investigate.

"Better to die fighting than to live in fear."

It was, along with other pithy proverbs, a phrase that Mr. Bennett shared with Nat and her three siblings, regardless of whether or not they wanted the unsolicited advice.

Nat sprang to her feet and slid on yoga pants, which were still on the floor from the previous day. Dressed in a long t-shirt and yoga pants, she removed the loaded Glock 19 from her nightstand and slid her cell phone into her waistband. The polymer and steel weapon felt familiar and comfortable in Nat's right palm. As a child, she hunted often with her dad and, more recently, spent hours at the shooting range each month in Alexandria, Virginia, with her Capital Police ex-boyfriend.

The carpet muted Nat's movement toward the stairs, and she stopped to listen for more sounds.

Doubt crept into Nat's thoughts.

Did I really hear something? Was it a person? Should I call 911 and wait up here until the police arrive?

Dread of the potential embarrassment of calling the police for no good reason won out over the fear of someone inside her home trying to harm her.

"I'm sure it's nothing. I'll go check it out so I can go back to sleep," Nat whispered to herself.

Her bare foot touched the second step, and that's when she felt it. The air pressure change caused by the door opening and closing caused the thin brown hair on Nat's arm to stand fully erect. Nat readjusted her grip on the Glock and covered the remaining nine steps in under two seconds.

At the landing at the bottom of the stairs, Nat pushed her back up tight against the wall to make herself small, like she'd heard her ex-boyfriend say many times in Virginia. She allowed one eye to sneak a peek of the dark family room and galley kitchen and retreated to the landing. Nat did not detect any movement or anything out of place.

Maybe I am hearing things.

Nat took a deep breath and checked again. Nothing.

A range of emotions circled inside Nat like a tornado. Nothing on the first level of her two-story townhome indicated another human being was present, but her gut was still sounding the danger alarm. She had to leave the safety of the landing and either confirm everything was okay or confront the danger lurking in her home.

She inhaled deeply, and during the exhale, Nat raised her weapon to the ready position and jumped into the living room. The silhouettes of her couch, coffee table, and chair were visible in the twilight coming through the windows, so she continued into the kitchen like a soldier in the point position. Nat poked her head in and quickly pulled it back in case someone was waiting to shoot her. She saw nothing or anyone, so she led with her pistol and entered the kitchen.

Nat couldn't see the stubby sight post at the end of her Glock in the dark, so she swept the barrel of the pistol across the room, ready to fire. Once Nat knew the room was clear, she flipped on the light and nearly screamed.

The kitchen door was ajar, and Nat was sure that she had locked it, even in her slightly drunk state, when she arrived home. She covered the length of the kitchen in three strides, slammed the door shut, and locked it in one motion.

Nat moved away from the door as if it could attack her, and that's when she noticed an odd smell. Her nose wrinkled with each sniff and tilt of her head to identify the source. A beat later, a faint hiss grew louder than her labored breathing, and Nat saw that all four gas burners on her stove top were on. She tossed the gun on the counter and lunged forward as her hands fumbled with each knob that she usually turned with minimal effort. The need to turn the gas off and remove the threat of an explosion overwhelmed her nervous system, causing her fingers to react slower than expected. Seconds later, Nat turned all four burners off.

She leaned against the counter, and her chest heaved as if she'd sprinted a quarter mile to reach the stove. Her eyes darted around the room, looking for answers to the unexplained open door and gas burners switched to the HI position on her range. Nat's head stopped at her thermostat. This time, certainty prevailed.

I know I never turned on my heat.

Nat considered turning on the air conditioning a few days earlier as temps in the Las Vegas desert reached the high eighties in early April. She hadn't turned on the heat in over a month and knew she wasn't responsible for the word HEAT blinking on her thermostat.

"What the hell is going on?" Nat asked aloud.

But she would never get the answer to her question.

A second later, she heard what sounded like the rumbling of the blower on the other side of the wall, followed by a blinding blue-orange light that suddenly filled her room.

Unable to grasp what was happening, she felt something squeeze around her chest, lifting her off the ground.

As the life drained from her body, she again asked the same question.

What the hell is going on?

Nothing made sense.

And then . . . her world went dark forever.

CHAPTER 14

Las Vegas, Nevada

Jason's eyes blinked open to the sun's rays casting a bright column on the wall through a slit in the curtains. Outside his hotel room, the golden glow of the sun illuminated the top portion of the Eiffel Tower outside the Paris Hotel, overlooking the Las Vegas strip. He checked his phone and let his head fall back into the pillow. It was the latest he'd slept since the Yuma bombing. Jason assumed his subconscious grew more relaxed to sleep past 6:30 a.m. The four beers from the previous night probably didn't hurt either.

He tossed the bed sheet off and placed his bare feet on the carpeted floor of the hotel room when his phone blasted an alarm that sounded like the warning of a nuclear meltdown. It was Clay's custom ringtone, and Jason immediately knew something was wrong.

"What's going on?" Jason answered.

"Get to my room as soon as you can."

Three minutes later, Jason met Clay standing in the open doorway of his hotel room. Clay's room was one door from Senator Conrad's suite on the 34th floor of the Paris Hotel in Las Vegas.

"Is the senator okay?" Jason asked.

Two doors opened further down the hallway before Clay answered. Central and Zee appeared and hurried to Clay's room. Jason noted the same expression of concern when they arrived.

Clay stepped into his room and held the door. "Come in, and I'll brief you."

The four former special forces operators assembled at the end of one of two queen-size beds. Clay ran his fingers through his short, blond hair and exhaled.

"I got a call from Crenshaw a few minutes ago. One of Congresswoman Duarte's staff was killed in an explosion at her townhome in Henderson ninety minutes ago."

"Holy shit!" Zee chirped.

Jason asked, "Was she involved in the POLAR Act? Do they know if it was the same explosives used in Yuma?"

Clay raised both palms toward his team as if pushing back all the questions. "Whoa. Slow down. They haven't got that far in the investigation. Crenshaw and Jasmine are on the way with more details, but no matter what they find, this changes everything for us."

The room fell quiet. It reminded Jason of diving underwater into a watery world of muted and muffled sounds. Everyone understood that the job of protecting the senator just rose to the highest level. 100% effort and attention to detail were no longer enough. Each man had to elevate their game, or more people could die.

A powerful knock on the door sounded like a bang in the silent room. Clay rushed to the door and opened it. Chief of Staff Julia Crenshaw and her deputy assistant, Jasmine Harris, stood in the hall with slumped shoulders and sullen faces.

"Come in. The security team is already here."

"What happened?" Central asked.

"I know this is not the ideal setting for a meeting, but I'd feel better if all of you took a seat," Crenshaw said.

Jason and Zee sat on Clay's messy bed while Central and Jasmine sat on the other one. Clay pulled a chair next to Crenshaw.

Conrad's chief of staff pushed back a black curl from her face and placed it over her ear.

"I got a call from Congresswoman Duarte's chief of staff about twenty minutes ago that Nat Bennett, one of their field reps based here in Henderson, was found dead at her home. The fire department quickly extinguished the small fire, but it was too late for Nat. They pronounced her dead at the scene. The fire department is still investigating, but their initial thought is a natural gas leak in the furnace."

Heads across the room dropped until Zee said what Jason was thinking. "No way. That's too big of a coincidence."

Crenshaw nodded and leaned against the entertainment center next to the TV.

"That's why Duarte's chief of staff contacted me, and I called Clay. It's plausible that it was a natural gas explosion. It happens, but to protect Senator Conrad and the rest of his staff, we have to assume foul play until the completed investigations prove otherwise."

"What now?" Jason asked.

"I've reallocated a portion of the communications budget into the security budget and authorized Clay to beef up local resources on future campaign stops."

"We'll bring in the ATF and their bomb-sniffing K9 units whenever possible," Clay added.

Jason stood and leaned against the entertainment center next to Crenshaw. "Does Senator Conrad know? Is he willing to alter his agenda to help us better protect him?"

He saw Crenshaw glance at Clay before she responded.

"He's unaware of the explosion, but we plan to tell him soon. I wanted all of you to know first."

Crenshaw turned to her deputy. "What's the Senator's first meeting today?"

Jason watched Jasmine scroll through several screens on her phone.

"He has breakfast at 8:30 in the Eiffel Tower restaurant with the head of the Natural Resources division at the Colorado River Commission of Nevada."

"Clay, how can we beef up protection for Senator Conrad until we get our new resources?" Crenshaw asked.

Clay stood, put his hands on his hips, and exhaled.

"I'll see if LVPD can spare another person to help watch this floor. Zee and Central, I need you to work with hotel security and have them review footage from the last three nights to see if anyone suspicious was poking around parts of the hotel or restaurants. Mulder, get with building maintenance and have them audit all their HVAC and water systems for explosives. Crenshaw, I need you to get the senator to clear his schedule of all public appearances until we know more about this recent explosion."

"I'm going over there now, but I don't think he'll do it. He said—"

Crenshaw stopped when her phone chimed. She tapped several keys and looked up.

"That's him. He's coming here."

Moments later, Clay opened the door, and Senator Conrad entered. He strode confidently into the room in a charcoal gray suit with his trademark crimson tie adorned with the West Point crest.

"What's going on?" Senator Conrad asked.

"We have some bad news, sir," Crenshaw started. "A member of Congresswoman Duarte's staff was killed in an explosion at her home a couple of hours ago."

Jason noticed Conrad stiffen at the news. "Wow, I wasn't expecting to hear that. Do you have more specifics about what happened?"

"Not yet. Details are still murky while the fire department is investigating."

"Was it intentional?" Senator Conrad scanned the entire room as if he wanted to hear from everyone.

"It's too early to tell, but after Yuma, we are assuming that it may have been intentional. We were discussing our new safety and security contingencies, and I was going to speak to you about your schedule," Crenshaw said.

"What about it?" Conrad's tone turned from conciliatory to defensive in a flash.

Clay jumped in. "Sir, we can best protect you if we alter certain aspects of your agenda, especially your events today that were shared with the public before we head back to DC. We'd like you—"

"Absolutely not. I'm not changing anything to appease a potential lunatic. Everything on my schedule is there for a reason, and I have one of the best PSDs in the senate, so I expect you to keep me and my staff safe while I conduct important business."

The former Army Officer sounded like he was leading men and women into battle. Although Jason was concerned about his upcoming breakfast in the Eiffel Tower, it was hard not to downplay the threat and follow him on the battlefield.

Should I say something or trust that the Senator knows what's best?

Before Jason could answer his question, Senator Conrad turned to Crenshaw.

"Please get Eva on the phone. I want to express my condolences about her poor staffer before I head to breakfast," Conrad said of his co-sponsor and Nevada congresswoman.

Senator Conrad turned to leave, so Jason stepped forward.

"Excuse me, senator," Jason blurted out. It sounded louder than he hoped to his ears.

Conrad turned toward Jason and tilted his head. "I have a tight schedule today. What is it?"

"Could you at least move your breakfast to another location?"

Jason saw Clay bristle at the question out of the corner of his eye.

"Son, I just said I'm not changing anything for anyone. If you'll excuse me."

"Senator, if a bomber is targeting you, you're a sitting duck in the Eiffel Tower. There is one way up and down from the restaurant, and we cannot evacuate you if you are in danger. I'm not suggesting you cancel the breakfast; just move the venue to another location. Mon Ami Gabi is on the main level, so we have multiple evacuation routes if needed. Plus, the spicy andouille sausage benedict is amazing."

Jason finished with a forced smile to add some levity to the thick tension in the room.

Senator Conrad stared at Jason for several seconds, which felt like minutes, and then nodded. "Spicy andouille sausage benedict sounds amazing."

He turned to Crenshaw. "Please change our reservation to Mon Ami Gabi, and I'll head down right after I talk to the congresswoman."

Clay followed Senator Conrad out of the room and gave Jason a quick fist bump as he passed.

Crenshaw turned to Jason and the remaining PSD members. "On another topic, before I forget, Senator Conrad is accepting the endorsement from the Arizona DPS union at the annual Back the Blue fundraiser in Phoenix next week. He said the event will have plenty of security by DPS, so all of you can take the night off and bring a spouse or significant other to the gala. I need your RSVP in two days if you plan to come."

"Open bar?" Zee asked.

"Only during the cocktail hour."

"Can I bring my six-month-old?" Jason asked.

"I don't see why not," Crenshaw replied. "Remember to let me know if you plan to attend. If you'll excuse me, I have to contact the congresswoman."

Everyone but Jason followed Crenshaw out of the room. He moved to the floor-to-ceiling window overlooking the calm water in the Bellagio Fountain.

Could the Yuma bomber be the same person who killed Duarte's staffer?

Jason considered the evidence Archie had shared in Yuma for the millionth time. He was sure law enforcement had the wrong man and wasn't looking for the real killer.

I'll have to investigate myself to ensure Senator Conrad isn't next to die.

CHAPTER 15

Terracotta-colored earth dotted with catclaw acacia and creosote bushes breezed by Jason's Ford truck as he descended toward Parker, Arizona. His eyes widened at the emerald oasis rising from the desert like a giant light and dark green checkerboard along the Colorado River. It was a welcome respite after driving through a landscape that looked more lunar than earthly for two and a half hours after leaving Las Vegas. Now he knew why some conspiracy theorists claimed the moon landings took place an hour to the south...and people believed them.

Clay, Zee, and Central escorted Senator Conrad and his staff back to Washington, DC so Jason could return home. While the Las Vegas strip was still visible in Jason's rearview mirror, he received a text from Archie. He'd found something new in Yuma and wanted to share it with Jason, so instead of turning southeast toward his home in Whispering Pines, he drove due south.

Jason slowed as he crossed over the Colorado River in Parker. He squinted in disbelief at the narrow stream of water responsible for the 19,300-acre Lake Havasu fifteen miles north and the more massive reservoirs of Lake Mead and Lake Powell further upstream. The cracked earth banks and barren sandbars in the middle of the river were a stark contrast to the class IV rapids he encountered during a guided raft tour through the Grand Canyon years ago.

He pulled into a gas station in Parker, filled up, and strolled inside to buy snacks. He placed a turkey sub sandwich, chili lime potato chips, and a can of half lemonade and half iced tea on the counter.

"Is the river always this low around here?" Jason asked.

The attendant looked over his glasses tucked into a few remaining tufts of gray hair above his ears. His bald head shone in the fluorescent lights as he scanned Jason's items.

"Well, it hasn't always been this bad, but it's gotten worse in the last eight or nine years. Some of the old-timers say it will be completely dry in a decade. Cash or credit?"

"Cash and I need a receipt," Jason said.

The attendant traded Jason a receipt for his cash.

"You think it will get that bad in ten years?"

The man shook his head. "Nah, I don't think so."

Jason nodded at the favorable prognosis.

"I think it will be dry in five years."

The response caused Jason to stare longer than he wanted at the attendant before he returned to his truck and resumed his journey to Yuma. He understood the need for the POLAR Act when Senator Conrad first announced it, but now he had more visual proof that the Colorado River was closer to life support than full capacity.

Five hours after departing the glitz and glamor of Sin City, Jason arrived on the outskirts of the winter lettuce capital of the world. He continued into the town center until he arrived at a contemporary, two-story brick building next to the Yuma International Airport. He parked next to a flagpole with Old Glory waving in the wind, exited his truck, and felt a rumble throughout his body.

Jason turned and looked through the security fence as an F-35B Lightning II, the Marine Corps variant of the Joint Strike Fighter, screamed down the runway and shot into the indigo sky. A smile tugged at his lips as the sleek fighter jet disappeared into the clouds.

"I never get tired of watching them take off," Jason said aloud.

He appreciated the strong military presence in the community. The Marine Corps Air Station, or MCAS, brought over 14,000 personnel and 600 aircraft to Yuma for training each year, making it the busiest air station in the Marine Corps. Not to be outdone, the US Army Yuma Proving Ground, northeast of town, was one of the world's largest military installations and Yuma County's largest civilian employer. Every year, tens of thousands of artillery and missile rounds were fired, 36,000 parachute drops took place, and 4000 air sorties were flown. Jason spent four weeks in Yuma at the Military Freefall School during his first year of PJ training. His smile evaporated at the thought of his involuntary discharge from the Air Force Reserve a half year earlier. He appreciated his current job on the private security detail for Senator Conrad, but it paled in comparison to the physical and mental challenges of being a pararescueman. Jason still thought of his PJ squad and former missions every day.

Jason turned back toward the Yuma FBI satellite office and entered. He signed in with security, and they called Archie. Minutes later, the FBI special agent arrived in the lobby.

"Thanks for coming down here. I have something I want to show you."

Archie escorted Jason through the secure doors and used his badge to call the elevator.

"Where are we going?"

"We're headed to the basement. This week, a forensic chemist and certified explosive specialist from the Phoenix ATF office are working with our bomb technicians downstairs. They found some interesting information on the materials used to make the bomb targeting the senator."

The elevator door opened to a long hallway surrounded by a dozen secure rooms on both sides. Jason noted that every room and its occupants were visible through thick Plexiglass. Archie swiped his card to enter a room down the hall, and Jason followed him inside. Stainless steel countertops lined with an array of precision instruments greeted them while cool fluorescent light illuminated the contents of each table. A muscular man in a black polo shirt stood alongside another man and woman in white lab coats. All three were bent over one table at the far end of the room. It looked as if they were conducting an autopsy, but instead of a human, they focused their attention on a mangled quarter panel of a pickup truck and a tray of dirt.

"I have someone I would like you all to meet," Archie said. He put his arm around Jason and nudged him toward the group.

"This is Jason Mulder. He's part of Senator Conrad's security detail and leads their internal investigation into the bombing. Jason is a former Air Force Pararescueman and DEA Special Agent, so he has the security clearance and bona fides to be in this room."

Jason sensed Archie was trying to quash any pushback to his presence in the room before it started. Archie spun and pointed to the tallest of the three.

"This is Raj Kapoor. He's a certified explosive specialist currently on loan to the Phoenix ATF from the Explosives Research and Development Division, based at the Redstone Arsenal in Huntsville, Alabama. Raj has forgotten more about explosives than I'll ever know."

At six feet, two inches, it was rare that Jason had to look up to make eye contact, but the explosive specialist was at least three inches taller than him. The CES extended his long arm to Jason.

"Nice to meet you."

Next, Archie pointed to a woman who appeared to be in her lower thirties with black hair fashioned in a bob style. "This is Dr. Emilia Betancourt. She's a forensic chemist with the skills and equipment to find a needle in a haystack. Dr. Betancourt is also from the ATF but hails from the Phoenix office."

Jason shook her soft, limp hand. "Pleased to meet you, Jason," she said, barely louder than a whisper.

Lastly, Archie moved next to a man with biceps, deltoids, and pectoral muscles that did not look happy to be contained by his tight black polo shirt. He extended his hand to Jason, and they shook before Archie could introduce them. Jason didn't know his name but knew he had one of the firmest handshakes he'd encountered.

"Now you've met Marcin Dobrowski with our bomb squad. He spent years at Redstone training other bomb techs and is one of the best in the business. We have something we like to tell new people around here about Marcin."

"What's that?"

"If you see him running, try to catch up."

Everyone laughed, and Archie took control of the group as he moved to the table's edge. "Let's bring Mr. Mulder up to speed here. Dr. Betancourt, what materials have you found in the bomb residue?"

She cleared her throat and pointed to the twisted quarter panel. "They used relatively standard materials that we see in agricultural areas. It was mostly ammonium nitrate or traditional fertilizer, readily available to any farmer and rancher in the area. However,

I also found nitromethane and methylammonium nitrate, which may indicate more advanced knowledge of explosives."

Dr. Betancourt backed away from the table. Jason looked around the room, and everyone else seemed to understand what the doctor had just said, but he had no clue.

"I'm familiar with ammonium nitrate and its use as a component in explosives, but I'm not familiar with the other two. What makes them unique and interesting?" Jason asked.

Marcin quickly responded, "Nitromethane is used to make a binary explosive. Neither is explosive by itself, but they pack a powerful punch combined. We see binary explosives most often in commercial applications because they are safer to handle. The bombing wasn't a hastily devised plan. Someone either had advanced knowledge of explosives or ample time to prepare for the senator's speech."

The room drew silent as everyone stared at the components on the table.

"Is that something you'd expect a typical farmer or rancher in the area to know how to do?" Jason asked.

"Not in my experience," Dobrowski replied.

Jason spun to face Archie standing behind him. "I need to see the crater again. Can we check it out now?"

"Wait, I found something else intriguing," Raj chirped.

All eyes turned to the certified explosive specialist with decades of experience examining the aftermath of explosions.

"We found blasting caps and PETN, which suggests they used det cord. The det cord vaporized in the blast, but we found traces of the blasting caps. They were military-grade blasting caps, and we traced them back to a manufacturer in Cologne, Germany."

"Can we track who purchased them in the United States?" Jason asked, his voice indicating hope of a quick resolution.

"Yes, that was easy. Only four US companies purchased blasting caps from the German manufacturer. One in New Hampshire, Nevada, North Carolina, and one in Florida."

The hum of the fluorescent lights overhead was the only sound in the room until Jason finally spoke.

"So we're dealing with an experienced professional who is buying materials on the black market. Am I reading this right?"

It came out as a question, but Jason already knew the answer. He knew he was reading things correctly, and that meant they had the wrong person in custody. Another threat—the real threat—was still out there. They had advanced knowledge of explosives. And soon they'd attempt again to take out the senator.

And anyone else associated with the POLAR Act.

Shit, Jason thought. *Time to get back to work.*

CHAPTER 16

Yuma, Arizona

Jason exited his truck and arrived at the edge of the field before Archie slid onto the dirt path. He gazed across the rows of lettuce until the seasoned FBI agent caught up with him.

"Whatcha thinking?" Archie asked.

"A jaded local farmer learning of the POLAR Act on Sunday and then coordinating an IED attack during a speech to kill a senator three days later makes little sense. Yuma County deputies checked every vehicle coming in, including the suspect in custody. Have you found anything yet that would suggest he's capable of building, transporting, and detonating the bomb, other than extreme dislike for a bill co-sponsored by Senator Conrad?"

Archie shook his head. "Nothing at this time, but my superiors want me to keep looking."

Jason crossed his arms and squinted at the FBI special agent. "Do they understand that each day they try to pin the bombing on the farmer, the real killer could plot more attacks? He may have already hit a member of Congresswomen Duarte's staff with a bomb that looked like a natural gas explosion."

"That's a lot of coulds, mays, and mights. I need more absolutes than that," Archie replied.

"Okay, let's talk this through. We don't believe the bomber sneaked all those materials past the Yuma deputies. Right?"

"Correct."

"So that only leaves one other option." Jason waved his arm across the greenery that stretched for miles in all directions. "The bomber had to come through these fields and plant the bomb while we were all distracted protecting the senator during his speech. You said the bomb had to be at least eighty pounds, so someone had to dress up like a farm worker and lug the bomb, plus all the other gear a worker needs to not stand out to the group. Does our sixty-year-old farmer in custody seem like he could do that?"

"Not really, but you'd be amazed at what someone determined can do."

"Agreed, but I used to train with that kind of weight in a ruck for miles, and it was taxing for me when I was in the best shape of my life. I think we're looking for at least one male that is extremely fit, large or both."

Archie nodded.

"Do you still have the contact info for the field boss working this field during the senator's speech?"

"I do. I've interviewed Mr. Ruiz twice since the incident."

"Let's pay him another visit to see if he noticed anyone on the crew that day that looked like he could carry nearly a hundred pounds of gear miles through the field."

Forty minutes later, Archie and Jason arrived at a lettuce processing facility eight miles from the bomb site. Shadows from the surrounding trees shaded the grounds as the workers ended their twelve-hour shift that started at 5:00 am. Jason followed Archie into an air-conditioned trailer yards away from a truck departing with thousands of pounds of fresh lettuce.

A haggard-looking man with skin that looked worn as an old baseball mitt sat at a table just inside the front door. He rose as Jason followed Archie into the trailer, and that's when Jason recognized the man from the field who helped him select the location for the speech. The field boss looked like he had aged a year for each day since the bombing.

"Mr. Ruiz, please sit," Archie said. "I know you've had a long day, so we won't keep you. My colleague and I have a couple of quick questions for you. Do you have a minute to help us?"

Mr. Ruiz removed his wide-brimmed hat, wiped his forehead with his shirt sleeve, and nodded.

"We met the day before the speech, so you know I work on Senator Conrad's security team. I have a couple of quick questions. First, did you have any new people on your crew on the day of the senator's speech?"

Mr. Ruiz looked up at the ceiling as if trying to picture the crew in his mind, and then he lowered his gaze back to Jason.

"We get new workers all the time, but I don't remember anyone new that day," Mr. Ruiz said.

Jason furrowed his brow. "Okay, what about the day before or the previous week?"

This time, Ruiz looked down at the table until his face popped up and revealed a wide row of teeth.

"Yes, we had three new men start two days before the bomb."

Jason pulled out a chair and sat across from the field boss.

"Great. Can you describe the men?"

"Um. They looked like everyone else with big hats to block the sun, long-sleeve shirts, and scarves over their faces."

"Were they taller or bigger than most of your other workers?" Archie asked.

"They were all a little taller, and one was the biggest man in the field. He was even bigger than him." Mr. Ruiz pointed to Jason and flexed his muscles as if he were a bodybuilder striking a pose.

Archie sat in the remaining chair across from Jason and Mr. Ruiz. "Where are they now?"

"I don't know. They never came back after the bomb."

Archie shook his head and let out a loud sigh. "You never thought to tell me that the last two times I was here?"

Mr. Ruiz shook his head innocently. "You asked if I noticed anyone else in the field or if I saw something suspicious. You never asked about new people on my crew."

Archie rocked from the chair and stood. "Thank you for your time, Mr. Ruiz."

"One last question," Jason said. "Did you notice anything else different about those three men?"

Mr. Ruiz gazed at Jason until his head bobbed up and down. "They were all very quiet. I'm not sure they spoke Spanish, but I heard them talking to each other in English and another language."

"Do you know what the other language was?"

"I'm not sure," Mr. Ruiz answered.

"Can you take a guess? Was it French, German, Arabic, Italian, Russian, Dutch or—"

"It wasn't a Latin language, and I couldn't understand a single word they said unless they spoke in English."

Jason extended his hand and shook with Mr. Ruiz. "Thank you for your time."

The first five miles of the ride back to the FBI satellite office in Yuma were quiet. The white noise from the road was the only sound in the truck cabin.

"Did you drive down from the main field office in Phoenix?" Jason asked.

"Nah, I flew in from DC."

"You work at the FBI Headquarters in the J. Edgar Hoover Building?"

Archie chuckled. "No, I work in the field office on 4th Street."

"Why did they send you out here?"

"Your principal."

Jason nodded. Archie must have felt it needed further explanation, so he continued. "My superiors always send someone from the District of Columbia to oversee crimes committed against sitting members of Congress, no matter where they occur. I'll work closely with all the field offices out here."

"I bet you're looking forward to solving this so you can get back to your family in DC," Jason said.

Jason's attempt to make small talk and get to know Archie better failed. The FBI special agent suddenly became interested in the rows of lettuce outside his window as white noise returned to the cab.

"I don't have a family to go home to."

"Sorry, I didn't know."

More white noise.

"I did it to myself. They're all still alive, but they cut me out of their lives."

Jason sensed a confession was bubbling inside Archie, so he kept his eyes on the road and listened.

"Six years ago, I was living and working in Huntsville, Alabama - my hometown. I was training recruits at the Redstone Armory when I got a call about a credible bomb threat at a local bank. When we pulled up, the bomber was sitting outside the front doors of the bank in a black Toyota Sequoia SUV with hostages in his vehicle."

Archie paused and looked straight ahead. Jason could tell the black Toyota was right before him again.

"Once we established communication, the bomber told us to back off. He said he had to blow up the building to cleanse the bankers responsible for his failed business or some bullshit like that. I couldn't get anything out of the guy on the hostages, but I got him to admit he had four hundred pounds of ANFO in the back of his SUV. Enough to turn the bank into a pile of rubble."

Archie shook his head. "I was standing behind our vehicle with my team about eighty yards from the SUV, and I thought we were progressing with him. Then suddenly, the guy loses it, and the next thing I hear is tires squealing, and all I see is three tons of SUV barreling toward my team. My training kicked in, and I fired all 17 rounds into the SUV."

Archie turned away from Jason and watched the rows of arugula pass by in a green blur.

"I killed the driver and saved my team, but also hit a nine-year-old girl and her mom that the bomber had taken hostage outside the bank. The review board said my shots were justified, but I've never forgiven myself. I started drinking, and I guess I treated my family like shit because my wife left, and my two boys disowned me. A year later, I got clean with some help from the union, but I needed a change, so I joined the Counterterrorism Unit. They're my new family."

Jason pulled into the FBI satellite office near the Yuma airport and parked his truck. "Thanks for letting me know. I would have done the same thing."

Archie spun toward Jason with a pained expression on his face.

"Pray you're never in that position. I've turned out the lights of more than one perp in my life with my service pistol, and I slept just fine, but the muffled screams I hear in my head from that innocent mother and daughter still haunt me every single night. I wouldn't wish that on anyone."

Archie strode toward the building's entrance while Jason felt the emotion telegraphed in his voice. He liked to believe he would do the right thing in a similar situation, but he knew the immense stress and the need for a rapid response to stay alive made every person react differently. Little did Jason know the test of his own response to a similar dilemma waited for him just around the corner.

Chapter 17

Scottsdale, Arizona

Senator Conrad watched the cloudless sky bid farewell to the sun in a brilliant display of oranges, pinks, and purples. The gentle breeze stilled as if it were turned off by the sunlight, taking with it the aroma of mesquite and agave. The senator stood alone on his back patio and swirled the chestnut-colored bourbon in his glass before he drained the last of the liquid.

"That never gets old."

The sliding glass door opened, and his wife, Melinda, emerged on the patio.

"Are you coming in? The guests will arrive soon."

Conrad lifted his arm to view his watch.

"Yeah, I wanted to catch the sunset and the waning moments of silence before the chaos ensues."

"Chaos? This time, it's a small gathering, and most of them are your staff and admirers at the clubhouse."

"They're not admirers. They want something from me, and my campaign hopes they'll donate, so I guess we're using each other tonight."

Conrad walked past Melinda into the dimly lit family room and stopped. "Five hours on the golf course is one thing, but entertaining them until the wee hours of the morning will take every ounce of strength I have in me. Maybe I'll hide out with Stella and Scarlet tonight. By the way, where are the girls?" Conrad asked about his fifteen and thirteen-year-old daughters.

"I told them to stay in the movie room tonight. I gave them money to order a couple of pizzas."

"Now, I'm definitely going to hang out with them."

Melinda playfully slapped her husband of twenty-four years. "Don't you dare leave me alone to entertain your guests."

"But you're so much better at it than me."

The doorbell rang. Melinda and James Conrad looked at each other as if the sound was a surprise.

"You get the door, and I'll pull the appetizers out of the oven."

Conrad opened the door to his chief of staff, Julia Crenshaw, and her deputy, Jasmine Mitchell, by her side. Crenshaw wore stylish wide-legged trousers paired with an off-the-shoulder blouse, while Jasmine arrived in a matcha green knee-length dress with matching sandals. Clay and Jason hurried up the sidewalk to the house to the open front door in their best business casual attire.

Senator Conrad greeted them with a welcoming smile. "Are Zee and Central coming?"

"No. Central and Zee are at a concert in downtown Phoenix," Clay said.

"Sounds fun. Please come in."

The quartet of staffers stepped into the house and lingered near the senator.

Conrad noticed and made a pushing motion toward the family room.

"None of you are on duty tonight, so make yourself at home. I'll come find you after the rest of our guests arrive."

Conrad's staff huddled together like cattle as they moved through the spacious foyer adorned with desert-inspired artwork.

The warm, earthy tones of the walls complemented the rich wooden furnishings in the grand family room, creating an atmosphere that was both luxurious and inviting.

Crenshaw led the rest of the staff onto the senator's outdoor patio, where they encountered breathtaking views of the Sonoran Desert. Towering saguaro cacti stood sentinel in the distance, their silhouettes painted against the dim sapphire hues of the twilight sky. Next to the patio, the senator's rectangular in-ground pool cast shimmering light onto the guests from the underwater LED lights. Majestic palms and strategically placed boulders surrounded the pool area. The gentle sound of water cascading from a travertine stone fountain added a soothing undertone to the serene setting.

Conrad's staff stopped at the far edge of the patio, which overlooked the twinkling lights of Phoenix thirty miles to the south. Senator Conrad walked up behind them, frozen on the edge of his patio. He noticed their eyes were directed past the fourteenth hole of the golf course toward the clubhouse illuminated by string lights, which looked like a medieval Spanish Castle carved in the valley below his home.

"You can close your mouth now, Mulder," Conrad said with a chuckle.

"Sorry, Senator. I've lived in Arizona most of my life and never witnessed a view from a private residence like this."

The senator moved next to his staff and looked out to the horizon.

"Melinda and I are very fortunate. We have families who decided five or six decades ago to buy land, which helped us achieve all this," Conrad said with a wave toward the desert.

"After my grandparents sold their tractor repair business in Germany in the 60s, they moved here with my parents and together bought land. They started with orange and pecan orchards in

Gilbert, then cotton and potato fields in Chandler. I worked on the family farm from when I was old enough to walk until I went to West Point. Melinda's grandparents did the same when they moved from Virginia, but they bought land in Scottsdale. Instead of planting crops, Melinda's father turned that land into commercial properties as new homes stretched farther into the desert. After I retired from the Army, my parents sold all their farmland and orchards to new home builders for millions. Not to be outdone, Melinda's father sold his properties to large out-of-state developers for tens of millions."

Conrad turned toward his staff.

"So what's the moral of those stories?"

Jasmine Mitchell quickly responded. "That family values and hard work can lead to amazing success."

"I think you've been hanging around the campaign copywriters too long," Conrad chuckled. "You're not wrong, but that's not what I was thinking. Anyone else?"

The remaining three staff members shook their heads.

"The moral of the story is to buy land and plant strip malls instead of crops."

Everyone laughed and turned to see five couples, who appeared to be in their early to mid-sixties, following Melinda onto the patio. Senator Conrad tilted his head toward the guests.

"Those are our neighbors and guests for the evening. Melinda and I are considered new money in this area, so we're still outsiders. They're old money from the West Coast, New York, and Texas. I love the house and area up here, but I'm not sure this neighborhood is right for us."

"Why is that?" Crenshaw asked.

"I have teenage daughters, and the oldest, Stella, will be sixteen in a few months. All her high school friends got cars, trucks, and

SUVs from brands like BMW, Audi, and Land Rover for their sweet sixteenth birthdays. Melinda and I told Stella and Scarlett that we'd help them buy their first car, but they'll have to work to cover a portion of the cost and pay for their maintenance and gas. We won't get them clunkers, but they won't have the same emblems on the hood as their friends' vehicles. A sweet deal, in my opinion, and a lot more than I got growing up."

The senator shook his head as his eyebrows pinched above his nose. "Stella told one of her friends about our deal, and her mother read me the riot act when dropping off her daughter. She told me I was out of touch by forcing my children to work for basic needs when I could easily afford to give them more. I smiled politely and shut the door, but it was more evidence that we're the oddballs in our little bubble up here. Melinda and I know the value of land and hard work and still believe in it, and occasionally, that puts us at odds with some of our higher net-worth neighbors."

"Honey, our guests are here," Melinda called out to her husband.

"I have to go, so grab something to eat and drink. Take advantage of a night off."

Conrad sipped his drink slowly with the wealthy men and women as they discussed classic car auctions, five-star ski lodges, and the recent stock performance.

I better not drink too much tonight. I can't get tipsy with this crowd.

With each additional drink, one of the guests grew louder and more obnoxious about his opinions on politics and politicians. Vern Walker, a 72-year-old former resident of Waco, Texas, boasted that he owned eleven thousand head of cattle on his 92,000-acre Goliath Ranch at the peak of his business. Throughout the night, he made multiple passive-aggressive remarks about the POLAR

Act, and Conrad wondered when Vern would consume enough liquid courage to broach the subject directly with him. That moment arrived just before midnight.

"Senator, I have a burr in my saddle that's been nagging at me all night, so I have to come right out and ask you," Vern started. He held his glass steady even as his speech slurred. "Why the hell are you targeting ranchers and farmers with your new bill? Did one of those liberal environmental groups make a large contribution to your campaign or something?"

Senator Conrad acknowledged the question with an amused smirk. Half a decade ago, the question would have spiked his blood pressure, but he'd met a thousand Vern's over the last five years and could respond without a hint of anger.

"Vern, I'm sorry you've received bad information, but I've neither received money for my campaign from environmental groups nor chosen to do anything other than preserve water in the Southwest for future generations. As a new resident of the Grand Canyon State, I thought you'd understand that."

Vern did not seem used to being challenged in public. His face flushed red as his index finger rose to Conrad's chest.

"I heard on the news that you're going to tax alfalfa farmers that grow the feed cattle ranchers depend on to feed their herds. That sounds like you're targeting ranchers to me."

Senator Conrad noticed Clay and Jason approaching with concerned looks on their faces. He raised his hand to stop them.

"Hold on fellas. I've got this."

Clay and Jason stopped as the senator turned his attention back to the angry Texan.

"Okay, Vern. What would you propose we do to solve the water crises in the West? Or do you claim that no crises exist because that may impact your personal agenda?"

Vern stared back at Conrad for several beats before he took another drink and cleared his throat.

"I don't have all the answers, but I know doing the bidding of environmental extremists isn't the answer. I was at Lake Havasu a few months ago, and it didn't look that low to me."

Conrad stared at Vern for a beat, waiting to see if something more compelling would emerge from his lips. When it was clear that was his full rebuttal, Conrad responded.

"Let me be clear, Vern. I'm co-sponsoring a bill to fix a problem that Congress should have addressed decades ago. I'm not putting my personal and political neck on the line for a check to my campaign or to boost my poll numbers. I'm doing it for them."

Conrad pointed to his two daughters with their feet in the pool and Melinda standing over them.

"If we do nothing, the Colorado River will become the world's longest mud puddle, and nobody will want to live or do business in Arizona. I won't let my kids and grandkids deal with an apocalyptic water crisis. That won't be my legacy."

The patio fell silent until Conrad checked his watch.

"It's late, so let's call it a night."

Clay and Jason were the last to exit the patio. Before they entered the house, they both turned to Senator Conrad and raised their glasses. The senator raised his glass with his left hand and made a fist with his right. He was just getting warmed up for the fight ahead.

Chapter 18

Tempe, Arizona

Modern buildings with glass facades and historic brick university structures flanked both sides of Jason's vehicle as he drove deeper into the heart of the Arizona State University campus in Tempe, Arizona. Students walking and rolling on skateboards hurried along the sun-drenched pathways intermittently shaded by stately palm trees. Maroon and gold banners fluttered from lampposts, promoting university achievements and upcoming events.

He arrived at Gammage Auditorium, the location of the Arizona senatorial debate between Conrad and his two challengers for his US Senate seat. Jason parked his truck near the Frank Lloyd Wright-designed circular building with fifty white concrete support columns guarding the glass-walled lobby. The three-thousand-seat multipurpose theater rose like a flamingo pink island among a sea of bleached asphalt.

Jason came to scout the venue, so he walked the perimeter of the property, often stopping to take notes of high-risk corridors to address with the Tempe police department. Once he completed his perimeter assessment, Jason examined the theater's exterior while circling the structure.

Jason turned his attention inside as the sun rose to its peak directly overhead. He met with the facilities management team to review building schematics and their emergency response plan. The sixty-year-old theater had hosted many high-profile plays, political debates, and music acts over its six decades, which made Jason feel more at ease. Although he'd been trained to identify security weaknesses, he was still new to private security. He welcomed the experience of previous security teams with decades of safe and successful events at the theater to ensure everything was covered.

Jason drove six blocks to the Tempe Police Department for a meeting with the sergeant in charge of debate security for the city. After he checked in at the front desk, a short man in his forties wearing his black service uniform arrived and waved for Jason to follow him to his desk.

"I'm Sergeant Campos. Please have a seat."

Jason sat in a plastic chair beside Sergeant Campos' desk at the far end of a sea of busy workstations. It was slightly quieter than the constant buzz of conversations in the center of the room.

"I'm Jason Mulder with Senator Conrad's security team. I've already inspected the Gammage Theater, so I'm interested in learning what you expect for tomorrow's debate."

"We're expecting protests at some point during the debate, some of which could be large," Campos replied.

"Protests?"

"You bet. ASU has the third largest university population in the country here on the Tempe campus, and each candidate is proposing unpopular legislation. We expect students and local activists to show up to the debate to exercise their First Amendment rights."

I wonder how many from SFA will show up?

Jason nodded. "How many protesters are you estimating?"

"I'd guess a thousand. Maybe more. We're putting up concrete barriers and closing down Mill Avenue outside the theater to separate the groups."

Jason jotted down notes and looked up at the sergeant.

"Anything special my team should plan for before or after the debate tomorrow?"

Sergeant Campos leaned back in his chair.

"Keep your head on a swivel and pack some patience, especially after the debate. Hang tight with the senator in a secure area until we inform you that it's clear to transport him from the theater."

The next day, Jason raised one of two cups of coffee to Clay as his boss approached from the Gammage Theater parking lot. He handed the coffee to the PSD head and turned toward the sprawling university campus.

"Are you ready for tonight?" Jason asked.

"I'll be glad when it's over. All the late hours in debate prep has Conrad in a shitty mood, and it's rolling downhill to Crenshaw and the rest of the staff."

Clay sipped his coffee. "Are the ASU campus police and Tempe PD ready for tonight? I heard on the news we may see some protests outside the debate."

"Sergeant Campos over at Tempe PD told me to expect protesters, and they're ready."

"Good."

Jason continued his pre-debate security checks as the media trucks arrived, followed by the other candidates. After snagging a quick gyro for dinner at a local Mediterranean restaurant, Jason returned to the theater as the first audience members arrived. He stood at a distance and observed each person as the contents in their purses and pockets went through metal detectors. A wide smile emerged at the sight of a familiar face.

"Hey Archie, what are you doing here?" Jason asked. He slapped the FBI special agent on the back like an old friend.

"I thought I'd hang out in the back of the audience and see if anyone suspicious catches my eye."

"You think the bomber could show up here tonight?"

"Serial bombers have been caught trying to blend in with concerned citizens to learn more about what the police knew about them. I don't have anything better to do tonight, so why not?"

"I'm glad you are here. I'll find you after the debate to see if you spotted any potential suspects."

The Republican candidate for US Senator stood at a podium to Conrad's left while the Democrat candidate took a position to his right. Jason positioned himself backstage to see the faces of the audience in the first twenty rows illuminated by the bright stage lights. Once the debate started, Jason heard the candidates speaking but ignored what they were saying. He was focused on the audience near the stage, and they all appeared engaged but calm.

An hour into the ninety-minute debate, everything had changed. The candidates started interrupting each other and occasionally shouting over their rivals. The moderator had lost control over the debate, and the audience reacted like feral dogs. The crowd collectively groaned and booed as the candidates attempted to respond, while some individuals yelled insults at the candidates on stage.

Jason felt the change in the audience as it happened. It was like an electric wave of contempt and negativity passed through everyone in the theater.

This debate can't end soon enough.

When Jason thought the night couldn't get worse, Sergeant Campos crackled over the radio.

"Protesters are gathered outside, and it's larger than expected. One group is throwing bottles at another, so security teams keep your candidates inside until I let you know it's clear to move them."

Jason looked across the stage at Clay and saw him shake his head at the radio transmission. He couldn't see Central or Zee in the back, but Jason assumed they'd have the same reaction. Simple tasks like a civil debate among candidates vying for the most stable, continuing body of Congress had become frustratingly difficult and dangerous.

The debate ended, and Clay guided Senator Conrad to a secure dressing room where his chief of staff and her deputy waited for him. Minutes later, Jason, Central, and Zee arrived.

Senator Conrad slammed his fist on a table. "That was a disaster!"

"I thought you did well. Most of the comments I've seen from the media so far have pegged you as the winner," Crenshaw replied.

"I'm not talking about my performance. I'm talking about the debate overall. That moderator lost all control. We'll never participate in another debate where he's the moderator."

The room fell silent, and Jason heard the protesters outside.

"I just want this night to end. Can we go now?" Conrad asked.

"Not yet," Clay replied.

"Why not?"

"The protesters outside are pretty rowdy right now, senator. ASU police and Tempe PD are working to disperse the crowd. They've asked us to hold tight for a few minutes until they give us the all-clear."

Once again, the room grew quiet, and the noise from the streets surrounding the theater seemed to have gotten louder, and the shouts were angrier.

Senator Conrad seemed to calm down ten minutes after his initial outburst. "Do you think it's safe to go now?"

"Tempe PD hasn't told us it's safe to leave, but we'll check. Jason, go outside and see if it looks like the crowd is breaking up."

When Jason left the dressing room, he heard the rhythmic beating of drums and whistle blasts. The roar of the protesters rose and fell with each step, like the crowd had swelled into one growling beast. As Jason drew closer to the metal door in the service entrance, the first muffled directives shouted by law enforcement could be heard.

He pushed the door open and froze.

The scene outside was worse than he'd imagined.

CHAPTER 19

Jason watched as translucent white smoke from tear gas canisters drifted over the crowd while German Shepherd dogs barked incessantly as they assisted their K9 handlers scuffling with protesters. Dozens of protesters were lying face down behind the police line with their hands zip-tied behind their backs. Minutes later, the officers dispersed the large crowd occupying the street into smaller clusters like border collies herding sheep. The smaller groups of protesters moved onto sidewalks and parking lots as they rubbed their eyes and coughed to rid their lungs of tear gas.

Jason returned to the dressing room to find Conrad and his staff watching the media coverage of the clash between protesters and law enforcement on their phones.

"How is it out there?" Clay asked.

"We're going to be in here for a while."

Two hours after the debate ended, Clay received the all-clear message from Sergeant Campos to move the senator to his convoy. Jason was in the rear of the diamond-shaped pattern, shuffling Senator Conrad to his waiting SUV. He remained at the theater while Clay, Central, and Zee joined their principal in the convoy to his hotel.

Jason stood motionless and scanned the trash strewn across the parking lot amid the dwindling police presence. He heard someone approaching from behind and spun around, his hands curled into fists to defend himself.

"Sorry to sneak up on you. I just stopped by to see how you're doing," Archie said with his hands up in surrender.

Jason dropped his hands to his side and let his shoulders relax. "I'm better now that this is all over. I knew protecting a US Senator campaigning for re-election wouldn't be easy, but I never expected it to be this hard."

Archie placed a hand on Jason's shoulder. "I don't think I could do your job. All the candidates on stage seem to have a target on their back."

"Did you see anyone that caught your eye tonight?" Jason asked.

"No, not really. Nobody caught my eye, but once the moderator lost control and the audience started acting up, I think anyone inside that building could be a suspect."

"I know. I couldn't believe how rowdy it got inside."

The two men stood beside each other and stared at the nearly empty parking lot.

"I've had a long day, so I'm taking off now," Jason said.

"Try to get some sleep. You're going to need your rest."

Jason broke right while Archie turned left before he suddenly stopped.

"Mulder, why is that car still in that parking lot?"

Jason returned to Archie's side. "I don't know. All the media, audience members, and theater workers had to park in the garage next door. That lot was for candidates and candidate staff, but I think everyone else is gone."

"I'm going to check it out," Archie said as he stepped into the parking lot.

"I'll go with you."

"You don't have to. Go home and be with your wife and kid."

"I'll head home as soon as we confirm everything is okay."

The duo reached the compact Nissan sedan, and Archie shined the beam of his flashlight inside the car. He stopped scanning to highlight an ID badge next to an energy drink in a cup holder. Jason looked at the item highlighted in the wide circle of light.

"That's Jasmine's badge for the Scottsdale office, so this must be her car," Jason said.

"Who's Jasmine?"

"She's the deputy chief of staff. Crenshaw took her home because she didn't want to drive alone with all the protesters. It's probably okay for her to leave it here tonight and pick it up tomorrow."

Archie nodded but continued scanning the vehicle with his flashlight. "That makes sense, but I will check one more place before we leave."

He dropped onto his haunches and directed his flashlight under the car. He stood up and whistled at one of the Tempe PD officers in riot gear, standing guard on a sidewalk twenty yards away. When the officer looked, Archie yelled out.

"I'm Agent Woods with the FBI. Do you have any bomb-sniffing dogs here?"

The officer shook his head. "I don't think so. Only crowd control."

"What about mirrors to check under vehicles?"

"We had some earlier tonight. Do you want me to radio them and have them bring the mirrors over here?"

"Yes. Tell them to hurry."

The FBI special agent motioned for Jason to move away from the vehicle. "Take several steps back, Mulder, and then take fifty more."

"Did you see something under the car?"

"I'm not sure yet. I'll be sure after the mirrors arrive."

Fifteen minutes later, two Tempe PD officers appeared with a flat mirror on four wheels the size of donuts and a long handle.

"May I?" Archie asked as he reached for the handle.

"Be my guest."

Archie moved the mirror under the car in different areas and let his light reflect onto the sedan's undercarriage. He checked the rear passenger side a second time and dropped the handle.

"I need everyone to move out of this parking lot."

"Is there a bomb under the car? "Jason asked.

The two police officers were gone before Jason finished his question.

"Yes. I can't tell if it's triggered by a timer, cellphone, or car ignition, so it could explode at any time," Archie growled.

"I'll call DPS to send EOD," Jason said. Five minutes later, he returned to the sidewalk next to Archie.

"How long before they get here?" Archie asked.

"They'll send a team as fast as they can."

"It's eleven o'clock at night. They won't be here for hours."

The two men stared at the silver sedan resting at the far edge of the parking lot. Archie stepped forward and looked up at the twelve-story dormitory for Arizona State University students across the street.

"The students in that dorm are in danger if the bomb goes off."

Jason looked up and down at the structure and nodded. "Yeah. I'll have Tempe PD contact the ASU campus police and initiate an evacuation."

"We don't have time," Archie replied. Jason had never heard such a high degree of seriousness in Archie's voice before.

"What should we do then?"

"I'll disable it myself."

"What? EOD is on the way."

"Not soon enough for those kids."

"Archie, we have to wait for the EOD. You don't have the proper protective gear. I'll call EOD back and tell them it's urgent. It's too risky for you to do it," Jason warned.

"What's risky is for us to leave a car bomb next to a college dorm full of students."

Jason glared at the FBI special agent. His heart raced inside his chest, which felt tighter each minute. He had to stop Archie from escalating a potentially catastrophic situation.

"EOD is on the way. They know exactly how to handle a car bomb."

"What do you think I did for the last twenty years? Do you want to second guess your decision for the rest of your life if the bomb goes off before EOD arrives?"

Jason looked down at the pavement and then locked eyes with Archie. "No."

"Do you know how to defuse a homemade bomb or an IED affixed to a vehicle?"

"No."

"Then let me do my damn job," Archie barked.

The look on Archie's face and the tone of his voice informed Jason that the debate was over. The FBI agent removed his jacket and rolled up his sleeves. Jason knew there was no talking him out of it.

"Fine. How can I help?"

"Keep your ass away from this car and get those kids out of the building. I can't guarantee this will work," Archie said as he turned and strode toward the sedan.

Jason relayed the message to evacuate to the Tempe PD while Archie stopped beside the car and pivoted towards the group of law enforcement officers gathered fifty yards away. Using his hands as a makeshift megaphone, he yelled out to them.

"Everyone, move back at least another fifty to sixty yards! If this bomb goes off, the blast will be huge."

CHAPTER 20

Archie Woods wiggled until his head and chest were under the sedan's trunk. He pulled his shirt down to cover his back, exposed to the cold asphalt, as he retrieved his flashlight from his belt. The white beam of light exposed an intricate network of wires extending from a foot-long PVC tube duct-taped to the undercarriage.

That's the detonation device, now let's see what's supposed to go boom.

The FBI agent slid out from under the car, moved to the driver's side door, and pulled on the handle. The dome light appeared inside the car, and Archie leaned inside the vehicle.

Pop.

The trunk disengaged and raised an inch. Archie returned to the rear of the vehicle and opened it. He stood motionless for several beats and then leaned forward with his hands on the lip of the trunk.

"Can you disarm it?" Jason yelled.

Archie nodded and turned toward the onlookers, who seemed to collectively hold their breath. "I think so, but it's bigger than I thought. The device under the car is just the primary. The sticky wicket is the six bags of ammonium nitrate fertilizer in the trunk."

Gasps came from the crowd standing outside the parking lot.

"Are you going to wait for EOD?" Jason asked.

"Too dangerous to wait. If this goes off, it could level all the dorms around this parking lot. Hurry up and get those students out of the buildings."

"Evacuations are underway," a Tempe PD officer stated. "Can you remove the bags of fertilizer from the trunk?"

"It could be booby-trapped, so I don't want to touch it."

"Good point. So what's your plan?" the officer asked.

Archie ran his palm and fingers over the stubble on his cheek. "The fertilizer in the trunk is stable as long as the primary explosive device under the car doesn't explode. I didn't see a time or transmitter to detonate remotely, so it must be an ignition-based trigger. I should be able to remove the primary detonator from the vehicle."

"Should be able?" another officer asked.

"I don't have time to chit-chat about this to make you feel better. You guys need to focus on the evacuations and push everyone back another fifty yards."

Archie's head and torso disappeared back under the car as he clamped the MAGLITE compact flashlight in his mouth. Both hands worked the sedan's chassis like a concert pianist. He paused momentarily and peeked out toward Jason from under the vehicle. He was on the sidewalk outside the theater, pacing back and forth like a tiger in a zoo.

The quick glance caused Archie's pocket knife to slip and slam into the undercarriage, followed by a loud clang. The people watching him collectively jumped at the abrupt metal-on-metal sound.

"Sorry, bout that. My knife slipped," Archie yelled out from under the car.

Ten minutes after sliding under the sedan, Archie emerged with a foot-long piece of PVC pipe covered with gray duct tape and held it chest high. He took careful, cautious steps, like walking on a high wire, until he was in front of the vehicle. A gray work truck bearing the Arizona Department of Public Safety seven-point star logo on the door, towing a metal cylindrical trailer, pulled into the parking lot as Archie gently lowered the bomb to the asphalt.

Three men emerged from the truck and met Archie around the hood of their vehicle. After a minute of discussion and pointing at the sedan, the EOD team from DPS split up. Two men lowered a robot on four wheels with an extending mechanical arm to the parking lot while the third member of the team donned the 120-pound EOD 10 bomb suit. The Kevlar and ceramic plates inside the suit would protect him from a blast from a one-pound block of TNT.

The person in the bomb suit waddled toward the PVC pipe with a hand-held X-ray while the robot followed close behind. Once the EOD tech scanned the explosive, he gave the robot operator a hand signal. A minute later, the robot snared the PVC pipe with its metal fingers and transported it to the trailer with the steel cylinder. The robot lowered the PVC pipe inside, and an EOD tech carefully closed the lid.

Archie returned to the sidewalk through a crowd of Tempe police officers who patted him on the back. "Good work" and "great job" rang out from the officers.

Jason nearly hugged the FBI special agent once he was close. "Are the students safe now?"

Archie turned, scanned the empty twelve-story structure, and nodded. "Yep. They're safe now."

The suddenness of the unexpected car bomb and witnessing Archie successfully disarm it left Jason with a fleeting sensation of relief. It didn't last long. Seething anger swept over Jason as he stomped away from Archie.

"I'm going to kill that son of a bitch. He could have killed Jasmine, you, or any of those students."

Jason paced back and forth on the sidewalk several times until he returned to Archie.

"Eckhart can't get away with this. We should drag him out of his house right now!"

"Whoa, whoa, whoa, Mulder. We don't know that Eckhart had anything to do with this."

"Archie, the guy's office is a mile from here, and he told us in our meeting with him that we'd be in for a fight if Conrad didn't change his bill. He may not have personally planted the bomb, but he surely knows something."

"Mulder. Let it go. We all want the animals behind these bombings locked up, but we have to follow protocol and do it the right way. He'll walk if we go charging into his home or business like the Wild West."

"Somebody is trying to kill my friends and coworkers. I can't just pretend that's not happening."

"I understand, and I'm frustrated too, but your reaction seems over the top, given that the bomb has been defused and everybody is okay. Is something else going on?"

Jason stared back at Archie with a pained expression splashed across his face.

Should I tell him?

The Yuma bombing triggered fresh memories of Josh and Gaby that he thought were forever stored in the depths of his mind. The sting of suddenly losing his high school sweetheart and little brother got less painful over time, but only a little. Jason blamed himself for their deaths even though every person, including Shanna, told him that it wasn't his fault. How could it not be his fault? If he'd known some of the most basic first aid procedures he learned early in Pararescuemen training, he might have saved Gaby, and if he'd gone with Josh into the forest on his biology project, Jason was sure his little brother would still be with him today. The anguish of second-guessing himself with Josh was almost as bad as the void of living without his little brother. Jason thought he'd buried those bones of regret deep inside, but the stress of three bombs aimed at people he knew dug them up like a persistent archaeologist.

Jason opened his mouth to speak but stopped. He didn't just respect Archie as a law enforcement professional but liked spending time with a guy three decades his senior. He sensed that Archie may even understand him after his incident in Huntsville.

Archie put his hands in his pockets and leaned against the Tempe PD cruiser beside him. It was clear Archie would not let Jason off the hook without an answer, so he let some of the steam out that was building up inside him like a pressure cooker.

"I lost two people very close to me, and lately, I've been thinking about them a lot more often. I guess watching you charge under that car to disable another bomb after others have been killed in explosions must have jarred some of the feelings. It won't happen again."

Archie placed one hand on Jason's shoulder and looked him in the eye. "I appreciate you telling me. I know it wasn't easy, but I understand. Don't beat yourself up for being human."

Jason inhaled and nodded. "Okay, now what?"

"Find the bomber. We got lucky this time, but he will kill more people if we don't catch him soon."

CHAPTER 21

Jassim Al-Rashidi tapped his finger on the steering wheel to the beat of his favorite Saudi musician as his truck exited Interstate 10 onto the highway leading to his family farm. After the five-hour drive from Culver City, California, the deserted two-lane road allowed him to stretch his stiff back and neck. Jassim was exhausted from the trip and long drive across the Mojave Desert, but it was a good tired. He had returned to the King Fahad Mosque in the Los Angeles suburb for the first time in months. Jassim had felt the stress weighing heavily on him dissipate like fog in a valley as he laid eyes on the white marble two-story building with its grand dome flanked by double columns. He prayed among his Sunni Muslim brothers in the cavernous prayer room oriented toward Mecca, which was adorned with Arabic calligraphy and mosaics from handmade tiles from Turkey. It allowed him to unwind and relax for the first time in weeks.

Praying in the Mosque built by the late King Fahad was revitalizing, but the time with his former Saudi Arabian National Guard comrades replaced the persistent scowl on his face. A sense of peace coursed through Jassim's veins until he saw the TV news van parked outside the main farm office of Al-Rashidi Farms.

"What is this?" Jassim roared.

He slammed his Chevy truck into park and stalked toward the reporter and cameraman amid a cloud of beige dust. Jassim focused his ire on Amir, standing in the office's open doorway, talking to the female reporter.

"What is going on here?"

Jassim wanted to know the answer, but more importantly, he didn't want Amir to say anything else while the camera was rolling.

The brunette reporter turned to face Jassim. "Hi, I'm Ally Rutledge with Fox in Phoenix."

The scowl returned to Jassim's face as he put his hands on his hips and looked down at the reporter, nearly a foot shorter than him.

"We're here to get your side of the story on all the complaints from neighbors that your farm is using more than your allotment of groundwater and buying surrounding land to hoard Colorado River water rights."

Rutledge turned to her cameraman. "Start rolling."

She raised the microphone in her hand toward Jassim's face.

"None of that is true," Jassim replied curtly.

"That's not what your neighbors with dry wells are telling us. According to La Paz County, Al-Rashidi Farms has purchased 3,200 acres of land with Colorado River water rights that haven't been touched. Do you plan to expand your farming operations to that part of the county or hold those water rights hostage during a drought?"

Jassim slowly calmed down after the shock of the TV reporter and cameraman staking out in his parking lot. Instead of anger, which he was sure the reporter hoped to capture on film, he replied with a radiant grin that had surprised and disarmed verbal attackers for years.

"Everything we do here is completely legal. Al-Rashidi Farms abides by strict rules and regulations from many local, state, and national government agencies. As for the land purchases, yes, we've made some speculative purchases like many other businesses. Al-Rashidi Farms is healthy and growing, so someday we may expand to that land."

The farm's general manager tilted his head and relaxed his shoulders, satisfied with his response.

"You're shipping most of the alfalfa harvested here to Saudi Arabia, correct? What do you say to the people who think you're taking advantage of our water resources because it's illegal to grow forage crops in Saudi Arabia?"

Jassim cleared his throat. "I understand the concern, but my family purchased this land at a fair market price, and we employ a dozen local workers on our farm. We buy all our supplies and equipment from US companies, so we give back far more to this community than we take. The people who disagree don't like to see foreigners succeed in their land. Now, if you'll excuse me, I must return to work."

Jassim waved and walked away with a satisfied smirk. He was proud of himself for controlling his temper and delivering a response to the camera that few could dispute.

"Excuse me, sir, I have one last question," Ms. Rutledge yelled as she followed him.

Jassim continued to strut toward the maintenance building, where he could escape from the pesky reporter.

"Do you have a comment on the POLAR Act bill co-sponsored by Arizona Senator Conrad? It would impose a steep export tax on your alfalfa shipments overseas and add new fees to the excessive amount of groundwater your family farm uses."

The mention of Senator Conrad stopped Jassim in his tracks like he'd hit a brick wall. Hearing the senator's name triggered Jassim every time since he heard of the proposed legislation from Brock Eckhart during an SFA event several months earlier.

Jassim couldn't contain the fury swirling inside him at the thought of the government interfering with his family's business. The fake smile vanished, and cordial replies were dead. He spun around with rage radiating from his body, stopping the reporter from advancing.

"The POLAR Act is an outrage. It's government interference at its worst and an act of war on farms and ranches everywhere," Jassim hissed. "It's an assault on law-abiding businesses, and every voter should fight to see the bill never passes. It could mean the end of my family's business and many others like it. I will fight to ensure that never happens."

Jassim disappeared through the door before any more of his rage escaped into words he may regret.

A minute after he took refuge inside the maintenance building, he looked through the window. Jassim exhaled at the sight of the reporter and cameraman returning to their van. He waited until they were a mile down the road before returning to the main office to speak with his brother.

Amir wasn't at his desk when Jassim arrived. He stood by the window facing the departing TV van when the door opened, and Amir entered.

"What was all that about?" the younger brother asked.

"Reporters trying to drum up a story to feed more red meat to their dogs that watch that filth. I guess Saudis are on the menu this month."

"Did you straighten her out? Will they be back?" Amir asked.

Jassim took a deep breath and exhaled. "I don't know. This new bill by the senator is putting a spotlight on businesses like ours, so it may attract more reporters."

"Brother, we can't let them kill our family business. We need — "

"I am aware of that," Jassim interrupted with thunder in his voice. "I told you I won't let that happen on my watch, and I meant it. We didn't ask for this fight, but we're prepared to fight back with all our might. There is only one remaining question."

"What is it, Jassim?"

"What are you willing to do to win the fight?"

Chapter 22

Gila County, Arizona

Two golden aspen leaves drifted near Jason's fly, which he cast into the babbling stream on Upper Tonto Creek. Crows calling from opposite sides of the creek echoed throughout the shallow canyon. The last remnants of the setting sun filtered through the dense canopy, causing light to dance on the dark body of water. Jason repeated the process every time his artificial mayfly traveled between the sets of rapids thirty yards apart.

Jason had driven to his favorite spring fishing location, an hour from home, after an early dinner with Shanna and JJ. He wanted to get a jump on the trout feeding on the bounty coming downstream in the spring runoff. Jason also needed time in nature to decompress and process everything that had occurred over the previous month.

The sting of Archie's comments in Tempe two days earlier still weighed heavily on Jason's mind.

I can't believe I lost control like that. I need to slow down and focus, or I'll get someone killed.

A splash of water near his fly caused Jason to shift his attention to his rod, but the prize of a brown trout on his hook didn't materialize.

Am I focused on Eckhart because he's an asshole, or does the evidence clearly point to him?

Jason learned basic investigative skills at the DEA academy and during his first year on the job, but he was still a novice and susceptible to letting emotions color the facts. Jason's disdain for the SFA president was still too strong for him to answer honestly, so he compromised with himself.

Keep all my options open until we lock up the real bomber.

After the sun vanished behind the trees, Jason returned to his truck in the twilight. His headlights pierced the cooling evening air and illuminated the pine trees lining Tonto Creek near his parking spot. He had no fish on a stringer, but the expedition was still a success. Jason got his mind right.

An hour later, he pulled up to his house in Whispering Pines, and Shanna burst from the back door onto the patio. His initial thought was that she missed him and couldn't wait to see him again, but panic quickly supplanted that misnomer. He saw the hurt on Shanna's face and realized something was wrong. Jason's mind immediately went to JJ, and his heart skipped a beat as acid roared in his stomach. Images of his family's anguish in the hospital room when he heard about Josh's death flooded his mind.

Jason skidded to a stop and leapt from his truck.

"What's wrong? Is JJ okay?"

"JJ is fine. It's my mom."

Shanna reached for Jason and tightly wrapped her arms around him as she buried her face into his chest. She shook with quiet sobs.

Jason gently peeled her away and ducked several inches until their eyes were level.

"Take a breath and tell me what happened," Jason said. His voice was calming and reassuring.

"My mom was in a car accident with her date. The doctor said she was going to be okay, but they were taking her into surgery to repair a broken leg. She said my mom would need plates and pins, so it was a bad break. The police are also there."

"The police? Why?"

"Her date is getting a DUI. The idiot got smashed before he picked her up for dinner," Shanna said. Her face looked like she had just eaten the most disgusting food on the planet.

Shanna covered her mouth with her hand as more tears rolled down her cheeks. "I feel so bad for my mom. She's had a rough couple of years."

Jason moved beside Shanna and rubbed circles on her back like his mom did for him when he was upset as a little boy. "I know. She deserves better."

Shanna sniffed and turned back toward Jason. "I'm going to Whiteriver Hospital to be there when she gets out of surgery, so keep an ear out for JJ. I just put him in his crib."

"We're going with you."

"Jason, I don't want to wake up JJ, and I don't know how long we'll be there."

Jason retrieved the car seat and returned to Shanna. "We're all going together, and the longer we stand here talking about it, the later we get there. JJ will sleep in the car the whole way."

Shanna rocked JJ in her arms after he woke up in the waiting room. Jason stared at the clock every few minutes as his knee bounced impatiently. Forty-five minutes after they arrived, the surgeon entered the waiting room, so Jason took JJ from his mother.

"Are you Nancy Dosala's daughter?"

"Yes, I am. How is she?"

"The surgery went well. She has a plate and two pins in her femur, along with eight stitches above her eye where she hit her head. Your mom is going to have a long recovery, but with physical therapy, she should make a full recovery."

Shanna exhaled, and her entire body relaxed. "When can I see her?"

"You can see her now, although she may still be sleeping. The nurse will escort you to her room."

Shanna, Jason, and JJ spent the rest of the night and most of the next day with Nancy. Twenty-four hours after Shanna's mom was T-boned by a car a few blocks from home, her doctor discharged her with instructions to rest and start physical therapy in one week. Jason helped his mother-in-law up the three steps to the front door of her house and into her bedroom. The pain medication made her drowsy, and she desperately wanted to sleep in her own bed.

Once Nancy was secure in bed, Shanna made food for JJ and dinner for her and Jason. They shared a meal at the same kitchen table that Shanna had eaten her family dinners at since she was fourteen years old. The only sounds in the room were the clinking of silverware on porcelain plates and the ticking of an old clock above the sink until Shanna abruptly rose from her seat.

"Was that my mom?"

"I didn't hear anything," Jason replied.

"I better go check on her."

Shanna disappeared into the dark hallway and returned a half minute later.

"She's still asleep. I know she's going to be in a lot of pain when she wakes up, so I guess I'm a little on edge."

Jason squeezed her hand and reassured her. "Your mom is going to be okay."

"I know, but I will have to take some time off to help her."

She stared at Jason, and he could tell Shanna was trying to read his reaction to the revelation.

"Absolutely. She will need help for a couple of days."

"She's going to need more than a few days. Kai is living on his own now, and Ethan is at NAU. Nobody else can help her, so now is the best time to quit my job. Her rehab could take months."

Jason put down his fork. "I agree your mom needs you, and you should be here for her. I only request that you don't resign but take the full twelve weeks off through the Family Medical Leave Act. Between your accumulated vacation time and FMLA, we can get closer to the election so that you can get your job back in case Conrad loses. If he loses, I'm unemployed and don't know how long it would take me to find another good-paying job. If that happens, I'd like us to have the backup option of your income."

Shanna stood, leaned toward Jason, and kissed him. "Thank you. FMLA makes sense, so I'll take a few vacation days and then submit my paperwork for unpaid leave."

Jason moved JJ from his highchair to the couch in the TV room. Shanna turned on the TV, and the evening news appeared, but JJ's parents focused on his show of new skills. The little guy bounced up and down as if testing his stubby legs while he held on to the couch. After each bounce session, JJ looked to his parents for approval, which elicited warm smiles, encouraging another round of bouncing.

The flat-screen TV on the wall flashed to a scene in the desert that caught Jason's attention. The long-time investigative reporter for the local Fox affiliate, Ally Rutledge, stood in a dusty parking lot with her microphone aimed at a burly man with long, raven hair and a matching beard that obscured much of his weathered brown complexion. He seemed agitated by her presence. Jason's eyes fell to the headline at the bottom of the screen: Fights Over

`Water Continue in La Paz County`. He snagged the remote control and turned up the volume.

Ms. Rutledge asked the man about pumping excessive amounts of groundwater and buying land near the Colorado River with water rights when Jason learned the offending company was Al-Rashidi Farms. The man seemed to relax before the reporter followed up with a question on the shipment of their alfalfa to their parent company in Saudi Arabia. His reply, followed by a smirk, felt disingenuous, but his answer to the following question turned Jason's stomach sour.

The reporter asked the large man if he had a comment on the POLAR Act, which would tax his alfalfa shipments back to Saudi Arabia. The farm owner's body stiffened, and his expression grew cold. Jason stood and listened carefully to the man's specific words in his comment about the senator's bill. He called the bill an act of war and used more language of battles and fighting in his response.

"It's an assault on law-abiding businesses, and every voter should fight to see the bill never passes. It could mean the end of my family's business and others like it. I'm going to fight to ensure that never happens," the man said with a sneer. He escaped through a door before the reporter could ask any more questions, but his words continued to rattle in Jason's mind.

The man from Al-Rashidi Farms' contempt for the POLAR Act reminded Jason of Brock Eckhart from the SFA, but his words, facial expressions, and body language felt more personal to Jason. He guessed the man truly hated Senator Conrad.

Could the owners of Al-Rashidi Farms have something to do with the bombings?

Jason stood and ran his fingers through his hair.

Could they be willing to kill Conrad if they thought his bill would bankrupt their family business?

Jason turned his attention back to JJ and Shanna after a commercial appeared on TV, but his mind was still on the news story.

That's when it hit him.

A new suspect had emerged.

Chapter 23

FBI Special Agent Woods selected a table in the far corner of the first-floor café of the FBI office in North Phoenix. He sat near the windows with views of the McDowell Mountains, leaned back into his chair, and crossed his legs. The low hum of conversation washed over him as agency employees ordered breakfast and caffeinated drinks to start their day. Archie sipped his coffee and paid no attention to the beeps, hums, and hushed conversations around him as he scrolled through his phone.

After reading emails and several news articles, Archie tapped on the Contacts icon. His thumb guided him effortlessly to a name like his appendage had done hundreds of times before. The scrolling stopped on Gloria Woods. Archie stared at the eleven letters that reminded him of the good woman who had loved him for over three decades. He stared at her picture from the last time they were happy together during a weekend trip to the beach in the Florida panhandle.

We had so many good times, Gloria. Why did it have to end?

Archie continued the daily ritual by looking up both sons on his phone and letting his finger hover over the call button. It would be so easy to call his sons, Terrance and Thomas, with a tap of a finger, but Archie never let himself cross the line. His ex-wife and sons were clear during their last encounter that they no longer wanted

Archie in their lives. Although he was mentally well again and a better person today than he was back then, the bridge had been burned. Archie lost their trust and feared he'd never get it back.

A text notification pulled Archie back to the present. Marisol Bautista, FBI Intelligence Analyst, was ready to meet with him.

The elevator stopped on the third floor, and Archie found Bautista at the end of a hallway with private offices on both sides. Every door was closed, so Archie knocked. A petite woman opened the door. She was barely over five feet tall and wore a navy blazer over a white shirt. Her shoulder-length black hair was pulled into a ponytail.

"Special Agent Woods?"

"In the flesh."

"I'm Marisol Bautista. I got your message and have some new information to share."

"Great. Please call me Archie."

"Have a seat, Archie."

Bautista moved behind her desk and turned one of her three monitors so Archie could see from his seat across the desk.

"I've been digging into the Yuma Bombing suspect, John Barth, and I can't find any information linking him or his farm to the bombing. He's not in debt, his farm has made no unusual purchases, and I have found no sign that he's involved with any radical groups unless you count the Sustainable Future Alliance."

The comment about SFA caused Archie to look from the monitor to Bautista, but he said nothing.

"Sorry, but I couldn't come up with anything else to hold him. I think he's just an old farmer venting his anger about potential policy changes."

Archie nodded. He figured shortly after he landed in Arizona that the Yuma farmer in custody was due more to political reasons than hard evidence linking him to the bombing.

"Did you find anything on that Brock Eckhart character? A colleague insists there is some smoke worth investigating."

"Your colleague may be right."

"Do tell," Archie replied. He leaned back in his seat and turned his full attention to Bautista.

"The first thing that caught my eye is that he likes to play in the gray area regarding his finances. He owns several organizations that mix loans and investments with donations, which raises several red flags, but he has broken no laws that I could detect."

Archie rubbed his chin. "Interesting. Are there any outstanding debts owed to players we should be concerned about?"

"Nothing I've been able to find in our system, but he has a ton of personal debt, so I can't rule out the oldest motive to man. Money."

"Wait," Archie paused. "Is that a Tagalog accent?"

Bautista tilted her head. "How did you know?"

"I spent many months in the Philippines as a consultant on a special project. I loved it."

"Where were you?"

"I was with another three-letter agency, so it's classified, but if you know my history, I think you can put two and two together what I was doing over there."

Bautista smiled. "Got it. My parents moved from the Philippines to Martinez, California, in the East Bay and had my sister and me here in the states. I spoke Tagalog with my parents every day until I went to UC Irvine in Southern California and I never lost the accent."

"Never lose it. It's a beautiful country with amazing people."

"Thank you."

Bautista pointed to her monitor. "I kept digging, and this investment caught my attention. Eight months ago, his firm purchased two lithium mines in Nevada, giving him access to mining supplies and equipment, like blasting caps."

Archie leaned forward. "Really?"

"Blasting caps aren't unusual for mining operations, but purchasing them from Germany is not common. I found four cases of blasting caps on a manifest that came through Baltimore Harbor. The mines must file reports with local agencies for all blasting activities, and neither of his lithium mines has anything on record for the past three months. They could be storing them for future use, but—"

The eyebrow raised over Archie's right eye. "That's one heck of a coincidence."

"Coincidences don't exist in my world."

"Not in mine either," Archie replied. "Time to bring our boy Brock in to get some answers.

"Are you going to bring him in here?" Bautista asked.

"No. I'll have Tempe PD grab him at his office. I need to prepare because I'm getting answers from this joker. One way or another."

CHAPTER 24

Phoenix, Arizona

Archie fell into his rental car with a grunt and drove to his favorite coffee shop near the FBI office. He transported his black coffee to the counter, bisecting the floor-to-ceiling coffee shop windows overlooking the bustling Phoenix traffic, and opened the lid. He shook two sugar packets vigorously before adding them and copious amounts of creamer, turning his raven liquid light brown. Archie moved slower than usual for his routine third cup of Joe. His mind tried to connect all the dots with Eckhart as he mentally practiced his list of questions.

"Are you still using this?" a female voice interrupted Archie's thoughts.

The FBI special agent looked down and noticed that he still had the creamer carafe in his hand. He chuckled, returned the creamer to the counter, and moved to the side. "Sorry about that."

Archie secured the lid on his coffee and checked his watch. It was a quarter after ten and twenty-four hours had passed since he submitted his request to the Tempe PD. He'd hoped they'd bring Brock Eckhart in from his SFA office before lunch. The FBI office in Phoenix was less than a mile from his favorite coffee shop, so he figured he would wait there for the call. The phone buzzed in his pocket, and Archie placed his coffee on the roof of his Toyota sedan. It was the Tempe PD.

"Do you have Eckhart?" Archie asked after he answered.

"Yeah," the lieutenant answered. "He's in the interrogation room, and he's pissed."

"Good."

"You better get here soon if you want to talk to him before his lawyer arrives. I've met her several times, and she's a shark. The good news is that she's based in Cave Creek, so I'm guessing you have about ninety minutes before she arrives."

"I'm a minute away from the Phoenix FBI office. I'm bringing an analyst, so I'll be there in forty-five."

The interrogation room was stark, its fluorescent lights casting shadows across the bare tan walls. FBI Special Agent Woods entered the room, placed a briefcase on the table, slid both hands into his pant pockets, and fixed his gaze on the figure seated at the metal table in the center.

Brock Eckhart reacted to Archie's arrival with the relaxed confidence of an entitled man who'd experienced little accountability in his life for his words or actions.

What a prick.

"Mr. Eckhart, I'm Special Agent Woods from the FBI. Do you understand why you're here?" Archie's folksy southern accent, used to put suspects at ease, was thick and prominent.

Eckhart's lips curled into a smug smile. "I'm afraid I don't, Agent Woods. Would you care to enlighten me?"

Archie paused for effect and then pulled a file from his briefcase. He flipped it onto the table with a soft thud when it hit the surface.

"You've been very outspoken about a bill in Congress that may hurt some of your ranch and farm investments, and now we've evidence linking your blasting cap purchases in Nevada to recent bombings. Care to explain?"

Eckhart leaned back in his chair, seemingly unfazed by the accusation. "I'm a businessman, Agent Woods. I fight my battles in boardrooms, not with bombs. I have no need for violence."

Archie arched an eyebrow. "Can your German supplier of blasting caps make the same claim? Our BND counterparts in Berlin tell us they're under investigation for selling to extremist groups in Yemen."

"Pure coincidence, I assure you," Eckhart sighed. "We run a legal and legitimate business in our Nevada mines. You can check with the Nevada Division of Minerals since inspectors are crawling all over our operations. I can share the best contact at their Carson City office to get you a quick response."

"I'm not interested in your worker safety and dust abatement reports," Archie replied. He walked to the mirrored wall obscuring several members of Tempe PD and FBI Analyst Marisol Bautista and leaned against the reflective glass. "I would, however, like for you to share why you purchased blasting caps from an obscure provider in Germany over the plethora of suppliers in the good, ole US of A?"

"So let me get this straight," Eckhart started. "I'm a suspect in bombings targeting a US Senator because I like German engineering?" He held up his wrist. "Does my German watch make me a suspect in a bank robbery, or does my German car put me in a lineup for a hit and run?"

The interrogation was not going in the direction Archie had hoped, and he began to doubt Eckhart's involvement. He looked into the glass and asked Eckhart another question. "Where were you the day of the Yuma bombing?"

The door burst open, and a blond blur darted past Archie. "Don't answer that!"

Eckhart's attorney slammed her briefcase on the table and shot daggers at Archie. "Special Agent Woods," she said slowly. "We are done answering any of your questions. If you have credible evidence linking my client to any criminal activity, which you don't, I suggest you proceed with charges or escort Mr. Eckhart back to his place of business."

"I'll leave you two alone to talk," Archie said. "I'll be back in five minutes."

Archie found Bautista standing by the two-way mirror, observing the conversation between Eckhart and his attorney.

"We can't hold him," the FBI analyst stated.

"I know. The guy's a certified asshole and mixed bag of emotions based on his outburst in Henderson, but I don't think he's behind any of the bombings."

"I agree. The blasting caps were a link but not evidence of his involvement. We'll keep looking."

Archie listened to Bautista, but his focus was directed at the SFA president. The attorney gestured wildly with her arms while Eckhart relaxed in his metal chair, seemingly without a care in the world.

"You going to cut him loose now?" Bautista asked.

Archie checked his watch. "Want to grab lunch?"

"What about Eckhart? We can't just leave him in there."

"Are you sure?"

Bautista put her hands on her hips and tilted her head until her black locks covered one eye. "I'm sure. You have to let him go."

"Okay, if you insist."

Archie returned to the interrogation room. "You're free to leave."

Eckhart sprang to his feet.

"Stay in town," Archie warned. "We may have more questions for you."

The SFA president shook his head and sighed. "You guys are never going to find the bombers, are you?"

"Why do you say that? Was it one of your SFA members? Do you know who did it?"

"Brock, don't say anything else," his attorney warned.

"That's okay. I want to answer this question," Eckart hissed defiantly. "No, I don't know who did it, but I am sure you're wasting your time targeting someone like me just because I own a company with access to blasting caps."

"Oh, wise one. Please enlighten me on how to find the real bombers then."

Eckhart sneered. "Motive. Have you asked yourself who will lose the most if the POLAR Act is passed?" Eckart stepped closer to Archie. "Find the biggest losers, and you'll probably find your bombers."

"We're already working on that. What makes you think that will lead to the real bombers?"

Eckhart moved so close to Archie that he could smell his expensive but offensive cologne. "Agent Woods, I'm a predator, and I smell fear. Those bombs have fear written all over them. In fact, I'm sensing fear coming from you."

Archie puffed his chest, clenched his jaw, and stepped closer to Eckhart. "You think so?"

"Yes, sir. You're afraid I'm right."

Eckhart's attorney pulled on his arm until he turned and left the room with her.

Archie turned to the mirror, knowing Bautista had watched the whole thing. "Let's get back to the office. I have to let Mulder know that Eckhart is not our guy."

"Sounds good. I'll narrow down the list of new suspects as soon as we get back," Bautista added.

Archie nodded. "Until then, Senator Conrad and everyone on his staff are still in grave danger."

CHAPTER 25

Whispering Pines

A maroon tie, the same color as his PJ beret, tucked neatly under the three buttons on Jason's charcoal gray suit jacket. He ran his hands over the smooth fabric, a subtle grin appearing as he admired how his new suit fit him perfectly. His reflection beamed back at him as Jason stood tall in front of the full-length mirror in his bedroom.

Shanna yelled from the closet. "Can you get JJ dressed? I'm running a little behind."

"Sure. What do you want him to wear?" Jason yelled back.

"I put out a onesie that looks like a tuxedo. It's on the bed next to him."

Jason dressed his son and took a step back. "Look at you, little man. You look like a million bucks."

JJ pulled at his faux tux for a minute but then appeared to concede that it was his attire for the evening. Jason strapped JJ into a bouncy seat and turned on one of his favorite videos on his tablet so they could finish getting ready. Shanna stepped out as he passed the walk-in closet, and Jason stopped in his tracks. His lips curled up to his wide eyes at seeing his wife's beauty. She wore a full-length taupe dress that flowed gracefully over every curve. The dress perfectly complemented her high-heeled shoes of the same color, creating a stunning and cohesive look. The tan hues in the dress brought out the rich ebony notes in her hair, which cascaded down her shoulders in soft waves. He couldn't help but stop and admire his stunning wife.

"Wow."

Shanna's cheeks turned as red as her lips.

They stared as if they were seeing each other for the first time until Shanna put a hand on her hip. "Close your mouth, Honey. You don't want to drool on your fancy suit."

Jason pulled her into his arms and kissed her. "I'll drool all I want when I have the most beautiful woman on my arm tonight."

"Thank you," Shanna beamed.

The Mulders arrived at the Chateau Luxe event center in Phoenix after the sun retreated behind the western mountain peaks. Jason removed JJ from the rear cab after he parked near the exit for a quick getaway for the two-hour drive back north to Whispering Pines after the event ended. The trio passed through security provided by the Arizona Department of Public Safety and continued through the building until they reached the back terrace. The polished travertine tiled expanse provided a 270-degree view of the North Phoenix valley as the white stone glistened under the string of lights.

Jason looked around for other members of the PSD team. He spotted Central on the opposite end of the terrace, so he grabbed Shanna's hand and led her to the other side.

Central noticed Jason approaching and extended his hand. "Hey, Jason. I'm glad to see someone else here. This is my wife, Kim."

Jason raised JJ in his car seat to present him like a prized sculpture and introduced his family as Clay and Zee approached with their dates that had flown in from back East. Handshakes, hugs, introductions, and compliments by the ladies on their flowing dresses and sparkling jewelry followed until they were summoned to move inside. Conrad's PSD team and their dates moved into the ballroom to their assigned table in the back.

To celebrate the Arizona DPS event, the PSD team table was set with crisp white linens and a centerpiece of a dozen mini American flags with the Thin Blue Line. Stately chandeliers cast a soft white glow over the four PSD members and their dates as speakers stood at the podium and sang their praises of Senator Conrad.

While the senator took his turn at the podium to accept the endorsement, Jason inconspicuously scanned the faces of his teammates and their dates. The lights reflecting from their eyes and satisfied grins warmed Jason's heart. He liked everyone on Conrad's staff and enjoyed working with his PSD mates.

Could this be my new long-term career? I hope it lasts longer than a year.

After the event, the PSD team and their significant others stayed behind to ensure Senator Conrad made it safely to his secure limousine. They all stood under the port cochere as Senator Conrad followed the director of the Arizona Department of Public Safety into the back of the limousine under the watchful eye of his PSD. None of them had to be there, but Jason figured they all felt the same as him. He'd sleep much better tonight knowing the senator made it to the secure vehicle that would transport him to his hotel in Scottsdale.

It took five minutes for the quartet of former special forces operators and their dates to say goodbye and goodnight. Clay and his date broke away first into the parking lot.

"Is everyone okay to drive?" Clay asked.

"I'm good, boss. Only one drink," Central responded.

"Same," Jason followed.

All the eyes turned to Zee.

"What?"

"Give your keys to your date, Zee," Clay ordered.

His date smiled and put out her hand.

"She drives like a maniac. I'm not sure who's worse. Me after five beers or her sober."

Her open hand turned into a fist and pounded it into Zee's arm just below his shoulder. "I'm not that bad."

He raised his hands in surrender. "Fine."

Her open palm returned, and Zee placed the keys in her hand.

"If she kills me, it's all y'all's fault."

After the laughter died down, Clay turned back toward the parking lot. "Drive safe, PSD team. I'll see you on Monday."

Jason secured Shanna's hand with his left and held JJ's car seat with his right. They strolled to the edge of the parking lot near the exit. Jason opened the door for Shanna and helped her in. Jason started to shut the door but stopped. "Wait, I forgot something."

"What?" Shanna asked. She looked around the cab and back at her husband.

Jason leaned in and kissed her. "I've been waiting to do that all night."

Shanna's white teeth appeared through her ruby-red lips. "Let's get home."

Jason shut her door and strapped JJ safely in his seat in the rear cab. He jogged around the back of his truck when his phone dinged. Jason considered ignoring the text, but his curiosity got the best of him. He stood inside his open truck door and read the text. It was from Archie.

```
We had to let Eckhart walk. Yes, he's an
asshole, but I don't think he did it, so
```

```
that means the real bomber is still out
there. Be careful!
```

Jason scanned the parking lot and saw a line of cars passing a half dozen Phoenix police officers standing guard at the exit. He slid into his truck and reread the text.

If Eckhart wasn't involved, who could it be?

It was the first time Jason had thought about the bombers all night. It was a freedom he hadn't experienced in weeks, and it made his evening with Shanna and JJ the best they'd had together since he joined Conrad's PSD team. He put his foot on the brake but stopped before pushing the button to start the vehicle.

Why did Archie say to be careful? Does he know something?

Jason rolled down his window.

"Is everything okay?" Shanna asked.

Jason did not answer. He whistled to get the attention of a K9 officer from the Phoenix Police Department, who had checked all the vehicles entering earlier that evening. The officer noticed Jason and walked toward his truck with his tawny Belgian Malinois.

"What's up, man?"

"Can you do a quick sweep of my truck before we take off?"

The officer's eyebrows pinched above his nose.

"I'm part of the security detail for Senator Conrad. Just being extra cautious after Yuma."

The officer nodded. "Yeah, no problem. Give me a minute, and I'll let you know when it's clear."

Jason gripped the steering wheel, and his knuckles slowly turned white. He watched the K9 team start at his front grill and then pass the driver's side of the truck, the dog's black nose bobbing up and down along the vehicle like a ship in a storm. Jason watched the duo go behind the bed of his truck in his side mirror. Jason relaxed his grip on the steering wheel when they reappeared in the passenger door mirror.

JJ cried out from the backseat. He was probably wondering why he was detained in the back while the truck remained parked.

"We should go. He's going to start getting fussy," Shanna warned.

"A few more seconds, and we'll be on our way."

He saw it in the mirror before he heard the bark. The Belgian Malinois circled and darted toward the bed of his truck between the cab and the rear passenger tire.

At first, it was a single, high-pitched yelp, but then the K9 continued barking, which Jason thought sounded like panic. Jason didn't have time to question the alarm.

"Get out and get as far from the truck as possible," Jason yelled to Shanna. He unbuckled her seatbelt at the same time and watched her burst from the truck. "I'm getting JJ!"

The former PJ was so hurried that he fumbled to press the button to dislodge JJ's car seat. He trained for thousands of hours to remain calm under fire, but this was different. The two most important people in his world were in imminent danger, and everything felt different. He moved fast with rushed movements that required focus at a measured pace. Jason didn't know if the explosives detected by the dog were on a timer, remote detonator, or set to explode when he started his truck.

Finally, the car seat popped up, and Jason snagged the handle. He pulled his son from the vehicle as fast as he could. Once he was safely away from his truck, he looked around for his wife—a bolt of fear shot from his head to his gut. For a second, Jason thought he might throw up.

"Shanna?" Jason yelled.

"Over here."

Jason ran to her side and pulled her close.

"What's going on?" Shanna asked.

"The K9 got a hit."

"For drugs?"

Jason didn't want to alarm Shanna but couldn't lie to her. "No. That dog detects explosives."

"A bomb?"

"Maybe. Just stay back here, and I'll find out what's going on."

Jason kept a safe distance from his truck as he approached the Phoenix police and found the sergeant.

"That's my truck. What's going on?"

"The K9 team found explosives near the rear quarter panel. EOD is en route, so they should be here soon."

Jason turned toward his truck.

"You should take your family back inside and call for a ride or something. That truck's not going anywhere tonight."

He shared the update with Shanna and escorted her inside. "Find a hotel nearby and call an Uber. We'll have to stay in the Valley tonight until this is sorted out."

Jason returned to the parking lot as the same EOD team that disarmed the bomb in Tempe arrived on the scene.

What is going on? First, they target Jasmine, and now my family.

He watched them suit up, launch the robot, and remove the explosive from his truck, just like they did in Tempe. It felt like a bad dream. He still couldn't believe a bomb was only a few feet from his family, and he was seconds from starting his truck.

Shanna exited the banquet center lobby. "I got us a hotel, and the Uber is almost here."

"Okay. Give me one minute."

Jason approached the EOD tech as he removed his protective gear. "I don't know if you remember me, but I was at the bomb you diffused in Tempe last week."

The man stopped and looked at Jason. "You look familiar. How can I help you?"

"We found out in Tempe that the bomb was set to detonate upon ignition. What about this one?"

"It looked like the same setup as last week but with more explosives. Whoever owns that truck is lucky they didn't start it."

Jason swallowed hard. "Why is that?"

"Because if they started the truck, we'd be standing in a crater right now, hoping to identify their remains with dental records."

Chapter 26

Jason lay awake as streaks of light raced across the walls and ceiling as cars passed outside his hotel room. He was grateful for the white noise of the air conditioner, which muffled JJ's gentle snoring and the sound of doors occasionally slamming down the hallway. It was an hour before sunrise, and Jason was sure he hadn't slept all night. Hundreds of scenarios passed through his head, but none led to satisfying answers, especially the question that most bothered him.

How did they find my truck and place a bomb under it?

Jason grabbed his cell phone from the nightstand and rolled over so the light wouldn't bother Shanna or JJ, who slept together in the other bed. He scrolled through texts and emails from the PSD team, Crenshaw, and even Senator Conrad, expressing their gratitude that Jason and his family were okay after the near brush with death. He read the messages until he dropped the phone onto his chest and stared into the darkness.

His head hurt from stress and fatigue, so he closed his eyes tight, hoping sleep would come. Instead, his phone buzzed. It was a text from Archie.

`I just heard what happened last night. Text me when you're up.`

Jason quickly responded. `Why are you awake so early?`

I couldn't sleep. Do you want to meet for coffee? I can pick you up and drive you to your truck when we finish.

Jason forgot he'd left his truck behind and accepted Archie's offer.

Archie picked up Jason in front of the hotel, and they drove to a coffee shop near the FBI office in North Phoenix.

"I found this place when I first arrived in Phoenix," Archie said. "It has great Costa Rican coffee and is not as busy as some other places."

Once they both had hot cups of steaming coffee in front of them, neither man spoke. Nearing the half-empty mark of his cup, Archie finally spoke.

"How's your family holding up through all this?"

Jason shook his head and let out a loud sigh. "Shanna is tough as nails, so she'll probably be fine. Fortunately, JJ has no clue what's going on. The change in routine is messing him up more than anything."

"What about you?"

"I can't believe somebody is twisted enough to target my wife and son because I'm on the payroll of a senator who sponsored a bill that they don't like. It's messed up, and I can't get my mind around it. Are you sure Eckhart isn't behind this?"

Archie sipped his coffee and scanned the patrons standing in line nearby. He leaned forward and lowered his voice. "I hate that guy as much as you do, but he didn't put a bomb under the deputy chief of staff's car or your truck. Our first two suspects didn't pan out, so it's time to look elsewhere."

"Have you learned anything new about Jasmine's car or my —"

Jason paused for a beat. "My truck."

"I read the reports from the EOD Team that responded to both incidents, and the materials and ignition mechanisms are the same. It's not a lot, but they are clearly related, and now we know it's someone targeting the senator and his staff."

"I figured that," Jason said. "Do you have anything else?"

Archie waggled his head. "Not at this time, but I'm dedicating all our resources to narrow down a list of new suspects as soon as possible."

Jason leaned back and watched customers order their fuel to start their day. He noticed several men and women did a double take in his direction. Jason looked down and saw he was the only one in a wrinkled suit early on a Saturday morning. The disheveled hair, stubble on his face, and dark circles under his tired eyes surely made Jason look like he spent the night out on the town partying and not stressing over a car bomb planted to kill his family.

"I look ridiculous. Let's get out of here."

Archie looked at his watch. "It's almost eight. Let's go get your truck now."

Shanna, Jason, and JJ ate dinner together in Whispering Pines. JJ's parents were doing their best to provide a sense of normalcy to their seven-month-old child. He seemed content to be in familiar surroundings, with both parents giving him their full attention. Jason grew more confident that JJ would not be affected by the car bomb. He couldn't say the same for Shanna or himself. Shanna was quiet most of the two-hour drive from Phoenix to Whispering Pines. Jason asked her once if she was okay, and Shanna responded that she was "fine," so he never pressed the issue. His wife was a trained grief counselor and dealt with trauma and grief professionally and personally in her life. Jason understood that she needed time to come to terms with the fact that her family had almost been blown apart.

Shanna also helped Jason to become more self-aware and realize that he was not okay, but he dealt with pain differently. Jason pushed down his feelings until he felt like a shaken soda can ready to burst. According to Shanna, it wasn't the healthiest method of dealing with trauma, but it was Jason's way, and she accepted it. The goal was to control his explosion of frustration and anger productively once the pressure got too great. Now that the bombers targeted Jason's family, that wouldn't be possible.

After dinner, Shanna gave JJ a bath while Jason cleaned up. Once the dishes were put away, Jason slipped into the backyard and into his new shed.

Under the single bulb hanging from the ceiling, Jason penciled the design for the bookshelf he planned to build for JJ's room.

I will help him fill this with books like I had growing up.

He cut the first four boards with a circular saw and began to screw two of them together when he stopped. The primary goal of the shed was to help Jason take his mind off the daily stressors of law enforcement and security work through woodworking projects. It would offer that escape sometime in the future. Jason was sure of it, but it would not happen tonight. He didn't want to forget about the bomber still on the loose. He wanted to focus on identifying the person or people putting his friends and family in danger. Jason turned out the light and crept back to his back patio.

Jason always thought more clearly during a run or in quiet solitude under the stars. He walked to the back railing and watched the full moon rise over the East Verde River, flowing a hundred yards behind his house.

If not Eckhart, who could have planted those bombs? Who is sick enough to target a family with a small child?

Clarity of thought transitioned to fiery rage as the memory of his young son in the rear cab of his truck with explosives underneath him consumed Jason's thoughts. His skin grew warm even in the cool air as white-hot anger coursed through his veins. Jason's hands trembled from the intensity of his desire to quickly apprehend the bombers. He refused to attend another funeral of a loved one.

Who targeted my family?

A faceless figure emerged in Jason's mind as his latest adversary. Discovering the mastermind behind these attacks was vital, but how Jason handled this new suspect would be even more crucial. He'd waited patiently for investigators to identify and prosecute the suspects but to no avail. At this rate, Senator Conrad, his staff, and Jason's family would all be dead before the bombers faced justice. It was time for Jason to go on offense.

It was time to strike back.

Chapter 27

Jason hammered a nail into the wood plank as the shadows of the towering pines stretched across the patio of his childhood home. He pulled another nail from his work belt and drove it through the white oak riser to complete the top step. A bead of sweat on Jason's forehead fell to the plank like a solitary drop of rain.

"The steps are done. Dad, I'll need your help with the railing," Jason said.

Phillip stepped forward like an eager recruit with his matching tool belt. "What do you want me to do?"

"Hold the handrail over the balusters so I can attach it to the newel post at the bottom. Once that's done, your patio will be ready to use again."

"Great. We use this staircase every day. I couldn't believe it when Noah told me the second step collapsed.

"It was thirty years old, Dad. You got your money's worth out of it."

The father and son duo backed away after they attached the handrail and admired their handiwork.

The back door opened, and Jason's mom, Celeste, appeared on the patio.

"Thank you for coming over and helping. Your dad and I appreciate it."

"No problem. It gives me an excuse to see you and Dad on my day off and keeps me busy while Shanna and JJ are in Whiteriver."

"How's Nancy doing?"

"Her leg is recovering, but she still has to use her walker to get around. Shanna has been over there almost every day helping Nancy since she got out of the hospital."

"Do you want to stay for dinner? I can have Phillip toss some pork chops or steaks on the grill."

Before Jason could answer, his phone buzzed in his pocket. He noticed it was his mother-in-law, Nancy, and quickly answered.

"Hi Jason, I'm sorry to bother you."

"You're not bothering me. Is everything okay with Shanna and JJ?"

"Oh, yes. They're fine. They left about an hour ago, so they should be home soon. It's just that—"

Nancy tailed off. Jason could hear the trepidation in her voice.

"What is it?"

"Well," Nancy sighed. "That guy I was dating when I got into an accident is scaring me."

Jason covered the phone and whispered to his mom. "I have to take this. You can start dinner without me."

He walked behind the garage so nobody else could hear him.

"What's he doing?"

"He's been calling and texting me nonstop since he got out on bail from his DUI a few hours ago. I didn't answer his calls or texts, so he showed up at my door right after Shanna and JJ left. I wouldn't answer the door, so he yelled that he wanted to go for a ride and talk about what happened, but I'm never talking to him again. Plus, I think he's been drinking. Before he went back to his truck, he said he wasn't leaving until he talked to me. I don't know what to do."

Heat shot up Jason's spine at the thought of somebody threatening his hobbled mother-in-law. He clenched his jaw and gripped the phone tighter before he could respond.

"What about WMAT PD? Couldn't they come over and talk to him?"

Nancy cleared her throat. "I know what he did to me, but I don't want more trouble with him. I'm afraid if I call the police, it will just set him off even more."

"What's he doing now?"

Jason heard shuffling and the distinctive clacking of a walker moving across her wood floors. "He's sitting in his truck in front of the house."

"OK, I'll come over. Don't open the door or talk to him until I get there."

"Thank you."

Jason passed the lone grocery store and auto shop in Whiteriver, Arizona, ninety minutes later before turning off Highway 73 onto the road he'd traveled many times to pick up Shanna while they were dating. The headlights of his Ford Raptor illuminated a white Chevy pickup truck sitting in front of Nancy's house.

Jason killed his headlights and parked two houses down from Nancy's house. He texted his mother-in-law and told her he was approaching the door before he crept toward the parked truck. Jason noted the rusted-out bed and bald tires before he got a look inside the driver's window. The large man had thin, white hair touching his shoulders. His arms were crossed, and his eyes fixed on Nancy's front door, so Jason couldn't tell if the older man was all muscle, fat, or a combination of the two. The man didn't notice Jason until he approached his dented hood. Nancy opened the front door, and Jason saw the relief on her face through the storm door glass, but it quickly turned to fear when the man in the truck opened his door and rushed toward her.

Jason sprinted to put himself between Nancy and the angry man. He beat him to the front stoop by several steps and put his hand up in the universal sign to stop. The man stopped, out of breath from the brief burst toward the house, and Jason confirmed he looked to be more bluster than bulk. He was a few inches shorter than Jason but looked at least thirty pounds heavier, mostly from his bulging gut.

"Whoa, buddy, stop right there," Jason said calmly.

The man squinted into the porch light, illuminating his face. "I need to talk to Nancy."

He slurred all five words, and Jason knew the guy was shit-faced.

"Not tonight. You need to go home and sleep it off. Where do you live?"

"Who the hell are you?" His voice grew louder with every syllable.

"It doesn't matter who I am. Nancy doesn't want to talk to you, so it's time to leave."

The man pulled up his pants at the waist and curled his hands into fists. Jason heard the metal front door slam shut and lock behind him.

Nancy knows what's going to happen. Too bad this guy has no idea.

"I'm not leaving until I talk to Nancy. Get out of my way, or I'll move you."

Jason adjusted his feet in case the man charged.

"Don't do it, man. Go home now, or you won't like the outcome."

"Get out of my way!" the man yelled. He extended his arms and lowered his head. Jason saw he was trying to tackle him, so he clocked the man with an elbow cross to the chin as he charged past like a blind bull. The man's eyes rolled back, and his momentum continued toward Jason, so he caught the man and let him down gently. Jason put his fingers on his neck to check his pulse, and that's when he heard another door slam across the street.

Jason confirmed the man was unconscious but uninjured. He hopped onto the front porch and knocked on the door. "Nancy, it's Jason. Please get me a couple of towels for this guy. He's going to be out for a bit."

A minute later, the deadbolt clicked, and Nancy opened the door with two bath towels in her arm. "What happened?"

"We were having a pleasant conversation when he got mad and ran into my elbow. He's okay, but I want to prop up his head and feet until he wakes up."

After Jason put the towels under the man, red and white strobes lit up Nancy's house. A White Mountain Apache Tribe police cruiser pulled into the driveway. An officer exited the vehicle and put on his department-issued cowboy hat.

Shit! I don't need this.

"We received a call about a fight. What's going on here?"

Just as Jason was prepared to deny the fight, the man stirred and opened his eyes. He turned to his side and threw up. The stench of alcohol caused Jason to take two steps back to prevent himself from losing his lunch.

"Officer, this man assaulted me. I want him arrested," the drunk man bellowed.

Jason saw the officer's silhouette stiffen as his hands moved closer to his service weapon.

"Is that true?"

"Not exactly. He was harassing my mother-in-law and wouldn't leave. I wasn't going to let him break in and hurt her."

"He's lying. Arrest him!"

The officer tilted his head for a beat. "I don't think Jason Mulder would lie."

Jason moved to his left to let the front porch light illuminate the officer's face. "Officer Spencer?"

The officer stepped forward and pulled Jason in for a tight bear hug. "You saved my life, Mulder. I'm still grateful for what you did for me."

Jason returned the hug with a pat on the back. "I'm thrilled to see you active with WMAT PD again. You gave us all a scare back in the woods a couple of years ago."

"What's going on here?" the man on the ground shouted.

Officer Spencer shined his flashlight on his face. "Earl Jones, is that you? Didn't you just get out of jail for your DUI accident last week?"

"Yep," Jason answered. "He was on a date with Shanna's mom during his accident, and now she's nursing a broken leg. He said he wants to talk, but she wants nothing to do with him."

Officer Spencer called into dispatch with his radio and turned to Jason. "Take care of your mother-in-law. Mr. Jones is going back to jail."

"Thank you."

"No, thank you, Jason."

Nancy opened the door and let Jason inside. Together, they watched EMTs put the cuffed man into the back of the ambulance and leave.

"Thank you for coming over. I can't believe I ever went out with that guy."

"No problem. Maybe get off the dating apps for a while."

"I've already deleted all of them."

Nancy attempted to smile, but her voice shook, and Jason could tell the incident outside her front door still bothered her. He checked his watch and texted Shanna to let her know he'd stay with her mom for the night.

"Can you get me a couple of pillows and blankets? I'm going to stay on the couch for the night."

"I'm okay. You don't have to do that."

"I know. I want to stay."

Nancy stared at Jason for several seconds, nodded, and retrieved pillows and a blanket for him.

Jason lay on the couch, propped up two pillows, and put his hands behind his head.

"Jason, you don't have to do this."

"Good night, Nancy."

She turned out the lights and disappeared down the hallway. In the dark, Jason gazed up at the ceiling with a contented grin. His mother-in-law was a kind and caring woman who struggled to find a man who would treat her right. She'd already been through so much during the three years that Jason had known her and it felt good to help protect someone who needed him. It had been a while since he had successfully protected a person in need. The string of bombings and loss of life felt like failures that weighed heavily on Jason.

Protecting the senator is starting to feel like an impossible mission. Can I protect him when his life is on the line?

It was a question Jason would have to answer sooner than he expected.

CHAPTER 28

Washington, DC

Senator Conrad's mahogany desk bathed in the warm glow of late afternoon sunlight, streaming in through the windows that offered a commanding view of the bustling streets of the nation's capital. He leaned into his leather executive chair and loosened his tie, a furrow of frustration creasing his brow as he reviewed the latest report on his bill.

Support for the POLAR Act had slipped, and if he didn't do something soon, the bill would never see a vote on the floor of the House or Senate. The noise from other vital issues grew louder with each new political speech or interview on cable TV news. No politician, citizen, or reporter wanted to talk to Senator Conrad or Congresswoman Duarte about the Colorado River's dwindling water levels or conservation programs. They wanted to know about the Yuma Bomber, as the media named him or her. Like the FBI, the news media had figured out that the bomber was targeting Conrad, Duarte, and their staff at all levels. Conrad was vitally concerned for the safety of his staff and wanted swift justice for the bomber as soon as possible, but he couldn't lose focus on other important issues. Eventually, the Yuma Bomber would be caught and arrested, and the Colorado River problems would still exist. Conrad was committed to solving both issues.

Chief of Staff Crenshaw appeared in his office with a look of despair. Strands of her brunette hair waved wildly from her previously neat bun as she walked. Her eyes swept past the window of the cherry trees in full bloom, their delicate petals shimmering in the late April sunlight. Despite the idyllic scene outside, Senator Conrad's office was filled with tension and dread.

"Senator, I just got off the phone with the committee chair, and it's not looking good for the POLAR Act. It's stuck in committee, and he's about to kill it."

Senator Conrad leaned forward and drummed his fingers against the polished surface of his desk.

"Dammit," he muttered under his breath. "We've put too much into this bill to let it die in committee. We need to find a way to breathe new life into it."

Crenshaw nodded in agreement.

Conrad leaned back in his seat while Crenshaw snatched a gold and black Montblanc pen from the holder on his desk, which cost more than her car payment, and parked herself in a nearby chair. She twirled the pen while Conrad pursed his lips and sighed often.

Crenshaw leaped to her feet.

"I have an idea," Crenshaw said as she returned the pen to the holder. "We know that the committee chair has been under pressure from certain interest groups to squash our bill. What if we could sway some key committee members to our side?"

Senator Conrad leaned forward. "Go on," he urged.

"We need to identify the swing votes on the committee and target them with a carefully crafted strategy," Crenshaw explained. "We could leverage our relationships with other senators to gather support, offer concessions where necessary, and perhaps even drum up public support to put pressure on the committee chair."

"I think that could work," Conrad mused. "I'll get back out and stump for the POLAR Act. Time is not on our side, so I want to head back out next week. "

"I'll start contacting our allies in the Senate and draft an action plan," she said. "We won't let this bill die without a fight."

"Great, but we need one more thing."

"What is it?" Crenshaw asked.

"We need an event that will get the attention of the general public and every committee member. We need something big and bold."

Crenshaw's hands went to her hips as she slipped her right foot in and out of her shoe.

"We could do something in Alexandria along the Potomac. That would attract attention to river health and be easy for all the DC media to attend."

Conrad shook his head. "Not bold enough. Plus, it needs to be in Arizona."

He saw a brief frown flash on the face of his chief of staff. He knew Crenshaw wasn't a fan of the remote Arizona locations he was pushing her to consider.

"How bold are we talking?"

"Scary bold."

Crenshaw sighed. "Okay, I might have the perfect venue."

"Whatcha got?"

"When you think of the Colorado River, what places come to mind?"

Conrad rubbed the stubble on his chin with his thumb and index finger. "I think of Lake Powell, the Grand Canyon, Horseshoe Bend, Lake Mead, and Lake Havasu."

"Which of those places visually tells the story of the dwindling water levels on the Colorado River without saying a word?" Crenshaw asked.

"Umm. Probably the bathtub ring around Lake Mead. Every time I drive by, it reminds me how far water levels have fallen."

"Exactly! Lake Mead and the Hoover Dam provide the perfect backdrop for why passing the POLAR Act in this session is critical. Waiting is not an option."

"I love it. Let's book it."

Crenshaw tapped on her smartphone and put it in her pocket. "We'd be returning to Yuma Bomber territory, so I'll let Clay know to pre-scout the area and seriously beef up security. After that, I'll find a TV crew willing to do a live feed."

"I want more than one TV crew. I want them all," Conrad said, leaning against his desk.

Crenshaw wrinkled her nose and tilted her head. "I understand, sir, but then everyone will know your speech's day, time, and location. I'm not sure that's a good idea, considering the Yuma Bomber has not been arrested."

Conrad left his desk and straightened his tie. "What did we talk about a few minutes ago?"

"Be bold," Crenshaw replied—a hint of defeat in her voice.

"Not just bold, scary bold. I trust my security team to keep us safe while we tell the citizens of Arizona and the United States why the POLAR Act must be passed this session."

"I wish I shared your confidence."

The Arizona Senator crossed his arms. "You don't think the security team can do their job and protect us?"

"No. No. It's not that. I think they do a great job, but it's a monumental task to protect a large audience from all the possible threats in that environment. I understand it's the right location, and we need to do it, but I still don't like it."

Conrad placed his hand on her shoulder. "I appreciate the concern, but I'm sure everything will be alright."

Despite the confidence in his voice, it was a statement he'd later regret.

CHAPTER 29

La Paz County, Arizona

Bright sunlight transitioned to dim fluorescent light as Jassim charged into the maintenance building. He expected to see the tractor and mower in the alfalfa field harvesting their second spring crop, but the field was empty. After Jassim stepped into the building and the door slammed behind him, his ears had tuned into men arguing and metal banging on metal. He found a maintenance worker and manager bickering next to the tractor that should be in the field.

"Ibrahim, why isn't the mower in the field?" Jassim demanded.

"The John Deere blew a front tire, and we tried to replace it, but the crane arm is broken. It won't swing the tire where we need it."

Jassim stared at the large green tractor with one of its eight tires missing.

"I told him I could drive the tractor under the tire," said Hamza, the maintenance worker.

"That won't work, Hamza. The tire must line up directly over the bolts, and it's over 800 pounds. We must hook a chain to the arm to see if we can move it with the front loader."

"That arm won't budge, it has—" "Enough!" Jassim barked. He moved closer to the wheel hub and stared at it for several seconds.

"Hamza, pull the tractor as close as possible. Ibrahim, get ready to apply and tighten the lug nuts. I won't be able to hold it for long."

"What are you going to do?" Ibrahim asked.

"I'm going to push the tire on."

"It's too heavy."

"Do you doubt I can do it?"

Ibrahim stared at Jassim for a moment and shook his head. "No, I never doubt you. Hamza, get in the cab."

Once the John Deere 9R 590 tractor was in place, Jassim moved behind the tire a foot taller than him. "Ibrahim. Get the top nut on first. That will help hold it on."

The maintenance manager nodded, his eyes wide with anticipation.

Jassim pushed the tire until it hit the hub. His muscles strained, and his face flushed red. "Hurry!"

Ibrahim secured the top and bottom lug nuts. "It's on. You can let go."

Jassim backed away, panting, and put his hands on his knees.

A crackling call came over his radio. "Jim for Jassim."

"This is Jassim."

"Sir, can you come to the new drill site in the northwest?"

"I'll be there in ten minutes."

Ibrahim used the impact wrench to secure the remaining bolts.

"Get the tractor and mower into the field. I have to go," Jassim ordered.

When Jassim arrived at the northwestern end of his property, hollow metal cylinders at the end of a mobile drilling rig protruded from the parched earth two stories into the sky. Jim, the rig operator, stood with his hands on his hips as Jassim pulled up in his truck.

The oldest Al-Rashidi brother already knew why he was summoned to the drill. He hired a company to drill another well to irrigate his crops with groundwater, but the first three were unsuccessful.

"You told me to call you once I hit 250 feet. This one is dry, just like the last three."

Jassim paced around the rig and stared at the dusty earth around the well cylinders.

"I don't think you'll find water here, Mr. Al-Rashidi. Over the past year, I've hit several dry wells at the neighboring farms. The water table is too far down, or it's gone."

"My neighbors' fields are still green. What are they doing for water?"

"They're buying it from the canal. It's expensive, but what else can you do in the middle of the desert?"

"How expensive is it?" Jassim asked.

"I don't know the exact amount, but I know you have some neighbors paying five figures a month for water, and it's only going to go up more if that POLAR bullshit from Conrad gets passed."

I have to ship my alfalfa halfway around the world. If our water costs increase that much, we'll surely go broke.

Jassim marched toward Jim, stopped, and extended his hand. "That will be all, Jim. Thanks for trying."

Twenty minutes later, the door of the maintenance building slammed behind Jassim. He noticed the John Deere was no longer inside and called for his maintenance team. "Ibrahim and Hamza, where are you?"

Hamza opened the door to the parts closet. "The John Deere is mowing the alfalfa right now, Jassim."

"I know. I want to talk to you and Ibrahim about something else. Tell him to come here."

Ibrahim returned to the maintenance building, and Jassim launched into his tirade. He waved his hands wildly as Ibrahim and Hamza nodded approvingly. Jassim noticed a door to the building had opened, and he stopped talking. Amir stepped through the door into the maintenance building.

"What is going on, Jassim?"

"Nothing, brother. I'm just talking to our maintenance team."

Amir shook his head. "I don't believe you. You've been acting funny around me for weeks. You're always whispering and going away on trips. You took Ibrahim and Hamza to Yuma and left for Las Vegas and Phoenix for days. Why can't you tell me what you are doing?"

"I am protecting the family business, Amir."

"We are in this together, so if you're protecting the family business, I want to help."

"Not this, Amir. I must do this alone."

"Why? I'm willing to do anything to protect our business."

"Not like I am. Please go back to the office while I speak with my men."

Amir's gaze lingered on his older brother for a few moments, his expression filled with defeat before he turned and exited the building.

After Jassim confirmed Amir was gone, he returned to Ibrahim and Hamza. "As I was saying before Amir interrupted. We have a big problem, so I have a new mission for us."

The cyan spire protruded prominently above the King Fahad Mosque, slicing through the partly cloudy sky like a sharp spear. As soon as Jassim saw the magnificent white marble structure, he felt reinvigorated.

After mid-afternoon prayers, Jassim joined five other men from his old SANG unit at The Persian Room, a cafe and hookah lounge that felt more like home than anywhere else in America. The patrons spoke exclusively Arabic while families fed each other hummus through clouds of fruit-scented smoke. Jassim sipped his fresh mint tea and waited for the right time. Once Hamid, a former demolition officer from his SANG unit in Riyadh, stood, Jassim followed him through a wall of beads hanging from the ceiling and into a private hookah room. Hamid perched himself in a corner, lifted the ornate mouthpiece to his lips, and took a long drag of the flavored tobacco. The tip of the hookah glowed as sweet-scented smoke swirled around them. Hamid motioned for Jassim to sit.

Jassim sat across from Hamid, and he offered the hookah to the former soldier.

"Not today."

"What brings you to Culver City this time?"

"I need new explosives. Something that will penetrate reinforced concrete underwater."

"Underwater?" Hamid confirmed.

Jassim nodded.

"How thick is the concrete?"

"Very thick."

Hamid took another long drag from the hookah, leaned back, and exhaled a white stream of smoke. He returned the mouthpiece, folded his hands, and rested them on his thawb, the white one-piece garment worn by all the men in the mosque. Hamid stared at the wall adjacent to Jassim for several moments until he nodded.

"I think C-4 is the best plastic explosive for underwater blasting that I can obtain. The VOD is 50% greater than the ammonium nitrate you've used in the past." The former SANG demolition specialist spoke of the velocity of detonation, which measures a blast's strength.

"Okay. I will take C-4."

"How much do you need?"

"How much can you get?"

"Will you be transporting on foot or a vehicle?"

"It will be hand-delivered." Jassim always responded in short, concise sentences whenever he was angry, focused, or both.

"I can get you twenty kilograms."

"I need eighty."

"Eighty? Why so much?"

"I need to make a large hole."

Hamid switched to a different mouthpiece and inhaled deeply. When no smoke appeared after he exhaled, he searched for a lighter. Once he found one on a nearby end table, he lit the tobacco, took a short drag, and exhaled a cloud of smoke. He offered the mouthpiece to Jassim again. "Are you sure?"

Jassim shook his head. "The C-4?"

"I can get you forty—no more. Put the C-4 in shaped charges." Shaped charges are metal devices that look similar to the bombs dropped from World War II planes and are designed to focus the kinetic energy of explosives to better penetrate armor or hardened steel. "The shaped charges will make a massive hole. When do you need it?" Hamid asked.

"How fast can you get it?"

"I can get it in a week."

"That is too long. I need it in 2 days."

"That's impossible!"

Jassim rose to his feet and stood over Hamid. "I need it in two days, or you'll no longer be part of the lucrative land deals I secured in Arizona."

The former SANG demolition specialist stared back. "Fine, but don't do anything stupid with it when you receive it," Hamid said with nervous laughter.

The focused expression on the elder Al-Rashidi brother did not change.

"I'm doing what must be done."

Chapter 30

Scottsdale, Arizona

Seeking refuge from the midday heat, Jason moved to the shade of the mesquite trees dotting the black asphalt parking lot. The air immediately over the cars and trucks appeared hazy and distorted, like a mirage, as thermal waves rose from their roofs. Although it was relatively cool for Phoenix standards on the first day of May, Jason's body opposed the ninety-degree temperatures. Beads of sweat formed on his temples as evidence of his discomfort with the twenty-five-degree temperature change after driving two hours from Whispering Pines to Scottsdale. He wiped the perspiration away with his shirt sleeve as he approached Senator Conrad's Arizona office building.

Jasmine Mitchell, deputy chief of staff, summoned Jason to the office to attend a videoconference with the rest of the staff in Washington, DC., but wouldn't share why he had to attend in person. He hurried to the front door.

Jason pushed the button under the sign adorned with United States Senator James Conrad embedded in the stone facade. The door buzzed, and Jason entered. A United States flag held high by an indoor flagpole greeted him on the left, and the Arizona state flag with a prominent copper-colored star superimposed in the center of the flag surrounded by thirteen alternating red and yellow rays like a setting sun on the right. Photographs capturing moments from Senator Conrad's political career lined the walls, from campaign rallies to meetings with world leaders.

The front desk attendant, a young woman with a warm smile, greeted him. "Welcome to the office, Mr. Mulder. Everyone is in the main conference room in the back."

The lone PSD member in Arizona sat at one of four long tables occupied by home-state staff. He was surrounded by caseworkers, outreach coordinators, field representatives, constituent advocates, and state directors. They all worked full-time in the Scottsdale office to help constituents or act as liaisons between the federal government and local businesses, state and local governments, and nonprofit organizations.

Jasmine moved to the front with a remote control in her hand. She turned on the four monitors, which formed one large screen. "The DC staff will join us in a minute," she said.

Five minutes later, Jasmine's boss, Julia Crenshaw, came to life on the screen with a dozen additional members of Conrad's staff in the room. The camera's downward angle accentuated her curly black bangs and pointy chin.

"Good afternoon, and thanks for coming in on such short notice," Crenshaw started. "We've made an important shift in priorities, which will impact everyone on this call."

The chief of staff continued with details regarding Senator Conrad's aggressive push to drum up committee and constituent support for the POLAR Act. Twenty minutes later, everyone had their new orders, and Jason sensed that his drive to Scottsdale was a colossal waste of time.

"Okay, everyone," Crenshaw said. "You all have your marching orders, so get started on your respective tasks, except you, Jason. Please stay on the call."

Everyone left the room, and Clay appeared on the screen beside Crenshaw.

"Hey Jason, thanks for coming into the office for this call. I have a new list of objectives for you," Clay stated. "We have several new sites that require advance scouting for potential events for Senator Conrad. I'll send you the list after the call, but you'll see parks, schools, farms, and those types of locations on the list."

"How soon do they need to be vetted?" Jason asked.

"Everything needs to be vetted in a couple of days."

"Days? Do you have a plan to clone me that I'm unaware of?"

"Better," Clay replied. "I'm flying out later today to help. Central and Zee will cover for me back here."

Learning of upcoming fifteen-hour days was not good news, but hearing that Clay was coming out to assist brightened Jason's day. He always worked well with his former Air Force buddy and welcomed the chance to work alongside him again. Although they belonged to the same private security detail, the duo worked together far less than Jason had imagined when he started.

"Great, I look forward to seeing you again in Arizona."

"I'll break down who will visit each location on the list I'm sending you. See you tomorrow," Clay closed.

After the video conference ended, Jason's phone chirped as he stared at his reflection on the dark screen. It was a text from Archie.

```
Stop by the FBI office in North Phoenix
if you're in town. I'm going over some new
suspects with an analyst today.
```

Jason knew working with Archie might be more challenging once Clay arrived, so he quickly replied.

```
I'm in Scottsdale now. Does 3 pm work?
Yep. Meet me at the coffee shop down the
street and I can drive us to the office.
```

Archie shared his credentials with the security guards and signed Jason into the FBI building in North Phoenix. He escorted him to FBI Analyst Bautista's office.

"Marisol, this is Jason Mulder. He's former special warfare in the Air Force and spent some time as a special agent with the DEA. He's part of Senator Conrad's Arizona-based security team, with a strong interest in finding the Yuma bomber before he strikes again."

The analyst rose from her chair and extended her hand to Jason. "I remember your name from the report on the car bomb a few miles from here. I'm sorry that happened to your family and hope everyone is okay."

"We're fine. Thank you."

Bautista settled back in her seat, and the monitor light brightened her face.

"I'm about to analyze some new data, so as long as Agent Woods is okay with your presence while we discuss sensitive information, so am I."

"He's good," Archie said.

Bautista pulled out a chair next to her desk and motioned for Jason to sit. "In that case, gentlemen, let's get started."

Jason adjusted himself in his chair to better see the lines of data whizzing across the analyst's computer screen. Archie stretched his legs and leaned back in his seat next to Jason as if he might take a nap.

"Senator Conrad and the POLAR Act are the common thread among all the bombings, so I pulled financial data from various jurisdictions to see which farms and ranches may be impacted most if the bill passes," Bautista said without taking her eyes off the screen.

"I have land loans, business loans, utility company delinquencies, personal debt, and a half dozen other financial fields running through my algorithm. Once it's done, it'll narrow our list of suspects from thousands to a few dozen—at least suspects with a potential financial motive."

Archie continued to recline with his eyes closed while Marisol and Jason watched the screen until the scrolling lines stopped.

"It's done," Bautista said. "Damn it!"

"What?" Jason asked.

"We still have 164 suspects, far more than I thought."

Archie opened his eyes. "Eliminate everyone north of Las Vegas and east of Phoenix."

"Why?" Bautista asked.

"Our bomber goes where he feels most comfortable. He's struck Yuma, Las Vegas, and Phoenix. Twice. The bomber feels most comfortable in central and western Arizona."

She nodded and punched a few keys on her keyboard.

"Wow, that eliminated 80% of them. We're down to 31 ranches and farms."

Jason skimmed the lines containing the business name, address, and phone number. They all sounded like ranches and farms he'd seen around Arizona his whole life: McCann Farms, Lazy G Ranch, Mohave Produce Co-op, and an additional two dozen names that were just characters on a screen to Jason.

"How do we narrow down the list from here?" Jason asked.

"Do you want to tell him, or should I?" Archie asked.

"You can tell him."

"Good old-fashioned detective work, Mulder. Unless you have another way to drill down the list, we'll have to visit all 31 names on the list."

Jason bit his lower lip as his hands turned into fists.

The best chance of finding the bomber can't be to search 31 farms around Arizona. We're no closer now than when I pulled into the parking lot.

"Archie, there's no other way?"

The veteran FBI special agent looked sympathetic but shook his head.

Desperate for a better solution, Jason pressed closer to the screen. Near the bottom of the list, he passed a name and quickly moved his eyes back to the farm on the previous line.

"Al-Rashidi Farms sounds familiar. Is there anything else you know about them?"

Bautista leaned toward the monitor, and Jason pointed to the line with Al-Rashidi Farms. "I can get more, but it will take a little time. How are they familiar? Is it because they are the only name of Middle Eastern descent on the list?"

"No, that's not it. I've seen the name somewhere recently."

Jason gazed up at the ceiling, then down at the desk, trying to trigger his memory and figure out why he felt a sense of recognition. Suddenly, it clicked.

"I know. I saw them on the news. A reporter was interviewing them on the POLAR Act, and one of the family members that owned the farm seemed pissed. They were making negative comments about Senator Conrad and the POLAR Act, so it caught my attention. I still remember the fury in the eyes of the owner."

Archie seemed to wake from his slumber. "That's not a lot, but it's something. Bautista, can you do a deeper dive on Al-Rashidi Farms? Check for any unusual purchases, travel, known associates on our watch list, or anything else that could help us eliminate them or move them to the top of our list."

"Okay, I'll get started."

"How long do you think it will take?" Jason asked.

"I don't know. It'll probably take a few days. I'll go as fast as I can."

Jason stared back for a beat, opened his mouth, and then thought better of it.

Bautista crossed her arms. "Is that not fast enough for you?"

"It's not that. Senator Conrad is coming to Arizona next week for a whirlwind tour to revive his bill. I'm concerned that if the Yuma bomber is still on the loose, he'll try again to kill the senator or his staff."

"I'll go as fast as I can."

"Thank you."

Jason knew that Bautista and Archie were working diligently to obtain the requested information, but each passing day without a solid suspect increased the already high level of danger. The bomber was growing more desperate, and Jason was well aware that the PSD team could not protect Conrad and his staff from every attack forever.

Chapter 31

La Paz County, Arizona

Jassim knelt and ran his fingers across the cracks in the dusty soil. A cicada buzzing nearby dropped to the ground and scurried into his shadow for a temporary respite from the unrelenting sun. The intense summer heat was fast approaching, and their groundwater pumps had dropped from 120 gallons per minute to 35 GPM. Days after the decrease in well output, large swaths of green alfalfa stiffened and turned pale yellow under the cloudless blue sky stretching endlessly above.

The eldest Al-Rashidi brother clenched the dirt in his fist and let the breeze scatter the dust across the dry field. Jassim never wished for this day to come, but his mother always said he was the fighter in the family. His temper was lightning quick as far back as he could remember, which caused him grief in his teenage years but admiration from his SANG brethren for his willingness to always stand up for himself and others. Water was available for his crops at four times his current cost, and Jassim knew his current irrigation issues didn't require a war with sitting members of the United States Congress. However, the pain inflicted on him and his family was deeply personal, an offense that couldn't go unpunished. He'd worked too hard to make Al-Rashidi Farms successful and was unwilling to struggle again for decades at the whim of politicians.

Jassim returned to the maintenance building and inspected the new crate that arrived by courier early that morning. He confirmed it contained everything Hamid agreed to deliver, so it was time to test the explosives.

He made sure nobody else was around when he called Ibrahim and Hamza to the crate.

"It arrived, so now we must do a dry run."

Ibrahim leaned into the crate and straightened, holding a 1.2 5-pound brick of C-4 in each hand and a satisfied smile. "When should we do this test?"

"Today."

"Today? Why so fast?"

"We don't have much time. Our window of opportunity is closing, so we must strike soon."

A door to the maintenance building slammed, so Jassim quickly closed the lid on the crate. Amir sauntered around the John Deere tractor to the three men standing around a wooden crate the size of a treasure chest.

"I came out to see what had arrived in this crate. I didn't order anything for maintenance and need to verify they delivered it to the right address."

"It came to the right place. I ordered it," Jassim replied.

"I would have ordered it for you. What is it?"

Amir bent to open the lid, but Jassim placed his massive boot on top.

"What's going on, Jassim?"

"I told you. We have some personal business we must take care of."

Redness filled Amir's cheeks as his eyes bulged. "I demand to know what you all are up to. I'm part of this family business, too!"

Jassim saw the anger in Amir's eyes, but mostly he saw the hurt in his little brother from the exclusion of their activities.

"Are you sure you want to know? You're also involved once you know what we've done and you can never return."

"I want to know," Amir snapped.

"Consider your answer carefully, brother."

"I have."

Jassim turned to Ibrahim and Hamza before leaning against the green mower's giant tire. He cleared his throat and shared the life-altering news.

"Do you recall the bombing in Yuma that nearly killed the senator?"

"That was you?"

"Ibrahim, Hamza and I took jobs as farm workers a couple of days before the senator's speech and placed the fertilizer in the back of the truck. It would have killed him had it detonated ten seconds earlier like it was supposed to. There was a delay due to a weak cell phone signal."

"Do they suspect it was you?" Amir asked. His face shone bright with excitement.

"They took a local farmer and fellow SFA member into custody but released him. We'll eventually end up on their radar, so we need to act fast."

"What else?" Amir asked.

"Las Vegas, Tempe, and Phoenix," Jassim replied. His tone was cool and unwavering as if he was rattling off a list of vacation destinations.

"I don't think I heard about the bombing in Las Vegas. What did you do there?"

Jassim pulled Hamza by the arm and put him in a loose head-lock. He kissed him on the top of his head and let the smiling young man go. "You know how Hamza used to work for an HVAC company fixing furnaces and water heaters to prevent them from exploding?"

Amir turned to Ibrahim's young protégé. "Yes, I remember."

"Well, he can also fix them to explode when desired," Jassim replied proudly.

"And Tempe and Phoenix?"

"Ibrahim and me."

Amir took several steps from the crate, reversed course, and returned to the other men.

"That was all you?"

"Yes," Jassim replied. "Now that you know, you must swear to secrecy and cover for us while we test these explosives."

"I want to go with you. I want to be part of whatever you have planned."

Jassim slammed his fist on the nearby tractor tire, knocking day-old dirt clods to the floor. "Absolutely not."

"Why not?"

"We didn't want this, Amir, but they gave us no choice, and now we have blood on our hands. I don't want the same for you. Plus, we need you to stay back and run the farm if something happens to us."

"And if I don't help you, will there even be a farm to run?" Amir barked back.

Jassim began to reply, but Ibrahim raised his hand to stop him. "I don't mean to interfere, but perhaps we should include Amir in the plan. He has the most scuba experience, which is the most difficult task in our plan."

Ibrahim looked as if he expected a rebuttal, backlash, or worse from Jassim, but instead, the oldest Al-Rashidi brother looked to the sky, closed his eyes, and returned his gaze to Amir seconds later.

"Ibrahim is right. We may need your diving skills soon, so you can come with us today."

A wide smile formed on Amir's face. "Excellent. What is the plan?"

Jassim reached into the crate and loaded two bricks of C4 into a black gym bag. "We are going to test these new explosives."

"Makes sense, but what is the big plan? What's after today?"

"I'll tell you when the time is right?" Jassim replied coolly.

"I told you I want to be part of this. Everything. No matter what it is."

Jassim continued to insert the C4 explosives into his bag and did not respond.

"Why won't you tell me, Jassim? I'm ready."

Jassim dropped the gym bag and turned toward Amir. "I'll tell you when I'm ready! If you ask again, you can forget about going today!"

Nobody in the room spoke, moved, or breathed for several seconds. Amir raised his hands in surrender. "Okay. Okay. I won't ask again. What should I do to get ready for today?"

Jassim and Amir arrived first, with Ibrahim and Hamza close behind in a second truck. They parked near the Gillespie Dam Bridge sixty-five miles southwest of Phoenix minutes before noon. The quartet from Al-Rashidi Farms were the only cars in the small lot. Still, the historic bridge attracted occasional onlookers at the nearly 100-year-old truss bridge upstream from the old Gillespie Dam, so their presence wouldn't cause alarm. A heavy storm in 1993 breached the dam and was never repaired, leaving a portion of the old dam intact on both banks of the Gila River.

Jassim reached into the bed of his truck and handed the black gym bag to Ibrahim.

"We must act like tourists exploring the area if anyone drives by. Once we get to the dam, move quickly. Does everyone remember the plan?"

Jassim scanned the blank faces staring back at him and decided to repeat his plan to everyone.

"Find a section underwater about four feet thick. I want to verify the C-4, timers, and blasting caps all detonate under the water like they are supposed to and see how deep nine kilos will penetrate," Jassim said.

Twenty minutes later, they sat inside their trucks eating sack lunches like road-weary tourists when twenty pounds of C-4 detonated. Turbulent river water mixed with mud and jagged pieces of concrete shot thirty feet into the air before plunging back into the river in a flurry of splashes.

"Whoa," Amir shouted and opened his door, but Jassim stopped him. "Don't rush up there, but we need to be quick. We've come too far to get caught now."

The foursome reached the blast site, and Jassim's lips curved upward at the sight of the crater. It was two feet deep.

"Will this work, Jassim?" Ibrahim asked.

"Yes. We have to go four times as deep with four times the explosives, so we'll need to use a shaped charge to be sure the job gets done."

Jassim stood and admired his successful test for several beats.

"We are done here," Jassim said, turning to Ibrahim and Hamza. "I need you both to stay out of sight and hang around here the rest of the day to see how quickly law enforcement shows up to investigate. It'll be good to know what kind of response an explosion in the middle of nowhere generates."

The two men nodded.

"Stay hidden, and no matter what, do not get caught!"

Chapter 32

Jason scrolled through his phone as the engine's soft purr and the air conditioner's hum filled the cab of his idling truck. He angled his screen to remove the reflection from the morning sun beaming through the driver's side window so he could see the address on his phone.

Jason arrived at his first scouting destination on the list Clay emailed him from the plane last night. He wasn't sure how long it took to reach Oasis VertiFarms from his hotel, and now he was sitting in front of a building that looked like every other structure in the warehouse district area of West Phoenix. The number on the building matched the number in his email, so he approached the front door of the gray three-story structure.

Jason reached for the front door, and it was locked—a good sign. A moment later, the door buzzed, and a thin man with a neatly trimmed blond mustache that matched his styled hair greeted him. A shorter but stout man with wavy black hair that matched his black blue polo shirt stood beside the tall man.

"You must be from the security team for the VIP they called about yesterday," the man said.

"Yes, sir."

"I'm Brad Grimes. I'm the founder of Oasis VertiFarms, so I can show you around and answer questions."

"I'm Jason, and I won't take up too much of your time. Do you have a security officer who can help answer some questions for me?"

"Yes," Brad said, turning toward the man in the polo shirt. "This is Antonio. He's our head of security and can show you everything you need."

Jason shook hands with Antonio. "I'll follow you."

"Don't hesitate to ask questions you have on our operation," Brad yelled to Jason as he walked away.

Ninety minutes later, Jason and Antonio returned to the front entrance, with Brad blocking the exit.

"How was it, Jason?" Brad asked.

"Very impressive operation. I'll share all about your bioweapon grade filtration system and advanced security cameras in my report."

Brad flashed a quick smile and tilted his head. "Any other questions on the operation?"

"No. Antonio was very thorough."

"Did he share that Oasis VertiFarms is the state's most advanced aeroponics vertical farm? Our environment consists only of air and a nutrient-packed mist with no soil and minimal water. We grow the same amount of produce as an outdoor field with 80-90% less water. We grow kale, arugula, spinach, basil, dill, baby leaf lettuce, and strawberries in vertically stacked layers rather than horizontally in an open field. Your VIP will love this place if he or she comes to tour our facility."

Now Jason understood where Brad was going with his burning desire to answer questions. "I will share everything about your exciting operation in my report."

"I would sincerely appreciate it. I saw the call came from Washington, DC. I'm here to serve my country proudly."

Brad handed his business card to Jason. "I'm just a phone call away if you or anyone else in Congress has questions for me."

Jason took the card and looked at his watch. "I really must go now. Thank you."

Jason pressed harder on the gas pedal during his drive back to Scottsdale. He agreed to meet Clay for a working lunch at a sports bar within walking distance of Senator Conrad's state office and didn't want to be late. He beat Clay to the outdoor table with a view of the pedestrian traffic he knew his boss and friend would appreciate.

When Clay arrived, he pulled Jason in for one of his famous bear hugs. Spending one-on-one time with a close friend who had helped him so much over the past three years felt good. They ate wings as they discussed work, and the lunch was going well until Clay received a text.

Jason watched his friend's eyes flutter across his phone screen as his shoulders slumped and his face fell sullen. Clay returned the phone to his pocket and turned his attention to the cars passing by the restaurant. No words were spoken for several minutes until Jason asked a question.

"You okay, man?"

Clay nodded. "Yeah, I'm fine."

"Was it the text? Did you receive some bad news?"

Clay shook his head and looked away. Jason could tell he was hurting.

"Okay. I won't keep pushing, but you know I've got your back if you need anything."

"I know, and I appreciate it."

Jason let silence take over the table as Clay processed whatever news he'd received. He couldn't help his friend if he didn't tell him what was wrong, but he could let Clay know he was there for him.

Jason's phone buzzed in his pocket, and he considered sending it to voicemail, but he saw it was Archie, so he answered.

"Hey Jason, we just heard that the Maricopa County Sheriff's Office is responding to an explosion near Gila Bend, Arizona. The reports state it was a big blast, so I'm on my way to check it out. I thought you'd want to know about any suspicious explosions."

"Hell yeah, I want to know."

"I just left, so I'm not too far away. Would you like to go with me?"

Jason looked at Clay, who seemed to get the color back in his face.

"Yeah, but I'll meet you there. Can you send me the address?"

"Sure, but is my driving that bad?"

"No. I'm here with Clay Landry, the head of Conrad's security team. I want him to see this."

"Sounds good. See you there."

The parking lot was full of police vehicles with county sheriff and state police logos, so Clay parked their GMC Yukon behind another black SUV on the side of the road.

"I think that's Archie's SUV. Let's find him first."

Jason saw half a dozen people standing on a concrete platform about a hundred yards upstream from the bridge. It appeared they were investigating a section of the breached dam.

"He's out on the dam," Jason said. "We can reach him from this bank."

Clay and Jason followed the dirt path through waist-high weeds until they reached a Maricopa County Sheriff's deputy standing behind yellow crime scene tape. He raised his hand with his palm facing the duo. "That's far enough. This is an active crime scene, so you'll have to turn around."

Jason saw Archie talking to another man twenty yards away on the dam and yelled out. "Hey, Archie!"

The veteran FBI special agent looked around, excited to hear his name, until he recognized Jason on the bank behind the tape.

"Can we get a little help here?"

"They are with me, so they're good," Archie shouted.

Clay and Jason proceeded to the dam next to Archie. Jason recognized the other man as Marcin Dobrowski with the FBI bomb squad. He shook Dobrowski's hand and introduced Clay to both FBI members. All four men turned toward the light gray concrete rubble among a sea of weathered, dark gray. It looked like the sun appeared through dark storm clouds to highlight a section of the vast ocean of concrete.

Jason picked up a piece of crumbled concrete, pressed it between his fingers, and let it fall back to the dam.

"What do you think?"

"I think it's a dry run," Archie said.

"A dry run? By who? Why?" Jason asked.

"I read that Gillespie Dam has been breached since 1993 after a bout of heavy rains, so blowing it up serves no purpose. Based on the symmetrical blast, they used C-4 or something similar. Ammonium nitrate fertilizer, like the one used in the car bombs, has a more random blast pattern," Archie explained.

"Why test it, though?" Clay asked.

"It's new for them. They want to know exactly how it works on concrete and maybe underwater. Most likely, they have something bigger planned," Dobrowski replied.

Jason stepped back and sighed while Clay and Archie poked at the concrete. He examined the dam and then scanned the area during a 360-degree rotation. His eyes swept past the bridge, a marsh, and a bluff a quarter mile upstream. Jason swung his attention back to the bluff and then quickly knelt back down next to Clay, Marcin, and Archie.

"Don't look now, but there's a truck with two men looking at us with binoculars from a bluff on the west side about a quarter mile up the river."

Everyone maintained their faux interest in the dam. "Must be spotters checking to see the response to their test," Archie whispered.

"You think they may be the bombers watching to see who shows up to investigate?" Clay asked.

"Happens all the time with explosions and fires. Some people can't help but admire their destruction as a casual observer. There's a good chance they are the bombers."

"I say we pay them a visit and see what they know," Clay said.

"That's a better job for law enforcement. I'll ask one of the deputies to check them out," Archie responded.

"They'll bolt as soon as they see a police vehicle approaching."

Archie nodded, seemingly in agreement, but his protest wasn't over. "They may be armed."

Clay padded his jacket. "I have my sidearm, and I know I've trained Jason to know better than to show up at a crime scene unarmed. Plus, I have two HK 416s in my SUV. We're good."

Archie faced Jason, seeking his opinion with his eyes.

"We can handle this, Archie. We'll call you if we catch them and let law enforcement take it from there, but we have to get rolling now before they get spooked."

"I can go with them," Dobrowski chimed in.

"No, let those two handle it," Archie said, turning toward the PSD team. "Mr. Landry and Mr. Mulder, you two be careful with those guys and call me as soon as you catch them."

Clay and Jason casually walked back to the SUV and drove over the bridge to the west side of the Gila River. Jason spotted the dirt road leading to the bluff.

"Turn here."

Clay's massive SUV blocked the only way in and out from the top of the bluff. They approached the last curve before the truck and two men would come into view. As Clay rounded the curve, they spotted the truck, which was no longer parked. The pickup truck was barreling towards them at a dangerous speed as if playing a game of chicken. The driver's determined expression made it clear they had no intention of swerving or slowing down.

A head-on collision seemed inevitable.

CHAPTER 33

Jason saw the whites in the driver's eyes before Clay veered off the dirt path and into the thick foliage of catclaw and sagebrush north of Gillespie Dam. They came to a sudden stop as the two men in a Toyota Tacoma truck raced past them, kicking up a cloud of dust that engulfed their vehicle.

"They're getting away!"

"Not if I can help it," Clay barked.

Immediately after the dust lifted, Clay turned the wheel and slammed his foot on the gas, sending the Yukon hurtling down the paved road. The engine's roar and wind whistling across their windshield filled the cab as they raced north on Highway 80 past lush green, irrigated fields interspersed with barren patches of dry land. The gap between the PSD team and the fleeing suspects grew smaller by the second.

"Should I call Archie to get the deputy to help?" Jason asked.

"No. I want to talk to these guys myself."

The Yukon Denali model contained a 6.2-liter V8 engine with twice the horsepower of the Tacoma, so the smaller Toyota had no chance of escaping. Once they were a few feet from their bumper, Clay warned Jason.

"Hang on, I'm moving in for a PIT maneuver."

Jason and Clay had learned how to use the Precision Immobilization Technique in PSD school. Clay pulled alongside the fleeing vehicle so that his front wheels aligned with the Toyota's back wheels. He steered sharply toward the target, accelerated and slammed his right quarter panel into the white truck. The rear of the fleeing vehicle swayed left and right, but it recovered and sped up.

"You need to slam into them harder," Jason said.

"I know. I know."

Clay overtook the white truck again, aggressively turning the steering wheel into the Tacoma. The maneuver worked as intended, causing the white truck to drift onto the soft shoulder and spin one and a half times until the Tacoma stopped on the highway, blocking both lanes. Clay braked hard and stopped twenty yards away from the stationary white truck.

"What are they doing?" Clay asked.

"Just sitting there."

"You remember how to fire from a vehicle like we were taught during our PSD training?"

Jason's head snapped toward Clay. "Yeah, what do you have in mind?"

"I'm going to pull around to the driver's side, so be ready with your Sig if this gets hot."

Jason unbuckled his seat belt, rolled down the window, and brought his pistol to the ready, as he'd learned in Arkansas six months earlier.

Clay swung around the back of the Tacoma and pulled beside the two men, blocking further escape north on the highway. Jason put the red dot of his reflex sight on the tinted driver's side window only ten yards away.

He could make out two figures through the translucent tint. Details of the passenger's facial features were difficult to distinguish, but Jason observed a mixture of fear and determination radiating from the driver's body. It seemed like the staring stand-off lasted a full minute, but seconds after Clay pulled beside the two men, the Tacoma's tire squealed, and the white truck shot into the desert.

"They're taking the wash," Jason yelled.

"I see em."

The highway intersection and the dry wash started as a shallow rocky depression easily traversed by both vehicles. A quarter mile off the road, the wash transitioned to a labyrinth of jagged rocks and temporary sandbars surrounded by saguaro cacti and other sharp, prickly sentinels ready to stab and poke anyone violating their territory. The walls surrounding the wash rose several feet, forcing both vehicles into the central channel. The heavier Yukon sank several inches into the sandy soil, while the lighter Tacoma seemed to skip across like a flat stone on a lake. Clay, who grew up on the bayou outside Baton Rouge, Louisiana, had significant experience navigating vehicles over soft earth. Combined with his driving skills from PSD school, Clay stayed close to the white truck.

"I'll try the PIT again as soon as we get close enough!" Clay shouted over the roar of the engines. His knuckles transitioned from pink to white as he maneuvered the SUV through the rugged terrain.

Jason nodded. He never took his eyes off the tailgate ahead, lurching up and down like a bull rider on the back of a bucking rodeo bull. The white pickup truck swerved wildly, kicking up blinding dust and sand as it careened from side to side in the wash. Visibility was intermittent. The white truck appeared briefly, and then a wall of brown dust and debris filled the whole windshield, making it impossible for Jason to see the fleeing vehicle.

As they barreled through the desert, the canyon walls surrounding the dry wash exceeded the height of the Yukon and transitioned from sand and shrubs to jagged granite. If the SUV or truck got too close to the wall, the stone fingers could destroy them like a giant meat grinder. The chances of surviving such a crash were slim.

"They're trapped now. There's no way out," Clay said, his voice satisfied.

Clay's jaw clenched, and his gaze locked on the target ahead. His boot pressed the accelerator to the floor, and the SUV surged forward, closing the gap between them and the fleeing truck.

"It widens a bit up there. Be ready to jump out. I'll try to pin them against the wall!"

The SUV's engine roared in response, and its bumper came within inches of the fleeing truck. Clay swung to the left and pulled past the Tacoma's bumper.

Jason put his seat belt back on, braced himself for impact, and prepared to leap from the vehicle to detain the fleeing men.

Pop!

A blast filled the cab as the SUV unexpectedly lurched upward. Then, the front end dove into the sand, bringing the vehicle to an abrupt halt inches from a potentially deadly granite wall. Shards of rubber flew in all directions, and several pieces landed on the hood.

"Dammit. We blew a tire!" Clay shouted. He slammed his fist on the dash.

Jason looked through the cracked windshield glass at the Tacoma taillights disappearing into the dust. His door swung open, and a beat later, he was in a full sprint into the brown cloud. The former PJ and DEA special agent didn't have a plan other than the unbridled desire to catch the men who tried to kill him and his family. He didn't expect to catch them, but he had to do everything humanly possible before quitting.

The dust began to thin, and two hundred yards past their blowout, Jason saw faint brake lights.

They must have thought that we gave up. They're in for a surprise.

Jason slowed to a trot, drifted beside the wall, and retrieved his weapon from its holster. Concealed by the dust, he got within twenty yards of the white truck when the driver exited. Jason pressed himself against the granite.

The driver's black hair curled over his ears, and his matching beard reached his chest. He took several steps from the truck and squinted into the dissipating dust. Jason heard the men speaking in a language he didn't understand, but he knew what they were discussing. They wanted to know if they were in the clear.

No!

Jason aimed his red dot at the driver's chest and stepped away from the wall.

"Freeze. Don't move!"

The driver's hands shot into the air, allowing Jason to scan his hands and waist for weapons. None were visible, but Jason learned after multiple tours in Afghanistan to never assume anything.

"Tell the passenger to get out of the truck with his hands up. Do it now!"

The driver relayed the message, and the passenger popped up on the other side of the truck with his hands up. The man was taller and more muscular than the driver. Jason could see the hate in his eyes as he inched closer to the two men.

"Who are you?" the passenger asked.

"I'm taking you into custody for the bombing of the dam back there." He watched their faces for any sign of recognition, but neither flinched.

"We had nothing to do with that."

"Then why were you watching us with binoculars and then fled when we tried to talk to you?"

"We work at the farm about a mile from here. We heard the blast and wanted to see what was happening but didn't want to get too close. We didn't know you were the police. We thought you were the bomber and ran."

It was a plausible story, and doubt crept into Jason's thoughts for the first time.

"You are the police, aren't you?" the passenger asked.

"I'm working with the police. They'll be here any minute."

The two men exchanged glances, and the passenger spoke again in a language similar to what he had heard in Afghanistan but different. Then, each man dove back inside the truck.

Jason ran alongside the Tacoma as he heard it shift into drive.

"Put it back in park, or I'll shoot!" Jason yelled. His red dot hovered on the driver's chest through the open window.

The driver stared back at Jason, expressionless. Their eyes in a standoff.

Jason's finger moved into the trigger guard, and he slid the tip of his index finger over the trigger. While he felt confident that the men knew something about the explosion at the dam, he couldn't be 100% certain, nor could he prove it, and that limited his options. Shooting innocent, unarmed men would send Jason to prison. *That* he was certain of. But were they really innocent men?

He didn't think so. But it was a tough call to make in the moment.

"Turn off the engine!"

The driver took his eyes off Jason and peered through the windshield. Jason could sense the questions going through his head that would ultimately lead to a decision to surrender or flee. An image of Archie appeared in Jason's mind. He recalled the pain the FBI agent suffered after taking the lives of innocent people when confronted with a similar situation. Archie told Jason he hoped he'd never be put in the same situation, yet here he was.

The engine revved, and the truck lurched forward. Jason braced for recoil but couldn't pull the trigger as the Toyota Tacoma truck fishtailed in the sand, gained traction, and sped away.

Jason's head fell to his chest as his gun lowered to his side. He knew he'd narrowly avoided the disaster of shooting innocent men or, on the other hand, let the people trying to kill his family and Senator Conrad escape. He hoped he didn't make a huge mistake that would come back to haunt him forever.

Chapter 34

Whiskey is for drinking; water is for fighting.

The official author of the quote is unknown but is often attributed to Mark Twain.

Parker, Arizona

Jason drove the first of two black SUVs as dust swirled behind their vehicles, speeding up the highway along the Colorado River north of Parker, Arizona. Houses, mobile homes, and RVs dotted both shorelines for miles, only to be interrupted by a formidable mountain of rust-red granite. Crenshaw sat next to Jason in the front seat, and Jasmine and Zee were in the back seat. They were followed by a vehicle with members from the Subcommittee on Water and Power within the Senate Committee on Energy and Natural Resources. Crenshaw, Zee, and the rest of the committee contingency had arrived on a chartered flight early that morning after Conrad convinced them to spend a day on the Colorado River before the upcoming committee vote on the POLAR Act.

"Who are we meeting at the Parker Dam?" Jason asked.

"His name is Greg Hammond. He's a civil engineer specializing in hydropower, so he's familiar with every dam and reservoir in the country. I invited him to give the committee members on the fence an overview of the current health of the Colorado River and its reservoirs. I've seen him speak, and he's very knowledgeable. Cross your fingers that he's also convincing."

Jason slowed as the massive eggshell white reinforced concrete structure came into view. Five square cutouts rose into the sky like giant open garage doors against the amber backdrop of the surrounding mountain range. The openings allowed dam operators to raise the spillway gates vertically to control the flow of water held in captivity behind the dam. He guided the SUV into the downstream parking lot across from the power generation station on the California side of the river—the second SUV of committee members parked beside them seconds later.

Conrad's team joined the senators and committee staff, and together, they walked toward a man standing alone on the sidewalk near the dam. He had a circle beard with shaggy medium hair that touched the collar of this purple polo shirt with the University of Washington logo on the chest.

Crenshaw marched ahead and shook hands with the man. She introduced everyone from Senator Conrad's staff and the committee to him.

"Please introduce yourself."

"Hello. I'm Greg, a civil engineer specializing in hydropower. Julia Crenshaw asked me to meet you here and give you more information on the Colorado River, its dams, and reservoirs. I can also answer any questions I don't cover at the end."

"Any questions before we get started?"

Jason watched the senator from Oregon step forward and point to the logo on Greg's shirt. "How frustrating is it knowing that your Huskies will lose to my Ducks in football this fall?" the senator asked with a wry smile.

Greg's lips remained straight. "If that happens, I'll drink this lake behind me."

The banter between long-time college football rivals elicited some "oohs" from the crowd.

"I can't wait to see that," the Oregon senator replied.

"Now that we've got that important business out of the way, let's get started."

Greg pointed to the concrete surrounding them. "This is Parker Dam. It's a concrete arch-gravity dam that sits 155 miles downstream from its much bigger brother, the Hoover Dam. The Bureau of Reclamation completed the dam in 1938 on the Arizona and California border to generate hydroelectric power and create a reservoir, Lake Havasu. The beautiful lake behind you stretches forty-five miles from north to south and covers thirty-two square miles. At its capacity, Lake Havasu has a storage capacity of over 200 billion gallons."

"How many Olympic size swimming pools can that fill?" the senator from New Mexico asked.

"A lot," Greg quipped. Chuckles from the group followed his answer.

Greg spun and marched toward the parking lot. "Follow me. We're going two minutes upstream to show you a critical component of this reservoir."

Minutes later, Jason parked the SUV and joined the rest of the audience at the Parker Dam boat launch. Everyone followed Greg to the water's edge overlooking the azure waters of Lake Havasu. A gentle breeze generated ripples on the surface as miniature waves lapped at their feet. Greg extended his arm and pointed to the north.

"You see those towers just beyond the bend of the river?"

Jason's eyes, along with a dozen others, squinted in the direction of Greg's index finger.

"That's the pumping stations for the Colorado River Aqueduct and one of the primary sources of drinking water for Southern California. The water district paid for the construction of Parker Dam and pumped this water 242 miles to its terminus at Lake Mathews near Riverside, California. Arizonans weren't happy with the dam or all the water going to California, so in 1935, the Arizona Governor sent the National Guard to halt construction of the dam. They were prepared to go to war over the dam, and it worked. The US Secretary of the Interior negotiated the Central Arizona Project that supplies water to Phoenix and Tucson, and Parker Dam was completed."

Jason turned to Zee beside him. "Arizonans have been eager to fight over water rights for the last century."

Zee spit between the boulders below his feet. "Yep. Sounds like it."

"Does anyone have questions for me?" the engineer asked.

The senator from Idaho asked about inflows and outflows on the Colorado River, which led to a five-minute response from Greg that Jason tuned out. He was interested in hearing the response to the next question.

"I keep hearing about the dead pool at Lake Mead. What exactly is *dead pool*?" Crenshaw asked.

Greg took a deep breath and exhaled. "Okay. If the water level at Lake Mead falls below 895 feet of elevation, it will be below the intake towers, and therefore, no additional water could pass through Hoover Dam."

"How close are we now?" Crenshaw asked.

"We have over 150 feet to go before we hit the dead pool in Lake Mead."

"What happens then?"

"Davis Dam is seventy miles downstream from Hoover Dam and forms Lake Mojave. If Lake Mead falls to a dead pool, Lake Mohave will dry up in about thirty days. Flows out of Davis Dam would slow to a trickle, and within an hour, the stretch of river that runs past Laughlin, Nevada, between Davis Dam and Lake Havasu would dry up. Within a few hours, the water level would fall below the pumps to the Colorado River Aqueduct, cutting off two-thirds of the water supply to the Greater Los Angeles Area. The same thing would happen to the Central Arizona Project a few hours later. Three to four days later, irrigation in western Arizona shuts down, and within a few weeks, Phoenix loses forty percent of its freshwater, and Tucson gets pinched a few weeks after that. Soon, every downstream canal that irrigates anything green in Southern Arizona and the Imperial Valley of California goes dry. Don't even get me started on the loss of hydropower generation," Greg added. "Dead pool in Lake Mead would be catastrophic to the region, country, and the world if crops in Arizona and California can't be irrigated."

Jason heard murmurs from the senators to his left and a whistle from Zee on his right. Crenshaw snapped toward Ruben Zambrano with a deep scowl.

Zee tossed up his hands in surrender. "What? That's some scary shit, man, but what's the chance that happens in our lifetimes? That dead pool is just worst-case scenario shit, right?"

A grin formed beneath Greg's whiskers on his face. "The water level fluctuates every year based on winter and spring snowpack and rainfall, but the long-term trend of Lake Mead elevation is heading lower. If nothing changes with the amount pumped from the Colorado River downstream, the dead pool is a matter of when, not if, it will happen. It's like a checking account for you and me. If we constantly withdraw more money than we put in, we eventually run out of money, but instead of getting hit with an overdraft fee, the Colorado River basin gets hit with a natural disaster for the ages."

"How can we avoid it?" Crenshaw asked.

"In theory, it's easy. Irrigators and cities must take less from the river, so less water has to pass from Lake Mead and Lake Powell through the dams that created them. The hard part is getting anyone to take a gallon less than they have the right to use based on a ninety-year-old pact, but I guess that's why you're here."

The group was quiet for several beats. "Any more questions?"

Crenshaw stepped forward. "Thank you, Greg. I think we all learned a lot today. I know I did. We'll be in touch if we have any future questions."

The SUV was mostly quiet, except for Zee singing to the melodies in his earphones, as Jason drove them to Phoenix to catch their flight back to Washington, DC. Jason grew up in Arizona but had no idea of the dire state of the Colorado River water supply that tens of millions of people relied on for their livelihoods. Now, Senator Conrad's relentless determination to see his bill passed by Congress and signed into law made more sense.

He didn't realize until now that the consequences of doing nothing could turn his family's life and millions of others into a living hell.

Chapter 35

Jason increased the speed of the hotel treadmill from six miles per hour to seven. A drop of sweat fell to the belt after he surpassed two miles and breathed heavily, but he couldn't hear anything over Guns N' Roses blasting over his earbuds. Over the past month, the significant events Jason endured were piling up inside him like sediment in a river. It wasn't just one thing, but the constant pressure of protecting a high-profile individual with a target on his back was taking its toll. Talking to Shanna usually helped, but she already had her hands full with JJ and her mom. Jason didn't want to bother his busy wife, so he turned to the thing that always helped clear his mind—a hard run to sweat out the stress.

Did I let the Yuma bombers escape after their test at the dam?

He thumbed the button, increasing the speed to eight miles per hour.

Stop beating yourself up over the past. You can't change it, so forget about it.

His calves, thighs, and chest burned, but Jason maintained the sprinter's pace.

Focus on the future. Work with Archie to find the bombers.

The treadmill slowed after Jason completed his third mile, and he walked until his breathing returned to normal. He stepped off the treadmill and wiped the sweat off his head and face with a towel. Jason scrolled through his phone as he continued to cool off before returning to his room to shower.

Ding.

Clay texted Jason, inviting him to breakfast, so Jason walked gingerly to his room. Thirty minutes later, Jason strolled into the hotel restaurant and found Clay eating alone in the corner. Jason stopped and watched Clay for a half-minute. Clay's body language made it clear that something was bothering him.

Is he still upset that the two suspects got away?

"Hey Clay, can I crash this party?"

"Sure," Clay replied. He looked up for a split second and then returned to the pancakes on his plate.

"Okay, I'll grab something at the buffet."

Jason filled his plate with toast, eggs, and bacon and then topped it off with a mug of coffee. He sipped the black liquid and expected to hate it, but it wasn't half bad.

Clay continued to scroll through his phone after Jason returned. Neither man said a word until Jason's plate was almost clean.

"You still pissed the two bombing suspects got away? It still bothered me this morning, so I went for a run to clear my head."

"Nah, that's not it. I just have a lot on my mind."

"Is it the stress of all the locations we have to scout in the next week? I could take a few places on your list to give you a short break," Jason offered.

"No, it has nothing to do with work."

"Is there any way I can help?"

"I wish you could, but unfortunately, neither of us can fix my problem."

Jason stared at his hurting friend. "Okay, I may not be able to fix anything, but just know I'm here for you. No matter what it is. I'm all in, just like you were for me when Josh died."

Clay nodded but didn't look up. Jason opened his phone and checked his emails until a cloth napkin flew into the center of the table.

"It came back," Clay whispered. His eyes glistened, and his lower lip quivered.

"What came back?"

Clay licked his lips and inhaled deeply. "My mom's ovarian cancer. She went to the doctor a couple of days ago after she unexpectedly lost a lot of weight. This morning, she found out that it came back."

"I'm sorry, Clay."

The former Air Force Special Recognizance operator from Louisiana shook his head. "She beat it six years ago after they caught it early. The radiation therapy eliminated the tumor, but her doctor said if it came back, they'd have to operate on her to remove the cancer. She's almost seventy and will probably need surgery."

Jason was stunned and didn't know what to say. He wanted to help in some way.

"Are any of your sisters around to help her?" Jason knew Clay had three older sisters and that he was born later in life to parents in their forties. His father was an alcoholic who died in prison when Clay was twelve after killing a young couple in a DUI accident, forcing his three sisters and Clay to take care of their mother and the large expanse of property passed down by their grandparents. During one of their stints in the Arizona pine forests, Clay told Jason that it was hard for him to leave his mom in Louisiana when he joined the Air Force, but she knew how important it was to him and practically kicked him out. The guilt for leaving his mom behind still ebbed and flowed like the tide in the Louisiana bayou. Jason understood the guilt that he'd been unable to shake.

"My youngest sister lives down the street and stops by several times a day, but she has her own family to worry about," Clay said.

"Go home and see your mom."

Clay looked like he'd bit into something awful. "I can't do that, and you know it. We have way too much going on here for me to sneak back home. In fact, we're wasting time talking about this. We have a few more locations to scout, so let's get rolling."

Clay stood, but Jason remained in his seat.

"Come on, Mulder, let's go."

"Not until we finish this conversation. Sit back down."

Clay removed the plastic straw from his lips and leaned closer to Jason. "You no longer outrank me, Mulder. You report to me now, and I said we're leaving."

Jason didn't react to the command. He moved to the end of his chair and looked Clay in his eyes.

"This isn't about rank, Clay," Jason said calmly, like a parent trying to console a hurt child.

"It's about respect, and I have too much respect for you and your relationship with your mom to let you march out of here like everyone is fine. Sit down. Please."

Clay's jaw and lower lip quivered again as he fell back into his former seat.

"Okay, what?" Clay asked, like an exasperated teen.

Jason sighed. "You have to go home and see your mom. Zee, Central, and I can hold down the fort until you return."

"Jason, did you not see our schedule for next week? Conrad is giving a speech at the bottom of the freaking Hoover Dam. It's practically a ready-made kill zone, and we're already short-handed for that kind of event. I won't do that to you guys."

"Could the speech be moved or delayed?"

"No chance. His baby is dying in committee, and he's pushing all his chips in on the speech to revive the POLAR Act. Changing anything with that speech is not something the senator would entertain."

Jason looked into his cup as if it provided the answers to his dilemma, and then he downed the rest of his coffee.

"Zee, Central, and I can handle it. I'll contact local and state police for additional resources and see if Congresswoman Duarte's PSD can help. They're just up the road in Vegas."

Clay exhaled, and his shoulders appeared to relax. "That may work."

"Of course it will. The bottom line is that you need to go home to your mom, and we'll take care of everything else. I promise everything will be fine."

Clay's look did not scream that he was convinced, but Jason sensed he was close.

"What would you say if Zee, Central, or I came to you with the same issue?"

"That's different," Clay said with a wave.

"No, it's not. We're a PSD family, and we support each other when our real families need us. It's your turn this time, so go home and be with your mom in her time of need. You know it will make her feel better to see your face."

The ends of Clay's lips tilted upward for a split second. "Okay, I'll go home, but I'll be back as soon as I confirm she's okay."

Jason stood and reached out his hand as if challenging Clay to an arm wrestling match. The big Cajun cupped Jason's hand and pulled him in for a hug.

"Thank you for the push. I needed it today," Clay said.

"Anytime."

Clay turned toward the elevators to return to his room while Jason watched his friend depart. He meant every word he said to Clay but knew his promise was flimsy. Keeping Senator Conrad safe would be a monumental challenge, especially with the bomber still on the loose. Jason hoped his push for Clay to return home wouldn't turn into a regrettable disaster.

The stakes were higher than ever, and if he failed, many people would die.

Chapter 36

Phoenix, Arizona

Jason gripped the steering wheel as his knuckles gradually turned as white as the freeway lines passing under his truck in a blur. A barrage of thoughts and possibilities bombarded Jason's senses while he drove to the FBI office in north Phoenix for a meeting with Archie. Angst and unease coursed through his veins.

After Clay left for the airport, Jason scouted an elementary school in Chandler, Arizona. Now, he felt as if a steel band was constricting his chest, tightening with each passing hour. It was hard for him to take a deep breath and fill his lungs.

It was similar to his pool training in the PJ pipeline when an instructor harassed Jason and a fellow trainee while buddy breathing. After Jason held his breath for a minute while his partner breathed, an instructor knocked his mask off. It fell to the bottom of the pool, forcing Jason to retrieve it before he could suck in life-giving oxygen from the snorkel. As Jason pushed off the bottom with his mask, he saw flickers of blackness, and his chest burned like he inhaled lava. The blackness worsened during each foot of his ascent, but Jason trusted his training and himself. At that point in the pipeline, Jason knew he'd become a PJ and wear the maroon beret. Jason made it back to the snorkel, but he never forgot the throbbing in his chest nine feet below the pool's surface.

Stress reared its ugly head again; this time, no talk, run, or sweat could help. Senator Conrad's Hoover Dam speech, elusive bombers, Clay's absence to be with his mom, and his mother-in-law's injury, which also impacted Shanna and JJ, all contributed to the enormous weight crushing Jason's chest. He had to remove some weight, but almost everything was out of his control. The only problem he could personally impact was to find the bombers.

First, he called Shanna. She picked up on the second ring.

"How are you and JJ doing?" Jason tried to sound upbeat.

"JJ sat by himself on the floor today for five minutes. I think he'll be crawling soon," Shanna shared. She sounded excited by their seven-month-old son's feat, but it had the opposite effect on Jason. Now, he had another stressor on his list: missing out on the first year of his son's life.

"How about your mom? Is she getting better?" Jason changed the subject, and his upbeat tone faded with the new question.

"Yeah, slowly but surely. She ditched the walker and graduated to a cane. Her doctor said she may have to use the cane for a while. Yesterday was the first time she could shower and dress herself."

"At least she's heading in the right direction."

"Yeah, and Mom is still talking about how her favorite son-in-law saved her from a disorderly date," Shanna chuckled.

Jason appreciated the comment and his wife's attempt to cheer him up, but he couldn't summon a positive response - they were buried too deep. He didn't respond, and Shanna must have expected a different reaction.

"What's wrong?"

"Nothing. Just a long week."

"I can tell something is bothering you. What is it?"

Jason couldn't lie to his wife, and Shanna was too smart even if he tried.

"Clay had to leave. He went home to visit his mom. Her cancer is back."

"Oh my gosh, that's awful," Shanna said. "Is she in the hospital? Are they treating it?"

"He just left for the airport, so I don't have all the details, but now I'm responsible for Senator Conrad and his staff's safety while they are in Arizona. I told Clay he should go, and I support him taking as much time as he needs, but losing a quarter of our team is a lot with everything else happening right now."

This time, Shanna was quiet. Jason listened to the road noise penetrating the cab as he neared the exit for the FBI office.

"Jason, I know you're probably stressed out because you're not home taking care of JJ and me, but we're okay. What can I do to help?"

"No, Hon, you're already doing so much. I'll admit I'm a little frustrated that I'm not home more often, but knowing you're with JJ more now makes it a little easier."

"Of course, we're a family and a team. We always support each other, so if I can help, let me know."

"Can you convince a stubborn senator not to give a speech in a hard-to-defend place or get the FBI to catch the people who seem to want him dead?" Jason joked.

"They still haven't caught the people that put the bomb under our truck?" Shanna's tone turned serious and accusatory.

"Not yet, but they will. I'm going to the FBI office now to review all the evidence with Archie. Hopefully, with everything on the table and everyone in one room, it will lead to a break in the case."

"Jason, you need to pressure the FBI to find the bombers as soon as possible. Nobody is safe until those monsters are behind bars," Shanna hissed.

"That's the plan."

"I know it will also take a lot of pressure off you, but you have to let the FBI do their job."

"Why do you say that?" Jason asked.

"I know how you get when you get your mind set on something. Does the La Palma cartel ring a bell?"

"That was different. Nobody else could find the people that killed Josh."

"I agree it was different, but these people already tried to kill you and your family. They seem ruthless and determined, so just be careful. Please."

Jason considered debating Shanna but instead agreed. "I will."

A cry from a young child came through the phone. "That's JJ. He's up from his nap, so I have to go. Be safe and call me later."

"I will. Love you."

"Love you, too."

Jason hung up as he pulled into the FBI office parking lot and stopped before the gate. It was the first time he drove to the FBI office without Archie and the increased security measures compared to the satellite office in Yuma were obvious. A man who looked about forty exited the guard station and motioned for Jason to roll down his window.

"Your business with the FBI today?" the security guard asked.

"I have a meeting with Special Agent Archie Woods."

"ID, please."

The guard took Jason's driver's license back to his station. Jason watched the man with his black uniform over a bulletproof vest and a utility belt with top-of-the-line radio, handcuffs, flashlight, pepper spray, and a Glock 17 peck at keys on a computer. Despite the mundane nature of his job, he looked engaged and ready to defend the people inside the building against harm.

Does he have as much stress in his job?

Jason watched with a hint of envy as the security guard returned with his license.

"Please pull to the front of the building and park in a spot for visitors' parking. Don't park anywhere else. You'll check in again with security inside the building."

Jason did as instructed and found a parking spot for visitors just outside the front doors of the FBI office. He studied the five-story building through his windshield as the American flag flapped in the gentle breeze on the flagpole. Jason ran his fingers through his cropped chestnut hair as he saw himself in the rearview mirror.

He leaned closer until only his eyes were visible in the rectangular reflection. "One way or another, I'm going to find the bombers and make them pay for trying to kill the people I've sworn to protect ... And the most important people in the world to me."

Chapter 37

Jason placed his phone, wallet, and keys in a plastic tray while a security guard motioned him through the metal detector. A second security guard, with an AR-15 rifle slung over his neck, retrieved his items from an X-ray tunnel and examined his phone as if he were seeing an iPhone for the first time. It was just like passing through airport security but with heavily armed agents.

"Please take a seat in the chair until your escort arrives," the security guard commanded.

Archie arrived before Jason sat down.

"Mulder, follow me."

They passed a bank of elevators and continued on the first floor into a corridor of conference rooms.

He followed Archie into a bright room and nodded to familiar faces, FBI analyst Marisol Bautista and FBI bomb squad expert Marcin Dobrowski, as they stood around the cherry wood table large enough to seat eight people. Dobrowski leaned over the table like he was doing a push-up while Bautista squinted at something in her hand.

The table was covered with a collage of photos and plastic trays with the word "evidence" stenciled on the ends.

Jason joined the group around the table, his gaze sweeping over the array of evidence. Photographs of the bomb sites were strewn across the tabletop, each one a stark reminder of the danger still lurking outside the building. Mulder leaned forward, his attention drawn to the Gillespie Dam and the last known bomb site.

Bautista was the first to speak. "All right, thank you all for coming. I invited everyone here to review the evidence and share what we know so far."

She held up her index finger. "First, the bomb in Yuma was made of ammonium nitrate, a readily available substance on farms and ranches. The last bomb was constructed with C-4, a more advanced explosive material, showing a progression in capabilities and tactics."

"C-4 is a highly regulated and closely monitored explosive," Dobrowski stated. "The suspects must have access to mining, construction, or law enforcement personnel. They may not even be farmers or ranchers."

Archie stepped closer to the table with his hands in his pant pockets. "Marisol is right. It suggests new resources and increased planning for something much larger."

All eyes shot to Archie. He said what Jason was thinking and probably Bautista and Dobrowski, but nobody else wanted to admit the threat posed by the bombers could get worse.

"The Al-Rashidi brothers are now the top suspects. What do we have on them?" Archie asked.

"The financial records I've been able to obtain of Jassim and Amir Al-Rashidi show substantial debt," Bautista said. "Since our last meeting, I've also found evidence of large farmland purchases in rural western Arizona. One farm was twelve hundred acres, and the other land purchased contained over two thousand acres. That's over five square miles of highly speculative land with little resources other than the water rights that come with them. The value of other farmland in the area with water rights has been rising rapidly but could also plummet if proposed legislation like the POLAR Act passes. The financial motive looks more likely with each piece of new information I uncover."

"That's good, but we need more," Archie interjected. "Can you do a deeper dive into Al-Rashidi Farms? Check for any unusual purchases, travel, known associates on our watch list, or anything else that could help us solidify their spot at the top of our list."

Dobrowski interrupted before Bautista could answer. "Also, see if you can find out where they obtained the C-4. That may provide a clue to their intentions. Do we have enough to get a warrant to search their farm?"

"Not yet. We need something to tie the Al-Rashidi brothers directly to any of the bombings to secure a warrant to search their property. Until we have that, we're just pissing in the wind," Archie replied.

Mulder sat in a chair beside the table and leaned back, his mind racing.

The other three continued to pore over the evidence until the room fell silent.

Archie cleared his throat. "Well, if that's all for today, let's —"

"Wait!" Jason interrupted. "Can one of you take me back to my truck?"

"Your truck?" asked Archie. "Why?"

"I have something that may be directly connected to the bombers, and I need one of you to come with me so I don't get strip-searched when I return."

"I'll take him," Dobrowski volunteered.

Ten minutes later, Jason and Dobrowski returned to the conference room. Archie and Bautista were sitting at the table, discussing another case. Jason placed the medallion between them on the table.

"I found this in the field near the bomb site in Yuma. The ornate designs look old, and I think the inscriptions are Arabic. I don't know what it is, but I'd bet it came from one of the bombers."

Archie picked it up first, examined it, and then placed it back on the table. Bautista did the same, but her eyes widened in possible recognition.

"I've seen something like this before, but I'll run it through the system to confirm. Give me twenty minutes."

Bautista went to her workstation on the third floor while Jason listened to Dobrowski and Archie share tales of misfires and bomb-defusing attempts that went very wrong. Dobrowski was finishing a story when Bautista returned. "And I think he literally shit his pants. I never laughed so hard in my life." The three men roared as Bautista waited patiently for the laughter to end.

"Are you done?" she asked.

"Yes," Archie replied. "Did you find anything?"

"I was right. It's an ornament from a jambiya."

"A jambiya?" Jason asked.

"Yeah, it's a dagger with a large handle and a short, curved blade. The double-edged jambiya originated in Saudi Arabia centuries ago and expanded to other parts of the Middle East. The steel blade is stored in a sheath decorated with ornaments that signify the status of the individual or tribe."

Jason stared at the ornamental medallion and nodded.

"They affix the sheath to a leather belt and wear it to cultural events and —"

Bautista stopped talking. Jason looked up from the jambiya ornament at the FBI analyst. "And?"

"And for battle."

Jason's eyebrows raised above his wide eyes.

"That's it! The Saudis wore jambiyas when they carried the explosives through the field in Yuma. They were going to battle with Senator Conrad. Can you get a warrant now?"

Archie inhaled deeply and leaned against the table.

"None of the evidence we have so far will hold up in court, and I doubt we'd get a warrant based on poor financial decisions and an ornament that fell off a dagger in a lettuce field. We still need more."

Everyone stared at the medallion as if it would reveal the solutions to their problems. Jason was sure the Al-Rashidi brothers were involved, if not the outright bombers.

We have to act now before it's too late. It's time to take matters into my own hands.

Jason stood abruptly, attracting all eyes on him.

"Give me twelve hours, and I'll get you the evidence you need."

"Don't break into their property or anything because that won't help get us a warrant, and any evidence you find won't be admissible," Bautista warned.

"I won't," Jason lied.

"How do you plan to obtain this evidence?" Archie asked.

"As a representative of Senator Conrad's staff, I plan to share details of the POLAR Act to gain support for the bill from Arizona constituents. Anything I find if invited on their property can be used to get a warrant."

Archie stood and crossed his arms. "I don't like it, Mulder. Those guys are dangerous, and you're walking right into the lion's den."

"He's right, though. As long as the evidence is legally obtained, we can get a warrant," Dobrowski added.

"Don't encourage him, Marcin. The young man is trying to get himself killed," Archie barked.

Jason moved in front of Archie and put both hands on his shoulders. He looked the FBI Special Agent in the eyes. "You're going to have to trust me on this one. I'll get the evidence you need to nail these guys."

He locked eyes with Archie for several beats, turned toward the door, and yelled over his shoulder. "Stay by your phone. I'll call with what I find soon."

Chapter 38

The engine of Jason's Ford Raptor roared to life as he pressed his boot harder on the accelerator to reach the summit of the pale brown ridge. At the peak, red-orange light flooded the cab as the two-lane desert highway appeared to swallow the setting sun. The visor shaded Jason's face from the blinding rays, but the intensity in his eyes cut through the darkness.

The GPS on the dash said he still had ten minutes until he reached Al-Rashidi Farms. Jason hoped he'd arrive before dark to recon the grounds, but he lost forty-five minutes of precious daylight in the treacherous rush hour traffic leaving Phoenix. Now, he'd have to learn as much as possible about the buildings and people under the stars and waxing moon.

Minutes before turning onto the road leading to Al-Rashidi Farms, Jason's phone buzzed on the seat next to him. He checked the caller ID and saw it was his boss.

"Hey Clay, how's your mom doing?"

"She's doing as well as one can expect. My mom's always been a fighter, and she has a lot of fight left in her."

"That's great news."

"Are you guys ready for Conrad's speech at the Hoover Dam in two days? Are you already in Vegas?"

Jason paused longer than he wanted before answering. He didn't want to lie, but also didn't want to alarm him.

"Not yet. I'm heading up there first thing tomorrow, but you don't need to worry about the speech. We got everything under control, so you can focus on your mom."

"Are you sure?" Clay asked.

"Yeah, we'll go over every inch of the speech venue tomorrow."

"Okay," Clay responded with a hint of concern in his voice. "Don't hesitate to call me if you need anything."

"I will."

Jason hung up, and a minute later, a sign for Al-Rashidi Farms appeared in his headlights. The white sign with navy blue letters rose prominently over a sea of alfalfa fields that stretched as far as he could see in the twilight. He slowed to a crawl on the rural street and noted multiple lighted structures at the end of a gravel road a quarter mile away. Jason opened the map application on his phone and chose the satellite view layer. He spotted a pull-off several hundred yards ahead and let his truck idle forward. Jason killed his lights as he pulled off under a cluster of overgrown mesquite trees.

The former PJ and DEA special agent ensured he had a round in his SIG Sauer P226 chamber with two additional full magazines before he slid from the truck. Jason's quick analysis of Al-Rashidi Farms before he left Phoenix indicated the farm did not contain any residential buildings, so he did not expect to run into anyone after dark. To be sure, he planned to approach on foot through the alfalfa fields in the dark to give him ample time to spot any people still on the property.

Jason snagged his backpack from the rear cab and entered the knee-high alfalfa field toward the lighted structures on the farm. He approached stealthily, like a lion hunting on the savanna, to hear any sounds coming from the buildings while concealing his presence. It took thirty minutes to cross five hundred yards, but Jason arrived at the field's edge undetected. He lowered himself into a prone position and removed binoculars from his pack. Jason swept the binoculars from left to right and then back again across the three nearest buildings. He never saw any human activity during his approach, and his magnified view of the structures confirmed no detectable cameras. Jason suspected the lack of security cameras was typical for a place dozens of miles from civilization.

The smaller building appeared to be an administrative office, while the one to its right was ten times bigger and two stories tall. The larger building looked ideal for storing ammonium nitrate fertilizer or a weapons cache, so Jason chose to investigate that one first.

He pulled his knees beneath him, looked both ways like he was crossing the street, and bolted for the door of the larger building. Jason stopped, took a deep breath, and slowly turned the handle. His lips curved upward when the handle turned, and the door pushed open into darkness. He slid inside, closed the door, and located the flashlight in his bag. Once Jason pressed the button, the metal Maglite torch turned the western half of the building into virtual daytime.

"Hello? Is anyone here to discuss the benefits of the POLAR Act?" Jason whispered. He chuckled at his ruse.

Jason continued deeper into the building. He inched forward, allowing the beam of light to illuminate two tractors and several pieces of equipment. Jason panned to the opposite side of the building and saw pallets of materials covered in tarps arranged in two neat rows. His eyes widened as he silently walked across the concrete floor toward the pallets. He raised the tarp on one side to view the contents underneath and was greeted with ammonium nitrate fertilizer stacked chest high.

Bingo!

Jason confirmed that all eight pallets contained twenty bags of fertilizer. He didn't know how big Al-Rashidi Farms was or how much fertilizer was needed, but it felt excessive.

Is this the evidence we need for a warrant? Should I call Archie now?

The answer to Jason's question came back to him quickly. He doubted a judge would issue a warrant for an active farm storing fertilizer. This wasn't the evidence he needed, so he had to keep going.

Another door was steps away from the pallets, so Jason turned off his flashlight and opened it. The building that looked like the administrative office was ten yards away. Jason exposed one eye to check for people. The farm grounds were still as quiet as when he first arrived, so he darted across the short expanse to the door of the single-story building. Jason tried the door, which was also unlocked, so he let himself inside.

Two computer monitors displaying the same image of a cloudless indigo-blue sky over a grassy meadow provided ample light to see the main room. It contained two desks pushed against the east and south walls, with one large desk in the middle. File cabinets and shelves covered the west wall.

"Jackpot," Jason whispered.

It was clear he'd found the farm's main office, so he searched the surface of each desk for anything that could be used to issue a warrant. Finding nothing, he moved to the top drawer of one of the file cabinets. He directed the beam of his flashlight to the file names as he pushed each file back with his thumb. Jason knew he wouldn't find a file named Yuma bombing or illegal C-4 purchases, but careless criminals could leave something incriminating behind, like an invoice for blasting caps.

Jason spent an hour going through every drawer in six file cabinets but came up empty. He put his hands on his hips as he pondered his next move.

I don't think they keep any incriminating evidence here. Keep searching for a few more minutes and get out of here before someone comes to the office.

Jason rolled his neck. It was stiff from looking down at the files for so long. He turned back to the north wall and noticed a door he missed when he first arrived. Eight steps later, he reached the door and tried the handle. It was the only locked door Jason had encountered all night, piquing his interest in learning what was inside the room. Jason retrieved the lock pick gun from his backpack and positioned the flashlight on the floor to light up the lock. He inserted a tension tool into the keyway and followed with the pick needle on the lock pick gun. It was a little larger than an ultrasonic toothbrush and vibrated like one when he turned it on. Less than ten seconds later, the lock opened.

Jason shone his flashlight on the nearest wall, and his jaw dropped. The room was slightly bigger than a bathroom in an average home, but every inch of the walls was covered with ancient weapons that looked straight out of medieval times. It was like a shrine to every device used to maim, torture, and kill for a thousand years during the Middle Ages. The left wall contained spears and swords, while the right wall held melee weapons like a war hammer, blunt mace, and studded club. The back wall displayed daggers of all shapes and sizes. Jason's wide eyes scanned all the weapons until one of them caught his attention. He stepped further into the room to better see an ornate jambiya with an empty circular area near the hilt. Something was missing and looked the same size as the medallion he had found in Yuma.

"That's it," Jason whispered. "They had that jambiya with them in Yuma."

Jason let out a long exhale and relaxed his shoulders.

There's no doubt now it was them. I'll let Archie know so he can get a warrant to put these pricks in jail.

The door creaked behind him, and Jason's hand instinctively snapped to his holster, grasping for his pistol as adrenaline flooded his veins. But before he could touch the cool steel, an intense pain exploded at the base of his skull, blinding him with white-hot sparks dancing across his vision. Struggling to stay upright, Jason's legs gave out, and he collapsed to the ground. He could make out the silhouette of a bearded figure looming over him but felt paralyzed to defend himself against another attack.

The assailant raised his arm high over his head and struck Jason again. His breath caught in his throat as darkness engulfed him, stealing his consciousness like a ruthless thief.

Chapter 39

The intruder slumped forward in the chair as blood ran down his face and neck to form a pool of crimson on his shirt collar. Jassim stood beside the man while Amir, Hamza, and Ibrahim crowded behind him to watch in the close quarters. He kicked the leg of the chair to stir the man, bound with zip ties on his wrists and ankles, from his unconscious slumber. The person was no stranger to Jassim, although he'd never met him. He's aware the man was on the security team for the evil senator trying to destroy their family business and that they called him Mulder. Jassim also knew that if Mulder had pressed the start button on his truck at the event center in Phoenix, he'd be in an urn or casket next to his wife and son instead of unconscious on a chair in his weapons room.

Jassim, Amir, and Hamza arrived before the sun rose after Ibrahim notified them that he'd knocked out an intruder. Fortunately for the Al-Rashidi brothers, their maintenance manager took it upon himself to sleep in one of the tractors after being chased by two men at the dam where they tested the C-4. Ibrahim saw the determination in their eyes and suspected they might show up at the typically deserted farm at night.

The member of Senator Conrad's personal security detail raised his chin several inches and let it fall back to his chest again. Jassim kicked his chair again, and this time, Mulder raised his head and blinked his eyes open. He scanned the room and settled his gaze on Jassim. Mulder licked his lips and spoke.

"I was right."

"Right about what?" Jassim asked.

"You are behind all the bombings."

"Why would you say that? We're simply interrogating someone who broke into our place of business. You'd be in a lot of trouble if we called the police."

Mulder closed his eyes and shook his head.

"You'd do the same if it were your business, no?" Jassim asked.

"You can stop playing games," Mulder said in a raspy voice. "The FBI has evidence of means and motive, and now I can directly tie you to the Yuma bombing."

"Oh, do tell, oh wise one," Jassim said with a chuckle, causing the others to laugh.

Mulder pointed to the wall of daggers with his chin. "I found the missing medallion on your jambiya."

Jassim's facial expression transformed into a scowl of recognition and anger as he locked eyes with Mulder. This seemed to empower the bound man.

"Now that I've got your attention, you should know it's not too late to turn yourself in. You can get a lawyer, and a jury may be lenient when they hear your side of the story."

Jassim turned to his men and saw the looks of concern around the room.

"Shut up!" Droplets of blood splattered on the floor after Jassim landed a right hook across Mulder's mouth, almost knocking the man from his chair.

"Everyone, out of this room," Jassim roared.

The four men shut the door to the weapons room and moved to the far end of the administrative building as the first rays of sun danced on the white walls. Jassim stared into the eyes of Amir, Hamza, and Ibrahim like a drill sergeant inspecting his men.

"Are any of you interested in turning yourself in now?"

The trio stood silent and still as statues.

"I need to hear you say it. Are you still committed to this mission until the end?"

Heads nodded, and three " yes " answers came from the men.

"What are we going to do with him?" Amir asked.

Jassim turned toward the window and peered outside for five or six seconds, considering his options.

"This man can never leave the farm alive. Ibrahim, call in Laslov."

A twisted grin stretched across Ibrahim's face. "Laslov will break him into a million pieces."

"I know. Tell him to come right away. The other workers will be here in an hour."

The men followed Jassim back into the weapons room. A new blood stain appeared on the front of Mulder's shirt from his swollen, bloody lip.

"Okay, now that I have your attention," Jassim started. "I want you to know that you'll be dead soon."

He stopped talking, studying Mulder's face for any signs of dread he was sure would be there. But the intruder stared back at him with cold, unblinking eyes and an air of calmness. After seconds of silence and no indication of fear, Jassim continued.

"You're going to die for the stupidity of your politicians. Many other people will also die, including the senator you're trying to protect."

This got a reaction from Mulder as his eyes narrowed and the muscles in his neck tensed.

"Why kill innocent people over a proposed Colorado River water bill?"

Jassim leaned forward until he was a foot from Mulder's face. "We were a normal family farm following all the rules of your local, state, and federal governments, but that wasn't enough for your politicians. They always want more from the people. The new bill and its excise tax on exports to Saudi Arabia will crush my family's business that has been around for generations."

"It will also make your speculative investments in all that farmland with water rights worth far less," Mulder stated calmly.

Jassim straightened and nodded. "I see you have done your homework, and yes, that is also true."

"How do you expect to stop the POLAR Act by blowing up its drafters and supporters?" Jason asked.

"I don't," Jassim quickly replied.

"Then why go to all the trouble with the bombs?"

Jassim's lips curled up menacingly, like a predator baring its fangs. "Pain. I have no chance of changing anything the politicians want to do in Washington, DC, but I can inflict pain. I want them to feel some of the suffering the people must endure due to their stupid decisions."

Mulder started to speak, but Jassim held his hand up to stop him. "Enough talking. Bring him to the storage shed."

Hamza cut the ties to the chair but left them around his wrists while Ibrahim pulled Mulder to his feet. With one on each side, they dragged him through the administrative office. Once outside, they stood him up.

"Now walk, or you'll get a jambiya in the gut," Ibrahim threatened.

Mulder shuffled with the two Saudis to another large metal building in the far corner of the grounds. Once inside, they pushed him to the dusty dirt floor, where he landed with a thud.

"Laslov is almost here," Ibrahim said.

"Good."

"The authorities will find my body, and all of you will go to prison for the rest of your lives," Mulder said.

"You're right, so we'll be sure your body is never found."

"The FBI knows I'm here. If I don't return soon, this farm will be crawling with agents."

"Is that so?" Jassim asked. "You see that pile over there?" All eyes in the building turned to his finger, pointing at the brownish, gray mound buzzing with flies.

"That's fresh steer manure. Do you know what we do with cows that die at our dairy back in Saudi Arabia? We bury them in a manure pile, and they fully decompose in under a month."

The revelation of the dishonorable burial seemed to rattle Mulder, and he groaned as he tugged at the restraints on his wrist.

"That's right, Mr. Mulder. Your final resting place will be in a heap of shit until we use you to fertilize our alfalfa next season," Jassim stated. His tone is as calm as someone sharing the weather forecast of a sunny day.

A door opened, sending a wide beam of sunlight into the dim storage barn until a shadow blocked all but a few rays of the sun.

"He's here," Ibrahim said.

Mulder's eyes widened as the hulking figure stepped into the barn, and the outline of a menacing man stood tall before him.

Chapter 40

Jason watched the silhouette transform into a man nearly half a foot taller than him and likely a hundred pounds heavier. He wore camouflage Army pants with a tan t-shirt ripped into a tank top that exposed the rippled muscles in his arms, chest, and neck. Jason wasn't aware of how well the man could fight and didn't need to know. His size alone would make him a challenge for any human to overcome.

"Meet Laslov," Jassim said with pride in his voice.

"He came with me from our dairy in Saudi Arabia after my family gave him a second chance. None of the farms in our town would hire him after he was released from a Turkish prison and he refused to say why he spent a decade behind bars. We understood a man of his size brought unique skills that are valuable to a business and took a chance on him. He impressed my father with his ability to operate all of our equipment, but I was most excited about his non-farm capabilities. I watched him catch a man trying to steal a horse from our ranch and beat him to death with his bare hands in under a minute. Laslov is a man of few words, so I still don't know why he was in prison, but he did share that he loves the sensation of snapping human bones in his hands."

Jason scanned the giant standing over him and swallowed hard.

I'm a sitting duck with my hands and feet bound. I need to do something to give myself a chance.

"You're going to cut these zip cuffs off me so I can at least put up a fight, right?"

The question seemed to surprise the Saudi leader of the group.

"Your job is to die, not put up a fight," Jassim replied.

"So you brought in a giant to kill a man with his hands bound in cuffs? Why not just do it yourself? Are you all cowards?"

Jassim's eyes narrowed into thin slits, and he stepped toward Jason. Instead of striking him, he turned to Laslov. He spoke to him in Arabic, and the massive man nodded with a grunt.

"Laslov is no coward, and he will kill you just as fast without your hands tied."

Relief swept over Jason, but he made sure not to show it. Taking on five men while bound would be a sure death sentence, but having the full use of his hands and feet provided a slim hope of making it out alive.

Laslov moved toward Jason, and his shadow engulfed the former PJ. The farm enforcer grabbed Jason by the collar and pulled him to his feet. Laslov remained ramrod straight and tilted his neck and face toward Jason until he could feel the heat of the giant's breath on his forehead and cheeks. He reminded Jason of a furious bull, seething with anger until it was ready to unleash its full force.

"Cut him loose and let Laslov take care of him. We are already late for the next step in our mission," Jassim stated.

Hamza cut Jason loose with Laslov close by and ready to pounce. The four Saudi men strode to the exit and turned one last time to see Laslov shove Jason to the ground.

"Good luck," Jassim yelled out.

Jason crawled away from the massive man as the door closed behind them. Now, it was just the two of them, and he wanted to buy himself more time.

I don't see any weakness in this guy. How can I beat him without a weapon?

Jason searched the storage barn and saw the manure pile on one end and bales of alfalfa stacked to the ceiling on the other. Nothing else.

Laslov appeared impatient with the slow pace of Jason's inevitable demise and lunged forward. Jason turned and bolted for the alfalfa bales.

Could I push some heavy bales on him to slow him down?

Jason assumed he could outrun the behemoth, but after multiple blows to the head, his legs let him down. Steps into his improvised plan, an enormous hammer fist struck him between the shoulder blades. The force slammed Jason back to the dirt floor and sent waves of pain throughout his back and chest.

Running from Laslov wasn't a viable option, so Jason leaped to his feet and moved into the ready position he'd practiced thousands of times in Krav Maga training. He'd fought men bigger and stronger than Laslov, and his years of training in combat self-defense had allowed Jason to prevail over those men. Although he would be a monumental challenge, Jason was confident his years of training would allow him to defeat the massive man.

Laslov's snarl turned into a grin when he saw Jason take a defensive position, revealing two missing teeth on his upper jaw. His meaty hands turned into fists, resembling the medieval weapons Jason saw inside the administrative building. Laslov reared back and launched a haymaker punch that Jason easily saw coming. He raised his left arm to block the incoming blow but to no avail. The punch was so strong it pushed Jason's arm into his head as Laslov's fist was redirected to the top of his skull. The glancing blow forced Jason several steps to his right to prevent him from falling to the ground.

I won't survive too many of those punches—it's time to go on offense.

Jason responded with a flurry of straight punches to Laslov's upper chest and multiple knees to his thighs, but the mammoth of a man didn't even flinch. He grabbed Jason in a bear hug and squeezed, preventing Jason from launching additional blows. Laslov turned, twisted, and slid one arm between Jason's legs. Jason felt his feet leave the earthen floor until his entire body was over Laslov's head. His feet dangled seven feet in the air, and the oversized Saudi held him there for several beats as if it were the calm before the storm. Then Jason felt his body descend at a high rate of speed as Laslov slammed him to the earth. Pain shot through every inch of his body like an electrical shock.

Don't let him get on top of me now. Get up!

Jason wobbled to his feet like a baby fawn and resumed his defensive position. Laslov wasted no time and launched a straight punch that Jason unsuccessfully tried to redirect away from his face. Four enormous knuckles collided with Jason's face, and the dark void that consumed him earlier was rapidly approaching once again. His legs turned to mush and his head felt impossibly heavy as he fell to the ground, kicking up a cloud of dust upon impact.

As he regained consciousness, Jason woke to Laslov dragging him across the dirt floor by his left leg. The destination didn't register at first, but then Jason understood.

No! No! No! I'm not getting buried in that shit.

Jason secured a fistful of dirt and kicked Laslov in the ass with his free leg causing him to drop his other leg. He turned and bent toward Jason with his arm cocked to deliver another blow when

Jason flung the dirt into his eyes. Laslov let out a sound that was a mix between a grunt and a howl as he thrust both hands to his eyes. He rubbed his eye sockets with both hands and stumbled back, so Jason took advantage of the small window of opportunity. He got to his feet and aimed for the alfalfa bales. Jason moved like a drunk, staggering to maintain his balance as he haphazardly crossed the storage shed floor, but it was progress. His momentum carried Jason into the first row of alfalfa bales when he heard Laslov lumbering toward him like a raging elephant. He looked around for a weapon like a pitchfork or metal hook used to grab heavy hay bales but saw nothing. Jason scanned the walls until he saw something that might help him defeat the Saudi giant.

He climbed to the fourth row of alfalfa bales until he was out of Laslov's reach. Jason crawled to the wall and grabbed the material as Laslov jumped up and grabbed his ankle. He yanked hard, bringing Jason and several bales down on top of the massive man, knocking him down. Jason jumped to his feet first with the bailing wire he pulled from the wall and extended it until two feet of metal wire was exposed. He swept it over Laslov's head as he was on all fours trying to stand up and pulled it taught across his neck, just below his chin. Jason pulled with every ounce of muscle in his body, cutting off all oxygen and blood pumping through the giant's neck. Laslov thrashed like a fish trying to dislodge a hook, but Jason held on. He moved his knees up his back and pulled so hard Jason thought he might decapitate the giant. A part of Jason hoped his head would pop off and bounce off the dirt floor.

Laslov pulled on the wire coiled around his neck like a metal python. His flailing arms and jerking legs slowed as his brain began to suffer from a lack of oxygen.

"Die, you son of a bitch!" Jason yelled.

The fight remaining in the giant drained like a dying battery and eventually stopped, but Jason continued to yank as if his life depended on it. A full minute after Laslov stopped moving, Jason let go and let the man fall to the ground.

Jason stood over the dead giant until he caught his breath. A minute later, he staggered toward the door and opened it to bright sunlight. The grounds were still deserted, so he returned to the weapons room inside the administrative building. He noticed cabinets and drawers under the walls of the weapons he had seen earlier.

His backpack was still in the corner of the room, so Jason unzipped it and saw everything was still inside, including his SIG Sauer P226 that they removed from him after Ibrahim knocked him out. After sliding his weapon back into its holster and placing his phone in his pocket, he started rummaging through the cabinets. Most of the drawers were either empty or filled with damaged weapons, but he hit the jackpot when he reached the bottom drawer behind a row of daggers. He found two blasting caps, a one-foot section of det cord, and empty green wrappers. Jason unfurled the wrapper to expose the stenciled yellow letters that said CHARGE DEMOLITION M112 1-1/4 LBS COMP C-4.

Jason held the wrapper in one hand and a live blasting cap in the other for several seconds before returning them to the drawer. He knelt to open the cabinet below the drawer and spotted several maps rolled up into tight scrolls. Jason grabbed the largest map and opened it on a desk outside the weapons room. His eyes widened at the circled areas on the map.

He removed his phone from his pocket and dialed Archie. The FBI special agent answered after one ring.

"Archie, do you have access to a bird?"

"Yeah. I can get to one just down the street at Deer Valley Airport. Where are you?"

"I am at Al-Rashidi Farms."

"Did you find anything?" Archie asked.

"Yeah, and it's worse than I thought."

"What is it?"

"Get here as fast as you can. You need to see this yourself."

CHAPTER 41

FBI Special Agent Woods peered through the helicopter's rear window as dust from the rotor wash billowed like tan smoke above the buildings on Al-Rashidi Farms. Once the blades slowed, Archie and FBI analyst Marisol Bautista jogged with their heads down from the helicopter into the parking lot.

"Holy shit, Mulder, what happened to you?" Archie asked when Jason emerged from the administrative building. His clothes were torn and dusty from head to toe. He had a purple bruise forming over his right eye and dried blood on his face and neck.

"You should see the other guy," Jason replied. He started to laugh but winced and grabbed his ribs.

"Did you catch the Al-Rashidi brothers?" Bautista asked.

"Not exactly. They caught me first, tried to feed me to their giant assassin, and left for somewhere else with a couple of their workers. There are a total of four men."

"You said they tried to feed you to a giant assassin. I assume we'll find him dead somewhere on the farm," Archie said slowly as if trying to wrap his mind around the statement.

"Yep."

"Where?" Bautista yelped.

"He's in the storage shed next to the hay bales, but we don't have time for that right now. The other four men are heading to the

Hoover Dam as we speak to blow it up during Senator Conrad's speech tomorrow. Come inside, and I'll show you."

Bautista shot Archie a concerned glance and followed Jason inside to the desk with an open map. It was a detailed blueprint of the Hoover Dam and its tunnels. Jason pointed to a flat area near a small parking lot below the dam with a red circle around it. "That's where Conrad will give his speech. He wanted all possible media to attend there so everyone knows the time and place of his big speech."

The FBI analyst nodded. "Why do you think they have a bomb?"

"Jassim Al-Rashidi is their leader, and he told me he planned to kill Senator Conrad and a lot of other people who support the bill. I shared that I suspected they'd use a bomb, and he never denied it. Plus, I found this," Jason said, holding up the C-4 wrapper.

"Okay, so we know who, when, and how," Bautista said as she leaned closer to the map. "Do you have any idea where they may place a bomb?"

"They have so many circles crossed out near the dam that I can't tell what they have in mind. It looks like they may have been debating several locations underwater and onshore. Maybe they won't even know until they get there."

Archie stepped forward. "It will be underwater."

"How can you be sure?" Jason asked.

"After you left the FBI office yesterday, we learned that Jassim and Amir have military backgrounds, and the younger brother was a combat diver in the Royal Saudi Navy. Their test at the Gillespie Dam and his scuba experience points to them placing the bomb underwater."

"It's clear they want to blow up the dam with Conrad and everyone else below, but how can they do that? They're not going to blow a hole in the Hoover Dam with a couple hundred pounds of C-4," Jason said.

Archie inched closer to the map and ran his fingers over the ink renders of the dam and contours of the canyon walls as if he were reading Braille. His index finger stopped at a long tubular outline that ran alongside the dam on the Nevada side.

"I'd put my money on the diversion tunnels. I'm sure the Department of the Interior secured them somehow after the dam was completed, but that may be a weak spot the brothers will exploit."

The trio stared at the map momentarily until Jason nodded and snagged his backpack from a nearby chair.

"I have to get up there and start looking. I'll take my truck to Hoover Dam and get the rest of Conrad's security team on the hunt for the Saudis and the explosives."

"We have a helicopter, so why don't you wait until we're done here and fly up with us?" Archie asked.

"How long will you be here?"

"Probably a couple hours."

"It's only three-hours away, plus I need my truck, so I'll drive. Once you finish searching the farm, can you take the bird to Lake Mead and secure diving gear for two people while I'm driving?"

Archie tilted his head as if searching for the answer on the bare wall and nodded. "Yeah, I have an idea where I can get scuba equipment and a boat. Call me when you arrive, and we'll connect with the gear."

Jason raced up US Highway 95 parallel to the Colorado River for the next two hundred miles. He considered dozens of possibilities about how the Saudis could use a bomb to kill Senator Conrad. Blowing a hole in an old diversion tunnel to let a torrent of water wipe out everything in its path below the dam was one option, but they could try another car bomb close to the senator during his speech, or they could blow up the top of the cliffs overlooking the speech area and pummel the senator and the audience to death in a rock slide. It was a horrible location for a sitting US senator to give a speech, from a security perspective.

I should have pushed harder to move the location or time of Conrad's speech. So many lives are in danger now.

He pressed the button on his steering wheel to activate the Bluetooth and called Crenshaw. The call went to voice mail, so Jason hung up and tried again five minutes later. This time, she answered.

"We're swamped right now, Jason. What is it?"

"We have a good reason to believe the bombers will target the Hoover Dam tomorrow during Senator Conrad's speech."

"What? I assume you're working closely with law enforcement to catch those lunatics before the senator's speech tomorrow."

"We are, but Julia, this is serious. The senator is in imminent danger. Can he move the location or delay it for a day to give us more time?"

Jason noticed Senator Conrad's voice in the background. He heard Crenshaw cover the phone, followed by a quick discussion he couldn't make out.

"He heard our conversation and wants me to put you on speaker," Crenshaw announced.

Jason had no time to protest before Senator Conrad's voice boomed over the speakers in his truck.

"Mulder, I understand your concerns, but I told Crenshaw and Landry that this speech is critical to the POLAR Act, so I won't cancel or change it."

"Sir, I understand the importance of the speech, but these terrorists plan to detonate a bomb targeting you during your speech.

Any explosion in that area could be catastrophic to you and everyone else in attendance. I hope you'll reconsider—

"Hold on right there, Mulder," Senator Conrad interrupted. "I'm never going to change my plans for terrorists. That's exactly what they want, and I'll die before I give in to terrorists. I need you and the team to work with every possible law enforcement agency in the area to ensure everyone at the speech is safe. Is that understood?"

Jason knew he couldn't argue with the senator, so he capitulated and agreed. "Yes, sir." He hung up as he rounded the last curves to Hoover Dam and pulled into a parking lot. Central and Zee leaned against their SUV and appeared to be having an intense conversation. Jason watched the two men talk and sighed. "It's up to us to stop the bombers now."

The shadows of the canyon walls crept over the Hoover Dam as Jason and Central descended to the shoreline on the Arizona side of the river to a waiting boat. Archie stood behind the wheel of the thirty-foot, fiberglass V-hull boat with a wide, flat stern tied off to a gigantic boulder. Jason boarded first while Central untethered the dive boat.

"You look good as the captain of this ship," Jason said as he shook hands with his FBI friend.

"I could get used to this," Archie said. "I picked up gear from the Lake Mead dive club. You have a couple of wetsuit options in the bow."

Jason and Central chose 3/2 mm thick neoprene wetsuits to keep them warm in the 59-degree water but reduce sweating in the warm spring afternoon. They donned the remainder of the scuba gear and tested their oxygen tanks and apparatus.

"Where do you think we should start?" Jason asked.

"I spoke with the SRF folks twenty minutes ago," Archie started. "They stopped a dive boat that got too close to a restricted area earlier today. The guy I spoke to said they were pretty close to the spillway intake on the Nevada side. The spillway is using a portion of one of the old diversion tunnels. SRF sent a boat out to check on it and said two Middle Eastern men were on board, and everyone checked out, so they didn't arrest anyone."

"What's SRF?"

"SRF is the Bureau of Reclamation's Security Response Force. It defends cultural resources and critical power generation assets like Hoover Dam and Glen Canyon Dam. They are a small but elite unit that doesn't tolerate people getting too close to critical infrastructure."

"They only saw two people in the boat? You know what that means?" Jason asked.

Archie pursed his lips and nodded quickly. "Yep. The other two were diving."

"Have we been cleared to search the area?"

"Yeah, and the SRF reminded me that they are actively producing hydroelectricity to power all the air conditioners that turned on after lunch in Las Vegas. Do not get within 50 feet of those intake towers, or your loved ones will be planning a closed-casket funeral next week."

"Got it. We'll check the old diversion tunnel closest to the dam."

Mulder checked his equipment as Archie guided the boat to the Nevada side and as close to the dam as SRF allowed. The rhythmic sound of his breathing echoed in his ears as he adjusted the straps of his mask.

"This is it," Archie said.

The boat drifted to a halt and rocked gently in the current. Jason turned to Central with his right thumb up, and the former Navy

SEAL nodded. Together, Jason and Central stepped off the stern of the boat and plunged into the cool water of Lake Mead with a splash. A few feet below the surface, the view through Jason's mask turned from a bright, clear day to a hazy shade of brown like an underwater dust storm.

Jason conducted a comms check on the radio with Central and Archie. After they replied affirmatively, the two descended deep into the lake. He switched on the flashlight attached to his mask to get a clear view of the craggy granite wall.

The hum of their regulators filled the silence until their flashlights highlighted the transition from granite to hardened steel forty feet below the surface. The gates prevented the river from spilling into one of four 50-foot-diameter tunnels, with two drilled through the canyon walls on each side. The tunnels could carry more than 1.5 million gallons of water per second. A breach of one tunnel would deliver catastrophic results to anything near the tunnel outtake area, which was precisely where Senator Conrad planned to give his speech.

"You take the right side, and I'll take the left," Jason radioed Central.

Jason searched every inch of the left edge of the gate and several feet of the stone wall around it with his eyes and fingers. He descended slowly until he reached the corner, and then he continued toward the light from Central's mask along the bottom of the gate. Moments later, he reached Central.

"Find anything?" Jason asked.

"No, what about you?"

Jason shook his head. "You double-check my side, and I'll check yours."

As both Central and Jason reached the top of the gate near their starting points, Archie's voice came over the radio. "Any luck down there?"

"Nothing, and we searched everywhere that leads to the spillway. Oxygen is getting low, so we're heading up," Jason replied.

The former Navy SEAL and Air Force Pararescueman surfaced and hoisted themselves onto the boat. They removed their gear and sat quietly in their wetsuits, looking defeated.

Jason stared at the dark water as the sun dipped below the canyon walls supporting the Mike O'Callaghan–Pat Tillman Memorial Bridge, which spanned the Colorado River to the west. He rested his elbows on his thighs while supporting his chin with his thumb as his mind raced with a million possibilities. Jason straightened and asked the question aloud that had haunted him since he surfaced.

"We know the target time and place of their planned attack and that they have explosives. The SRF saw their boat in this area, so they had the opportunity to plant a bomb somewhere around here. Are we looking in the wrong area, or did we miss it?"

CHAPTER 42

The morning sun rose over the sheer walls containing the Colorado River and warmed Jason's neck. He leaned against the concrete barrier at the summit of Hoover Dam and sipped his coffee. Jason gazed at the swirls in the river six hundred feet below and watched the water flow under the massive arch bridge connecting two states.

Jason left his hotel earlier that morning to see if a new day and perspective could help him pinpoint where the Al-Rashidi brothers and their two employees may have placed their bomb at the Hoover Dam. He parked at the visitor's center in Nevada, purchased tickets for a Hoover Dam tour, and walked to Arizona and back along the road on the dam. The cool morning air was invigorating, but nothing inspired a new potential place to search.

They were here, and I know they placed a bomb somewhere. Where did they put it?

He crossed the street and looked down at the intake tower devouring Lake Mead like a ravenous giant drinking through a straw. His eyes rose to the lake, and he thought about other potential search locations under the inky blue water. Lost in his thoughts, someone approached Jason from behind. He turned and stumbled backward in surprise just before the man reached him.

"Sorry to sneak up on you," Clay bellowed as he pulled Jason in for his classic bear hug. "I'm back."

Jason patted his boss and friend on the back and stepped back.

"I didn't expect to see you here. I thought you'd still be in Louisiana."

"I thought so too, but I'm concerned about this event, so I returned early."

"Why?" Jason asked. "We have it under control. You could have stayed with your mom."

"No, I couldn't. After I talked to you on the phone yesterday, I sensed something was wrong."

Jason shook his head. "You didn't have to do that."

"Yes, I did. My mom saw me pacing around the house, worried about this event, and practically kicked me out. Of course, Mama's pretty sick, but as you know, she's a fighter. Mama told me she'd beat back cancer until this was over, and then I could come back home. I believe her, so I hopped on the first flight this morning."

"Cancer picked the wrong person by messing with your mom."

"Damn straight," Clay replied. He fist-bumped Jason and turned toward Lake Mead behind the dam.

"What's going on here?" Clay asked.

"As you know, Senator Conrad won't change his plans. Archie received intel that our Saudi friends were in the area yesterday on a boat near the Nevada spillway. The youngest brother is a former combat diver in the Royal Saudi Navy, so Archie believes he planted a bomb underwater in an area where an explosion could send a mountain of water toward Senator Conrad and his audience. Central and I dove around where the SRF saw them and found nothing. I don't know where else to search."

Clay crossed the street, so Jason followed him back to the west side of the dam. Clay took in the view that Jason had absorbed earlier.

"It really is the ideal killing zone for the terrorists. They could blow a portion of the dam or put a sniper at the top of one of the canyons."

Jason looked up and down at the sheer granite walls soaring a thousand feet above them.

"Conrad's speech is on that flat area just past the bridge, right?" Jason asked.

Clay pointed. "Yeah, it's near the end of the old diversion tunnel at the Hoover Dam raft tour boarding port. The TV cameras will get a great view of the dam and bridge when Senator Conrad gives his speech, making Crenshaw happy."

The two men fell silent as they watched the water meander through the canyon. Jason's thoughts moved to Shanna and JJ at home, oblivious to the grave danger the senator, his staff, and dozens of supporters were facing later that morning. The former PJ would do anything to protect his family from physical harm. Still, he also wanted to protect them from living where disgruntled individuals could kill elected leaders when they disagreed with their decisions. Although his wife and son were safely out of range from any explosion at the Hoover Dam, he still had to protect them.

I need to find the bomb they placed soon. We're running out of time.

Jason pushed away from the railing and removed the phone from his pocket.

"Where are you going?" Clay asked.

"I have an idea. I'll bring you up to speed in a few minutes."

He scrolled through his contacts until he found Greg, the engineer who gave the senatorial committee a tour of Parker Dam. Jason tapped the button to dial the number and waited.

"Hello, this is Greg."

"Hi Greg, this is Jason Mulder from Senator Conrad's security team. Sorry for calling so early, but it's urgent."

"No worries. I've already been up for a couple of hours. What's up?"

"I have a quick question for you. The senator will deliver a speech below the Hoover Dam in a few hours. It's set up at the end of one of the old diversion tunnels on the Nevada side. Can the dam or tunnel be breached with a large amount of explosives?"

"Oh, that's not good."

"I agree, hence my concern and the reason for my call. What damage can explosives do to the dam or diversion tunnels?"

"Do you know what kind of explosives and how much they have?"

Jason didn't know how much the Saudis had but figured it had to be an amount they could carry by hand.

"It's a couple hundred pounds of C-4."

Greg sighed. "Good news. That's not going to make a dent in the dam. The crescent-shaped dam is forty-five feet thick at the road but is over 650 feet thick at its base. That's twice as long as two football fields. It rises over 700 feet from its foundation and is made with very sturdy material. There's enough concrete in the Hoover Dam to build a two-lane road from Seattle to Miami."

Jason paced along the road on the bridge. He was running out of underwater options for the Saudis to place a bomb and began to wonder if Archie's theory was wrong.

"Okay, they can't hurt the dam. What about the diversion tunnels? The senator's speech is near the outtake area of an old tunnel."

"Is it the one closest to the dam or the furthest one on the Nevada side?"

"It's the furthest one with the outflow just past the bridge."

"Okay," Greg said slowly. Jason detected a hint of concern in his voice.

Jason stared at the phone as if the next sound emitted from its speakers could change his life forever. It wasn't very far from the truth.

After several beats of uncomfortable silence, Greg responded.

"The outer diversion tunnel is sealed off with a steel 50 x 50-foot gate at the intake end and a concrete plug about a quarter way back from the entrance. The Nevada spillway uses the old diversion tunnel that dumps its water where your senator will give his speech. The water level in Lake Mead is way too low for the spillway to come into play right now, but if explosives are placed at a weak point, and the blast punches a hole through the gate, the surge of water could be enough to break through the eighty-year-old inner plug."

"Then what?"

"The result below the dam would be—"

Greg stopped.

"The result would be what, Greg?" Jason shouted. His face and neck were flushed red.

"Catastrophic. Nobody below the dam could survive the torrent of water in the fifty-foot diameter diversion tunnel."

Jason hung up and jogged back to Clay.

"I have to go, and I'm taking Central."

"What is it?"

"They're going to blow up the outer diversion tunnel. We only checked the inner tunnel yesterday. I have to find Central and Archie and get back into the water. How much time do we have?"

Clay looked at his watch. "It starts at eleven, so you have a little over two hours."

"That's impossible. It will take ninety minutes to get back into the water."

Clay shook his head. "You better find it fast, or we may all have the worst day of our lives."

CHAPTER 43

Jassim felt the difference on his skin before he experienced the dramatic change. The Land Rover's engine hummed as they navigated the undulating granite hills until the canyon walls quickly disappeared. The low murmur in the cabin was replaced by a hollow echo of 890 feet of open-air between the bridge and the Colorado River below. Jassim glanced back and forth while Amir, Ibrahim, and Hamza pressed their faces against the passenger-side windows.

"There it is," Amir said with the innocence of a child.

"It's even more beautiful than yesterday," Hamza added.

Nobody else spoke as they took in the natural beauty of the dam and lake in a flash as they crossed the second-tallest bridge in the United States. The instant the vehicle crossed into the "Silver State," the landscape transformed back into a lunar-like terrain. Although they crossed the same bridge the day before, everyone but Jassim stared straight ahead as if seeing a beautiful woman burned into their minds.

Several miles past the bridge, Jassim guided the white Land Rover off Interstate 11 onto the Hoover Dam Access Road exit.

"Are we going somewhere new today?" Amir asked.

Jassim responded with a barely perceptible nod.

"Where are we going?"

"You'll see."

Amir put his hand on the dashboard, leaned forward, and squinted as the Hoover Dam Security Check Point grew in the windshield. A large sign with shiny silver letters taller than a man read: WELCOME TO HOOVER DAM. The sign shone brightly on a menacing metal structure that provided shade during the day and light at night to four guard stands beyond the approaching traffic circle.

"We're not going through that security checkpoint, are we?" Amir asked. His eyes darted back and forth between the checkpoint and his brother.

"We'll never get through if they see four Middle Eastern men together. We may even get detained."

Jassim took the first right in the traffic circle, avoiding the checkpoint.

"No, we don't need to go through security where we are going."

Five minutes later, the oldest Al-Rashidi brother rounded the final switchback curve and turned off onto a spur in the road. He completed a three-point turn and parked so everyone had a perfect view of the Hoover Dam standing proud three hundred yards upstream through the arch spans of the O'Callaghan Tillman Memorial Bridge. They also had an unobstructed view of the Hoover Dam raft boarding port's parking lot, with a handful of TV news trucks already setting up for Senator Conrad's speech later that morning.

Jassim pointed to a concrete tunnel large enough to drive three double-decker buses side by side through it. "That's the end of the diversion tunnel right there."

Ibrahim and Hamza scooted forward from the backseat, nodding at the sight of the tunnel.

"Notice the location of the parking lot for the senator's speech at the end of the tunnel," Jassim stated proudly.

The statement generated looks of approval from Ibrahim and Hamza, but Amir crossed his arms as his eyebrows pinched above his nose.

"I did everything you asked of me yesterday when we dove and placed the explosives on the diversion tunnel gate," Amir reminded Jassim. "I deserve to know the full plan now."

Jassim glanced at Ibrahim and adjusted himself in the driver's seat to face his brother. "You are correct, Amir. You deserve to know."

After clearing his throat, Jassim began. "As you saw on the timers yesterday, this morning at eleven fifteen when the senator is at his podium delivering his speech, seventy-five pounds of C-4 in each shaped charge will explode. I've calculated that the blast will punch a hole through the gate, demolish the inner plug, and send millions of gallons in a torrent through the old diversion tunnel. Anybody below that opening over there will be swept away to their death, live on national TV. We'll send Senator Conrad and his supporters to hell with the same water they wish to deny our existence in the name of preservation."

Amir's face glowed with a childlike grin. "That's brilliant, Jassim. Thanks for including me on this honorable mission."

Amir turned his attention back to the news trucks setting up just below the diversion tunnel, but Jassim kept his eyes on his younger brother.

Was it a mistake to include Amir?

He couldn't shake the feeling he'd later regret getting his brother involved. His desire to destroy the man threatening his family's business was overwhelming, and now he may have sacrificed a family member to achieve his goal. The eldest Al-Rashidi brother wasn't worried about getting caught by law enforcement. He knew they'd be the focus of an intense manhunt the second the bombs detonated, and Senator Conrad and his supporters were swept to their deaths by the rushing waters. He'd spent years living off the land in the deserts of Saudi Arabia, so he knew he could outlast any search, but Amir was softer. His younger brother spent little time in the wilderness, so he'd have to find another way to evade capture once the hunt for them began.

"What will we do with all the pistols and rifles in the back?" Amir asked. He looked at Jassim with wide eyes and the eagerness of a child waiting for a surprise gift.

"Those are part of our backup plan if the explosions don't work as expected. We will drop Hamza and Ibrahim off on the Arizona side with the AR-15s so they can set up for a shot at the senator and his people if we need it. We'll return with the pistols and park along the access road. That's high enough to avoid any water coming from the diversion tunnel, but it's also at a choke point on the only road to and from the senator's speech. We may need to take matters into our own hands if the water doesn't take everyone out and Ibrahim doesn't shoot them first."

"So we may have to shoot the senator ourselves?" Amir asked.

Jassim exchanged another glance with Ibrahim and watched his brother closely. He questioned whether to include Amir in the plan because he wasn't sure his younger brother would be committed to the cause. His scuba diving skills forced Jassim to include him, but now he questioned his decision.

Amir seemed to sense Jassim's apprehension. "I am ready to be a martyr for the cause."

Jassim recoiled. "The goal is not martyrdom, but to kill the senator and as many supporters as possible and then escape so we can eventually return home to Saudi Arabia."

"That may be the case for all of you, but I'm prepared to be a martyr if that's what it takes."

Jassim turned his attention toward the future site of Senator Conrad's speech as the cab inside the Land Rover fell silent. He understood his brother was on board with the plan as much as any of the original three men.

Now, all four of them were ready to do whatever was necessary to ensure the senator died today.

Chapter 44

Hoover Dam, Nevada

Jason rushed to pick up Central at the Hoover Dam Security Response Force office, where he was coordinating plans with the SRF and Nevada State Police. Together, they returned to the Hoover Dam observation parking lot in Arizona to meet Archie again on the boat. Like a carbon copy from the day before, Jason and Central donned their scuba gear while FBI special agent Woods guided the vessel to the Nevada side of the lake. This time, they anchored fifty feet farther upstream to reach the gate to the outer diversion tunnel leading directly to the parking lot where Senator Conrad would deliver his speech in under fifteen minutes.

Archie left the wheel and returned to the stern, where Jason and Central completed their final equipment checks before diving into the lake.

"We're getting short on time, guys. Do you have a plan for this dive?" Archie asked.

"Yeah. Central and I will check the edges of the steel gate at the outer diversion tunnel intake like we did last time. That's all we have time to check, so let's hope that if the Saudis placed a bomb underwater, it's there."

"One of the SRF guys told me that we should focus on the bottom corners of the gate because they had to repair those areas thirty years ago due to corrosion from all the silt. If they corrode again, they may be the weakest points on the gates," Central interjected.

"Makes sense. Let's go."

Jason and Central lowered their masks and slid into the cool water. Visibility was slightly better than the previous day as the two divers descended thirty feet below the surface.

"There's the gate," Central said. "Fifty more feet to the bottom."

The sunlight helped some, but flashlights were essential to scan the gate for explosives at a depth of eighty feet.

"I'm approaching the bottom left corner," Central announced.

The only sounds were a quiet static from the radio and Jason breathing into the regulator, until Central shouted into his radio microphone.

"I found something!"

Those three words sent a torrent of adrenaline into Jason's gut, increasing his breathing and oxygen use. Once he gathered himself, Jason swam beside Central and saw the bomb for the first time.

"What do you see?" Archie asked over the radio.

Jason took several long, slow breaths, as he was taught in the PJ pipeline until he breathed normally again.

"I see a gray junction box that looks like the devices on every home in the south to program their landscape irrigation, but it looks waterproof," Jason replied. "It's attached to a metal cone about 50% bigger than the traffic cones used in construction sites."

Jason tapped on the metal cone with the hilt of his knife. "It feels thick and sturdy. I'm guessing iron or steel."

"That's a shaped charge. The C-4 is packed inside and is what goes boom," Archie stated. "Leave that alone for now. How's the gray box attached to the shaped charge?"

Jason illuminated the connection with his light and swam closer to the bomb.

"They're taped together with glossy black tape. It looks like the tape I've used to fix outdoor tools and equipment."

"Do you think you can cut it?"

"I think so. Give me a minute."

The knife's sharp edge moved back and forth across the plastic material until Jason cut through eight inches of tape. He tried to push the gray box away from the metal cone, but it wouldn't budge.

"Did you cut it?" Archie asked from the boat.

"Yeah, but it's still attached with some kind of cement or something. The box won't even wiggle."

"Can you get your knife between the box and shaped charge to see if you can separate them?"

"Negative. They filled the entire gap between the charge and box."

The radio went silent for a beat until Central spoke.

"Let me take a look."

The former Navy SEAL tried with his knife but quickly reached the same conclusion as Jason. "That adhesive is rock solid. That box isn't leaving the shaped charge. What's in the box, Archie?"

A deep sigh broadcast across the radio before Archie responded. "It has to contain the timer and an energy source, like a battery. To set off the charge, the trigger must be attached to the det cord and blasting cap."

"Are you sure it's a timer and not activated by a cell phone?" Central asked.

"A cellular phone signal would never reach a box that far below the surface. It must be a timer."

"Should I smash the box, let the water flood it, and short it out?" Central asked.

Jason thought it sounded like a good idea. At a minimum, they'd see the timer and know when it was scheduled to detonate, but Archie quickly disagreed.

"No! Don't smash the box! It may trigger the blast!"

Central and Jason floated a couple of yards away from the shaped charge loaded with nearly one hundred pounds of C-4 while they waited for Archie to formulate Plan B.

"Can you get your knife between the shaped charge and the metal gate?" Archie asked.

Central swam back to the charge and tried his blade in several spots. In one spot, his blade slid under three-quarters of the way. He applied pressure to the knife, and the shaped charge wiggled.

"It's moving!"

"Okay, we have to focus on the entire device. Do whatever you can to dislodge the shaped charge and bring it to the surface."

"Bring it to the surface?" Jason questioned.

Archie did not respond while Central maneuvered his knife back and forth. Soon, the shaped charge hung like a loose tooth on the diversion tunnel gate.

"It's coming off," Central said.

Jason swam next to him and held onto the shaped charge until he felt the total weight of seventy-five pounds of C-4 inside a lead cone in his arms.

"It's off. I'm coming up," Jason grunted.

The boat rocked gently with Archie inside as Jason and Central surfaced with the shaped charge. Archie leaned over the side and extended his arms to help, but Jason waved him off.

"It's heavy. I'll toss it on the stern."

The shaped charge splashed out of the water and landed on the stern with a thud. Jason removed his mask and breathing apparatus. "What are you going to do now?"

Archie stared at the shaped charge and attached timer, which contained enough explosives to blow up three city buses before he seemed to nod at the answer in his head.

"I'll drive it farther out on Lake Mead and away from the dam, so it won't cause any structural damage if it explodes."

"It can explode at any time!" Jason reminded everyone.

"Exactly, which is why I need to leave now," Archie barked.

Jason saw something in Archie's body language that raised alarm bells in his gut. He couldn't pinpoint exactly what it was, but it was sending ominous signals to Jason.

"You don't have to do this," Jason said.

Archie glared at Jason in a way he'd never seen in the short time he'd known the FBI agent.

"Yes, I do."

For several seconds, the only sound was the water lapping against the side of the boat.

"We can debate this until the bomb goes off, or I can rush this into a safer part of Lake Mead before anyone gets hurt."

Jason bobbed in the water as he watched Archie turn to the wheel and press the button for the winch to retrieve the anchor. The boat drifted away from Jason and Central in the current.

"I'll hurry out to a safe spot in the lake," Archie yelled over the engine. "Check the other corner for more bombs, and I'll be back in a few minutes to help if you need it."

"Archie, get to where you need to go, dump it, and hurry back. Don't hold it for too long," Jason choked out.

"I will," Archie said with a wink. "Goodbye, Mulder."

Chapter 45

Jason bobbed in the wake as the nose of the boat commanded by Archie rose and accelerated. The canyon filled with the roar of the inboard engines thrusting Archie and the bomb into the deeper waters of Lake Mead until he disappeared around a bend. Jason listened until the sound became too faint to hear. He swallowed hard and turned to Central. "Let's see if there are any more bombs down there."

"What time is it?" Central asked.

"It's ten after eleven."

Central's face turned ashen before he pulled down his mask and inserted his breather. They didn't have to say out loud that Senator Conrad's speech was underway and that a timed explosive would likely detonate at any second.

They descended into the cool water and resumed their search of the diversion tunnel gate. At the opposite corner of the last shaped charge at the bottom of the gate, Central radioed Jason. "I found another one."

Jason swam to Central and found a twin of the bomb in the back of Archie's boat.

"Let's do the same thing as last time. We have to get the charge off this gate," Jason said.

Central maneuvered his knife around the shaped charge like last time but struggled to find any points to wedge it between the bomb and the metal gate.

"They cemented this one even better. I can't get my knife in anywhere," Central cried out of the radio. Jason heard the panic in his voice and rapid breathing over the radio. The pressure to dislodge the shaped charge before it blew them to pieces felt like a python wrapped around his chest, and he knew Central was feeling the same thing.

"I found a weak spot. I got my knife in almost an inch."

The steel gate and granite walls around them rattled like an earthquake before Jason heard the thunderous blast through the water.

"That was the bomb! Swim away as far as you can!" Jason shouted.

Jason kicked hard to optimize the whip of the long fins on his feet while he pushed water behind him with each stroke to propel him farther from the bomb. He swam without stopping for at least two minutes toward the Arizona shore until he felt and heard the second explosion simultaneously. The proximity of the blast sent Jason into involuntary somersaults in the water. It knocked the regulator out of his mouth and sent his mask and radio to the bottom of the lake. Disoriented and unsure of his depth, Jason held his breath and let his training kick in.

The drown-proofing training as a PJ was designed for this type of predicament. Jason remained perfectly still and let his buoyant body guide him to safety. Once he knew the direction of the surface, he kicked slowly to increase his ascent, but he still wasn't reaching the oxygen his lungs craved.

I must have been deeper than I thought. Keep pushing. Don't stop.

As his chest burned, Jason sensed light through his closed eyelids. The dim light got brighter until he felt the sun and fresh air on his face. He gulped in oxygen and spun in the water to orient his position in the lake. First, he located the dam, then Jason rotated one hundred and eighty degrees, and that's when he saw Central floating face down twenty yards away. The former PJ kicked hard to reach Central and flipped him over so his mouth and nose were above water.

"Hang on, Central."

Jason dragged him across the surface to a flat rock raised inches above the waterline between two boulders on the Arizona shoreline. He pushed Central onto the stone platform, checked his airways, and began chest compressions.

"Come on, Central," Jason said as he continued the rhythmic compressions.

A half minute later, Central coughed and spit out lake water. Jason helped him turn to his side as he continued to cough.

Central propped himself up on one elbow. "Thank you," he said between coughs. "I took in a little too much water after that blast."

"Same. I felt like I was inside a washing machine with a half dozen bowling balls."

Central quit coughing but was panting like a dog on a hot day.

"I'll get you to the parking lot and call an ambulance."

"I'm fine. Just give me a minute."

"Central, you almost drowned. You have to get checked out by paramedics."

Central's head snapped up, and he scooted closer to Jason. "Terrorists just tried to blow up the Hoover Dam. We don't know how badly the tunnel was damaged, so the shit may be hitting the fan right now below the dam. They may need our help. Seriously, I'm fine. Just give me a minute. Please."

Jason knew Central was right and nodded. He stood tall on the river's edge, and that's when he noticed the black smoke wafting over the canyon walls into the indigo sky.

"Archie?"

He knew a C-4 explosion underwater wouldn't generate that much black smoke. It required fuel and materials to burn—the same ingredients found on a dive boat. Jason couldn't see the open lake but already felt the outcome.

Archie is gone.

Jason climbed several boulders higher and watched the billowing smoke for any sign that he might be wrong. A wave of sickness overcame him, and he leaned against a boulder and vomited.

"Are you okay?" Central asked.

Jason continued to stare at the smoke. He was in shock at the realization that another person he cared about was ripped from his life.

"Mulder?"

Jason wiped his mouth and turned to Central. "Yeah, I'm fine," Jason lied. He climbed farther up the boulders, out of sight of Central, and fixed his gaze on the transition of the dark black smoke to lighter gray smoke over the lake.

"They must be putting the blaze out. I hope they find his body," Jason said to the wind.

The smoke transformed into images of his high school sweetheart, Gaby, lying motionless on the road, and the helpless feeling that haunted Jason for years prickled his skin. Then, visions of his little brother Josh reaching out to him for help as he died at the bottom of a gully flashed in his mind like a persistent nightmare.

Why does this keep happening to me?

Jason couldn't move. He was frozen on the Arizona shoreline with water still lapping at the boulders from the nearby explosion.

"You should have thrown it overboard like you said you would," Jason said slightly louder than a whisper.

The smoke transitioned from Gaby and Josh to Archie. First, scenes of Archie ambling into the Yuma field and surprising Jason with his wit and skills appeared. Then, the time Archie crawled under a car in a Tempe parking lot to diffuse a car bomb with his bare hands flashed next.

Crack.

The unmistakable sounds of concrete and steel snapping, followed a nanosecond later by water rushing through the diversion tunnel, shook Jason from his thoughts. He heard the slurry destroying everything in its path as it plunged 600 feet to the bottom of the diversion tunnel.

The second blast punched a hole through the gate, letting millions of gallons of water into the sealed-off portion of the diversion tunnel. The old interior plug wasn't strong enough to resist a persistent Lake Mead that wished to escape captivity above the dam and race to the end of the diversion tunnel.

Thoughts of Archie switched to the utter devastation that Clay, the senator, and everyone else below the dam must be experiencing.

Jason bound back down to Central, who stood with his mouth open.

"We need to go *now!*"

Chapter 46

Clay stood still as a statue on the far edge of the platform that elevated Senator Conrad above the audience. The senator glowed in the sunlight, and after each pause in his speech, the sounds of cameras clicking and the audience clapping filled the raft launch platform. Fifteen minutes after the senator started, Clay scanned the audience and relaxed his shoulders. They were minutes from the speech ending and leaving the high-risk location.

During a brief pause in the senator's speech, Clay felt the platform shake and then, a moment later, heard a soft rumble like thunder rolling in the distance. He may not have noticed it if he wasn't on full alert, but Clay was sure it didn't sound natural, so he moved several steps closer to Senator Conrad. He tuned out the senator's voice and listened carefully, but the breeze in his ears was all Clay heard.

Did I really hear a rumble? Wouldn't Mulder, Central, or Archie have called if it was an explosion?

Clay convinced himself that his nerves were getting the best of him and continued to scan the crowd and canyon for other threats. Senator Conrad ended his speech by thanking his supporters.

Please don't offer to take any questions.

"I have a minute to take questions from the news media."

Dammit!

A reporter in her early thirties stood after Conrad pointed at her, but she never got to ask a question.

The sound of the second blast roared into the canyon. The ground shook, and shock waves bounced off the steep granite walls like a pinball. The sound was followed by chunks of granite, from small pebbles to baseball-sized pieces, tumbling from the cliff walls and splashing violently into the river.

Clay pressed his hand over his ear to hear the radio in his earpiece. "Mulder or Central — was that an explosion?"

White noise was the only reply.

"Mulder, do you copy? Central, do you copy?"

More silence.

The nearby diversion tunnel groaned and creaked like an old ship on an angry sea. Senator Conrad swiveled his head towards the noise, and all eyes in the audience followed suit. Clay sprang into action and sprinted toward the senator while everyone else remained frozen with fear and indecision.

"We need to get you to higher ground, sir."

Crenshaw rushed to the podium. "What's going on?"

Senator Conrad, Clay, and Crenshaw stepped away from the microphone. "I don't know, but we need to get Senator Conrad out of here."

"Aren't Mulder and Central up there? Do they know what's going on?"

"They're not responding."

Deputy Chief of Staff Jasmine Mitchell and policy adviser Ryan Kimpton joined the trio behind the podium.

"Is the speech over?" Kimpton asked.

"Not yet," Crenshaw barked.

Crack!

The deafening roar of rushing water was loud enough to drown out the noise of a jet engine. A blast of dank and musty air preceded the violent cacophony of water, debris, and metal hurtling toward them from the diversion tunnel.

The hair on Clay's neck and arm stood at attention, but it did not slow him down. He pulled Senator Conrad close and shoved him up a hiking trail he'd scouted before the speech.

"Everyone, follow me!"

The trio of staffers followed Clay and Senator Conrad from the platform at the end of the diversion tunnel up a steep incline on a path worn by thousands of hikers. They were twenty feet above the parking lot when the first drops of water landed on Clay's face and neck like the start of a thunderstorm. They still had to get higher to avoid being swept into the depths of the Colorado River, so Clay kept pushing up the trail and never turned around to see the water surging below him. Once they reached a curve in the path, Clay placed Senator Conrad behind a cluster of massive rocks.

"Everyone take cover behind one of the large boulders."

Clay looked down at the reporters and audience members for the first time. Several followed Conrad's staff up the trail, but many others did not react in time. Forty feet below, chairs, banners, and even vehicles churned in the frothy white water like they were in a blender. Despite the speed of the raging waters, everything slowed down for Clay. He saw elbows, hands, and feet among the scattered debris. But it was the expressions on their faces that stood out to him. The understanding of inevitable death etched a look of terror onto the men and women below, one that would be seared into Clay's mind forever. He swallowed hard and turned his attention back to the senator and his staff.

"Stay behind the boulders. We don't know if the terrorists are trying to flush us out or have already fled the area. Stay put until I give you the all-clear to leave."

"But what if the water comes up here? We should keep moving before we get swept away, too," Kimpton said, his voice cracking with fear.

"The water will not get this high. Don't go anywhere yet."

Senator Conrad turned to Clay. "Okay, what's your plan?"

Clay raised his index finger. "Zee, are you still in place?"

Two radio clicks confirmed Zee was still in position.

"Zee is at the top of the canyon with a sniper rifle in case the terrorists are trying to flush us out. I'll call the Nevada State Police to get us in a secure vehicle, so we have to hang tight here for a few more minutes."

Senator Conrad nodded in approval as his policy adviser, Ryan Kimpton, stood up.

"Get back down, Ryan," Clay yelled.

"I can't swim very well, so I'm going to take the access road out of here while I still can."

"No, don't— "

It was too late because Kimpton was in a full trot away from the rest of the staff. Seconds later, Kimpton's head exploded into a red mist, followed by a thunderous bang that echoed throughout the canyon. High-pitched screams came from behind the boulders when more gunfire erupted from both sides of the canyon.

The gunshots ended, and Clay received a transmission over the radio.

"I got 'em, boss. Two tangos down. I don't see any more, so you should be clear," Zee said excitedly into the radio.

"Good work, Zee."

Clay didn't want to take any chances, so he removed his phone to call the Nevada State Police when his phone buzzed. It was Jason Mulder.

"Jason, where are you?" Clay asked when he answered.

"Central and I almost got taken out by that second explosion, but we are both okay. We're en route to your location right now."

"Okay, we're hunkered down about fifty feet above the raft launch."

"Got it."

"Jason," Clay said with a sigh. "It's ugly, so please hurry."

Jason arrived at the upper parking lot above the flooded Hoover Dam raft boarding port two minutes later. Despite the urge to gawk at the devastation below, he resisted the temptation. He'd experienced enough heartbreak for one day.

They rushed toward Clay's location with the senator. They abruptly halted when they came upon a body twisted in an unnatural manner on the path leading to the parking lot.

"What happened?" Central asked.

"Ryan Kimpton tried to run to safety, and one of the terrorists shot him," Clay answered.

Central and Jason both ducked and looked around the canyon. "Zee took them out, but not before they shot Ryan."

Jason stood and rushed along the path until he reached Clay and the senator.

"Clay, come with me. We have to go," Jason said.

"I'm not leaving until the senator and the rest of the staff are safe."

"I passed a white Land Rover speeding away when I started down the access road. It was the Al-Rashidi brothers. They're behind all this, and I don't want them to get away. Central can stay here with Senator Conrad until help arrives."

Clay turned to the senator. "Will you be okay?"

"Yes. Yes. I'll be fine with Central until the state police arrive. Go get those bastards."

Clay's face revealed a look of determination. He reached into his pack, removed his backup earpiece and radio, and handed them to Central. "Call the Nevada State Police and tell them to send a team to pick up Senator Conrad and his staff. Zee has the high ground and a sniper rifle, so you two work together to keep everyone safe until they get here."

Clay started toward the parking lot but stopped and turned back to Central. "Also, have the state police call 911 and tell them to send as many ambulances as they can to help the injured and pick up the dead."

Jason ran ahead of Clay and hopped into his truck's driver's seat. Once Clay was in the passenger seat, Jason slammed the accelerator and squealed out of the parking lot onto the access road.

"What do you have for weapons in here?" Clay asked.

"I have two HK 416s in the back and my sidearm."

"That should work."

Fiery determination radiated from Jason as he steered his truck onto the northbound lanes of Interstate 11, toward Las Vegas.

"What's your plan if you catch up with them?"

Jason gazed out the windshield of his truck as he contemplated the best response.

"I'm not sure yet, but I know they're not getting away again. This all ends today."

CHAPTER 47

Jason raced up Interstate 11 at breakneck speeds up to one-hundred miles per hour to catch up with the fleeing Saudi brothers. The undulating peaks of the McCullough Mountain Range towered above the vast expanse of sagebrush, acting as a natural funnel between the Mojave Desert and the sprawling Las Vegas metro area. As they approached Henderson, Nevada, Jason had to slow down due to heavy traffic. The PSD duo rode in silence as they expertly maneuvered through the cars on Interstate 215 in Henderson. Jason was laser-focused on spotting the white Land Rover with Jassim and Amir Al-Rashidi.

"Do you see them yet?" Jason asked.

"Not yet."

"Do you think they fled into Arizona?"

Clay stared ahead at the brake lights on the freeway as if considering the answer. "It's possible, but finding them on that lone desolate highway leaving Hoover Dam wouldn't be difficult. They could easily vanish among the crowds in Las Vegas."

Jason nodded. His gut told him the same thing, but each mile they drove without seeing the Saudis allowed more frustration to build.

"Do you think they'd go to the strip or old town?" Jason asked.

"Both are good options. I'd head to the strip first."

The satisfied rumble of the engine and white noise from the road filled the cabin as Jason navigated the lunchtime traffic in Las Vegas. Speeds slowed to a crawl and stopped entirely as they approached Las Vegas International Airport and the famous Las Vegas strip. Jason braked hard and slammed his fist on the steering wheel.

"Come on, people. Let's move!"

The towering hotels and casinos on the Las Vegas strip looked tauntingly close across the airport's runways, but they still had several miles to go.

"Finally," Jason bellowed when the traffic started moving again.

"What happened back there?" Clay asked.

Jason looked out of the driver's side window so Clay couldn't see his face. He still couldn't believe Archie was gone, and a part of him expected to get a call and hear the slow twang from the FBI special agent at any moment. He smacked his lips and cleared his throat.

"We tried to disarm the bombs but couldn't. Archie insisted we put one of the shaped charges in his boat so he could race into water farther away from the dam and toss it overboard. He sped off, and I lost sight of him. The bomb exploded in the boat before he could dump it," Jason croaked.

Clay nodded. "I heard the first explosion but wasn't sure what it was, so I moved closer to Conrad. Those extra few seconds may have saved us."

Jason started to feel hot, so he turned up the air conditioner.

Clay's eyes drifted toward the cars ahead and then turned to Jason. "You know," Clay started. "In a weird way, Archie warned you and Central so that you could escape the second bomb."

Jason also considered it and agreed that Archie probably saved their lives, but he didn't want to talk about Archie anymore.

A stormy rage swirled in his gut, spurring Jason to make the Al-Rashidi brothers pay for their actions. He didn't want to lose that fiery determination before confronting them.

"What about you? What happened back there?" Jason asked.

Clay closed his eyes and bowed his head. "I saw them die. I saw the fear on their faces when they knew death was imminent, and I don't think I'll ever forget their faces."

Seconds later, his eyes opened, and he peered through the windshield. "I watched them get swept away to their death, and I couldn't do anything about it."

Jason had never felt so close to Clay. He'd experienced something similar more than once and knew exactly how it felt. Jason also knew no words could comfort him, so he kept his response short.

"I get it. I'm sorry you had to see that."

Clay nodded.

"Let's put the people responsible for all this pain in the ground."

The head of Conrad's PSD made a fist and moved it toward Jason until they fist-bumped.

"You should call Zee and see if they got the senator to safety yet," Jason suggested.

Clay dialed Zee and put him on speaker once he answered. "Is the senator and all of you safe now?"

"Yeah. The Nevada State Police picked us up and took us to the SRF building. We're all in the break room now, but nobody is saying much. Everyone seems to be in shock about what happened."

"I'm glad you're all safe. Zee, see if the state police have any information on the white Land Rover we saw fleeing the scene."

"Hang on. There's a sergeant right here."

Jason passed Allegiant Stadium for the Las Vegas Raiders NFL football team on his left and the azure pools at the Mandalay Bay Resort and Casino on his right as they waited for Zee.

"Guys, the Nevada State Police and Las Vegas PD are in a stand-off with the occupants of a white Land Rover right now."

"What? Where?" Jason shouted.

"They're on Las Vegas Boulevard just north of the New York New York and the MGM Grand."

Jason turned to Clay. "That's off the next exit on Tropicana."

"Shots have been fired, so everything is closed in that area," Zee added.

"Thanks, Zee."

Clay hung up, and the cab was quiet for the next quarter mile.

"I have an idea about how we can still get to the Al-Rashidi brothers," Jason said.

"What's your plan?"

"Are you cool with some highly illegal traffic maneuvers and maybe even some weapons activity that may get us shot?"

"Sure. What's the downside?" Clay asked with a smirk.

"Do you know any good defense attorneys?"

Clay tilted his head. "I believe we both work for a man that still sits on the bar in Virginia, so I feel good about our defense."

"Okay, then tighten your seat belt. It's going to get interesting real quick."

CHAPTER 48

Jason guided his truck toward his exit as massive billboards, parking garages, and hotels soaring over fifty stories into the blue sky flanked both sides of the freeway. He took the ramp to Flamingo Road and turned right toward The Strip on Las Vegas Boulevard. The Las Vegas PD had closed southbound traffic and blocked off access with two police cruisers, but they left the northbound lanes open for people to escape the gunfire – just as Jason expected.

Jason tapped on the steering wheel with his index finger while they waited at a red light that seemed to last forever.

"Are you sure you want to do this?" Clay asked.

Jason pursed his lips and looked down the street at the flashing lights from dozens of police vehicles.

"We wouldn't get too far with the 416s and the heavy police presence. We have to get as close as possible for this to work."

"You know we may go to prison for this," Clay said with a chuckle.

The light turned green, and Jason continued east on Flamingo Road, past the police cruisers. Once they passed the blockade, he yanked the wheel hard into northbound traffic and immediately confronted a taxi barreling toward them in the center lane. Jason veered left, running the driver's side tires on the sidewalk for fifty yards, and then pulled back into oncoming traffic as he picked up speed.

"Get out of the way!" Jason yelled.

The cluster of flashing emergency lights drew closer as Jason and Clay approached the standoff. Jason took his foot off the gas and leaned forward in his seat to ensure his eyes weren't playing tricks on him.

"Are they running toward us?"

"It looks like it," Clay replied with confusion in his voice.

The truck drifted forward, and Jason slammed on the brakes. "That looks like the brothers. They're running, and the police are in pursuit."

Jason watched in stunned belief as their targets were running straight toward them. Before he could react, the brothers turned off Las Vegas Boulevard.

"They're running up the Bellagio driveway. Get the rifles," Clay shouted.

"I'll grab them while you call Zee and tell him to let the Nevada State Police know a federal security detail is on site and that LVPD should hold their fire."

Jason opened the secure Pelican case, bolted to his truck bed, and removed two hard shell rifle cases, each containing an HK 416 rifle. With practiced skill, he swiftly handled the rifles, inspected the ammunition, and secured two tactical vests. After Clay returned from his call, he handed him a vest, rifle, and radio.

"There's two more full magazines in the vest," Jason said. "Did you call Zee?"

"Yeah, he's talking to the state police now."

Jason turned toward high-pitched screams coming from the vehicle drop-off area of the Bellagio.

"We need to move now. You go straight toward the fountain, and I'll go right about twenty meters to give us two angles," Jason barked.

"Roger."

Clay and Jason darted across the median, the closed southbound lanes of Las Vegas Boulevard, and took cover behind the stone railing surrounding the Fountains of Bellagio.

"Comms check," Clay said into the radio.

"I hear you loud and clear."

Jason raised his HK 416 to get a better look at the brothers through his scope, but all he had were the metal sights. He'd forgotten he ordered the Over the Beach or OTB features for an amphibious assault. It seemed like a good idea then, but now he had to rely on Clay to see what Amir and Jassim were doing.

"Clay, I don't have the electric scope on my rifle. What are they doing?"

A moment later, Clay replied. "They each have hostages. Two women. They have pistols pointed at their heads."

"Shit!" Jason barked. "Can you get a shot?"

"I can take out the skinny one if he moves a little to my left, but right now, I've got nothing," Clay announced.

While Jason aimed toward the eldest Al-Rashidi brother standing behind a bleach-blond hostage, a new voice behind him entered the discussion. "Drop the weapon!"

Jason turned his head slowly and saw an officer from LVPD with her service pistol pointed right at him.

"Clay, call Zee and tell him to give LVPD our radio frequency. Fast!"

"Okay, what's up?"

"One of them is pointing her gun at me. She wants me to drop my weapon."

"Got it."

Jason remained crouched, lowered his rifle to the sidewalk, and slowly raised his hands.

Come on, Zee. Hurry up.

The LVPD officer inched closer with her gun pointed at Jason's chest and screamed louder. "Get on your stomach."

"I'm with a security detail trying to stop the terrorists that have those hostages. Check with the Nevada State Police," Jason said. He hoped this would spark some cooperation, but it further agitated the officer.

"If you don't get on your stomach right now, you're getting a bullet. Get down now!"

He did as instructed and lowered himself to the sidewalk.

"Put your hands behind your back and interlock your fingers."

"Clay, any luck?" Jason asked over the radio as he complied with the officer.

"We're close. Hang on another minute," Clay replied. He remained close to the railing and out of sight of the officer.

"Hurry. I'll be in the back of a police cruiser in thirty seconds."

The LVPD officer drove her knee into Jason's back, knocking the wind from his lungs. Jason heard the clang of metal cuffs coming from her utility belt when a crackle came over the officer's radio clipped to her chest.

"Say again?" the officer said after clicking her mic.

"This is Commander Lewis with the Nevada State Police. We have two members of a senator's security team authorized to assist with the takedown of the terrorists. Stand down if you confront them."

A long pause felt like an eternity before the knee left Jason's back, and the LVPD officer vanished as quickly as she appeared.

Jason grabbed his rifle from the pavement and rushed back to his position along the railing. "What did I miss?"

"They're staying put with the hostages. I can't get a good angle for a shot. Mulder, can you take a shot?"

The area fell eerily silent except for sirens in the distance, which got louder as they approached the scene.

"Anyone know when the fountain is supposed to go off?"

"This is not the time for jokes, Mulder," Clay barked. "Do you have a shot or not?"

"The only option is from the bank on the other side. The boulders below the Jasmine restaurant have a good angle, so I'll swim across and take the shot."

"He'll shoot you the second he sees you doing the breaststroke across the lake," Clay said.

"That's where you come in. I can swim underwater to the other side, but I need you to distract them from me until I'm in the water. Can you do that?"

The microphone was silent for several beats. "I'll find a way, but they're getting nervous. We don't have much time before they start blasting away at everyone and everything. How are you going to get over there in time?"

"The fastest route is to go straight across, which means I'll go right over the fountain jets. If they go off, they'll blast me into the next state. Do you have any idea when the fountain is supposed to go off?"

"No clue," Clay said.

"Okay, I'll take my chances with the fountain. I'll get in position and let you know when I need the distraction."

"Roger."

Jason scanned the area. He noticed a solid block of concrete where the barrier railing connected with a semicircular observation platform protruding several feet into the water. It was the perfect entry point, so he high-crawled to the area and pressed his back against the wall.

"I'm taking off my radio, so I'll wait for your distraction and then go."

Clay clicked twice to confirm he'd heard the message. Jason pressed himself against the railing and concentrated on his breathing so he could get into the water and take one deep breath before he went under.

Pop. Pop. Pop.

His leg was over the railing as the third pop echoed off the surrounding buildings. Jason was already under the surface when he heard the return fire from the smaller handguns. He kicked and swam deeper until all he heard was water passing by his ears.

He swam with his eyes closed in the heavily chlorinated water until Jason guessed he was near the row of 1,214 nozzles across the 8.5-acre lake that formed the Fountains of Bellagio. The dancing water show, powered by computerized compressed air nozzles, could shoot water as high as 460 feet into the air. They could also cut a person in half, so Jason slowed his kicking until he was over the nozzles, and then he swam as hard and fast as possible.

He passed the danger of the activated fountain jets, but now he was in jeopardy of being detected by Jassim and Amir. The water was deeper than Jason expected, so he dropped to what he estimated was eight feet below the surface. He knew someone from one of the hotel rooms directly above the fountain could easily see his silhouette in the fountain water, but hoped the reflecting sun made it impossible for the Saudi brothers to see him. He heard his old instructor barking in the PJ pipeline, "Hope is not a strategy."

Come on, Clay. I need another distraction.

After a minute underwater, Jason figured he was three-quarters across the fountain lake when his lungs started to burn. He'd held his breath for nearly two minutes as a PJ, but that was years ago. His body inched closer to the surface as Jason exhaled small amounts of old oxygen his lungs could no longer contain.

His body involuntarily rose to the surface in front of Jassim and Amir. His most likely options were drowning or a potential bullet to the head the moment he resurfaced. Jason hoped for a third option—one where he survived. In seconds, he'd know his fate.

CHAPTER 49

Jason ascended with his eyes open as the beige sandstone façade and green windows of the Bellagio Hotel shimmered brightly above the surface in the midday sun. He didn't make it all the way across, rising twenty feet short of the cover of the boulders. Jason brought his rifle to the ready to aim and fire the moment he breached the surface. He emerged faster than intended, causing a noticeable splash by anyone looking in his direction. Jason stood in chest-deep water and raised his rifle as water washed over his face. It took a second to reorient himself with the Saudi brothers, which was too long. Amir let go of his hostage, sprinted from his cover to the railing, and aimed his pistol at Jason.

The former PJ anticipated a pistol report with the sensation of hot lead shredding his body at any moment.

Pop. Pop.

Jason flinched and expected to feel sharp pain or see blackness, but he didn't.

Did he miss?

Instead of listening to his own death rattle before expiring, Jason realized the report came from behind him. He pivoted to the Las Vegas Eiffel Tower across the street, looked up, and saw a sniper perched on the observation deck. The barely visible long gun had sent two high-caliber rounds that left holes the size of silver dollars into the younger Al-Rashidi brother's chest.

A Spartan yell came from the Bellagio driveway.

"Amir, no!"

Jassim dragged his female hostage close to Amir, lying on the cobblestone drive with two puddles of blood growing over the left and right side of his chest. Jason watched Jassim gaze at his dead brother for several long seconds until his face twisted into an expression of pure, primal rage. The older brother held onto his hostage and lowered his pistol toward innocent bystanders cowering behind parked cars. He sent 9 MM rounds into, under, and around the vehicles and quickly brought the gun up to the side of the hostage's head. Jason heard yelps and moaning from the direction of the vehicles. He knew that familiar sound and was sure several innocent bystanders were hit.

Additional gunshots rang out from the Eiffel Tower sniper and other members of LVPD toward the terrorist holding a hostage. Glass from nearby vehicles exploded into shards, and fragments of concrete and stone flew in all directions near Jassim. Still, none of the bullets hit their intended target during the chaos. The Saudi retreated behind a limousine bus with dark-tinted windows, obscuring his view from the LVPD shooters posted across the street. His empty magazine bounced off the pavement as he clicked in a full magazine.

Jason emerged from the fountain, bounded up the shore, and took cover behind a massive boulder. It was the only spot that offered a direct view of Jassim. He was the only one with an angle to take a shot at the oldest brother before he began killing again. It was all up to Jason.

The distraught brother held his hostage in a tight headlock pressed against his body as he swung his gun in all directions, seemingly looking for someone to shoot.

Jason slid his elbows across the smooth granite, turning his arms into a tripod to stabilize his HK 416. He was now grateful for the Over the Beach features and confident that it would fire as expected, even after being submerged underwater for a few minutes.

The forward metal sight post hovered over Jassim's head thirty yards away, but Jason couldn't pull the trigger. The Saudi had pulled the hostage's forehead tight against his cheek. The fear on the young woman's face caused Jason to think about Archie and his decision to fire at the oncoming vehicle, which haunted him for the rest of his life.

Don't let this become my Huntsville.

Jason held steady as Jassim's wild, wide eyes scanned the area. He guessed the grief-stricken brother was searching for law enforcement officers repositioning themselves for a shot at him. Jason maintained his aim at Jassim's head but still didn't have enough clearance for a clear shot that wouldn't also hit the hostage. He pictured Archie standing over him with his arms crossed and shaking his head.

Okay, Archie, I can do this. All those rounds at the range will pay off now.

Jason inhaled and let it out slowly as his index finger hovered over the trigger. Jassim loosened his grip on the hostage as he looked in every direction, giving Jason another inch of margin.

Give me one or two more inches.

Jassim stopped looking around and settled his gaze in one direction. He looked right at Jason, squinted, and raised his gun.

He spotted me.

Jason dove to his right as muzzle flashes and pistol reports filled the southern shore of Bellagio Lake. He heard another empty magazine hit the pavement and darted behind the boulder closest to the oldest Al-Rashidi brother. Jason eased one eye out and saw Jassim aiming toward the boulder where he'd previously been. He closed his eyes and saw Archie again.

"Have you tried to talk him down without firing a shot? He may not deserve to live, but a peaceful surrender is the best outcome for everyone involved."

Jason opened his eyes and considered the words of his old friend. *I'll give him one chance.*

"Let the girl go. This is between you and me," Jason yelled out from behind the cover of the boulder.

Jassim did not reply.

"You don't have to die over this. Let her go and drop your weapon if you want your day in court."

Jason thought someone like Jassim might relish spewing his manifesto to the media during prison interviews on prime-time TV and opt to surrender. He was wrong.

"You'll never take me alive," Jassim shouted back. His voice was surprisingly even. "I don't know how you survived Laslov, but now you killed my brother, so I must personally ensure you die today."

"That's not going to happen, my friend. You either let the girl go and drop your weapon, or you'll be reunited with your brother real soon."

"I am not your friend," Jassim hissed.

"Why'd you do it, Jassim?" Jason asked. "Why would you kill all those innocent people while attempting to assassinate the senator? You had other options to fight the bill. You had to know your choice would end like this."

Jason slowly leaned out again and saw Jassim thirty yards away, still pointing his gun at his previous position.

"The senator has the blood of those people on his hands as much as I do. He tried to destroy my family by bankrupting our business. Now, the senator and all his supporters must face the consequences of their choices."

"Remember. I gave you the choice to surrender."

A high-pitched yelp wafted over the boulder. Jason held his HK 416 at the ready with his back against the boulder. He leaned out again and saw that Jassim had his pistol pressed under his hostage's chin. She looked terrified and resigned to die.

Jason preferred more space between the target and the hostage, but he was out of time. A slug a few millimeters off could strike the woman, but that was the risk he was forced to take with any hope of saving her life.

He's still looking at my old position behind the other boulder. That may buy me a half-second when I leave my cover.

Jason exhaled and started his internal countdown.

Three, two—

The barrel of the HK 416 led Jason's body out from behind the boulder as he raised the rifle to shoot. He saw only two to three inches of Jassim's body and face not shielded by the hostage, so Jason moved the front sight post over the tiny target.

Jassim noticed the new location of his nemesis and adjusted his aim while Jason closed his left eye and applied pressure to the trigger.

Before a rifle report echoed off the buildings, a loud whoosh erupted across the lake. The Bellagio fountains sprang to life, and jets of water shot hundreds of feet into the air. Jassim looked up at the wall of water, and he loosened his grip on the hostage, doubling the size of Jason's target. Recoil pressed the butt of the

HK 416 into Jason's shoulder twice, and he lifted his eyes above the sights. A crimson haze mixed with brain matter appeared where the older Al-Rashidi brother's face had been before he crumpled to the pavement. Blood oozed from the mangled body, marking the cobblestones with the location of Jassim's last breath.

The female hostage stumbled toward the sliding doors of the Bellagio, screaming as Jason jumped the railing and marched toward the lifeless body with his weapon at the ready.

A half dozen LVPD members beat him to the dead body, so Jason lowered his weapon and stood over Jassim's corpse.

"That was for your choice to harm Shanna, JJ, and Archie. Don't ever mess with my family or friends."

Chapter 50

Six Weeks Later

Senator Conrad swirled the brown Maker's Mark bourbon in his glass but did not take a drink. He reclined on a sofa in his Washington, DC, office on Capitol Hill under the light of a single floor lamp. The TV on the wall that had filled the room with flickering light two hours ago was off as Conrad stared at the black screen. The House had voted on the POLAR Act bill earlier that evening, which was expected to be a tight vote after the Senate narrowly passed a lightly amended version the previous week. Senator Conrad was in no mood for drama and promised himself he'd wait until tomorrow to check on the result. He hadn't slept well in months, and a defeat in the final session of the House before their summer recess would keep him up all night.

Crenshaw knocked on his door and entered in one motion. "Congratulations, senator. What are you going to do to celebrate?"

Conrad's gaze snapped from the blank wall to his chief of staff. He wanted to bark at her for spoiling the news until the announcement sank in. He stood and moved toward Crenshaw.

"It passed?" Conrad asked. A wide smile followed the question.

"You didn't know?" Crenshaw blushed. "I'm sorry. I assumed you knew."

Senator Conrad waved her off. "I guess I was expecting bad news, so I was in no hurry to find out. What was the final tally?"

"272 yes votes, with a few abstentions."

"Really? That's over 60% of the House. It was able to garner bi-partisan support."

"Yes, it did. It's a testament to the bill and to you, sir. You won over several members with your tenacity in never giving in to the terrorists. Public support for the POLAR Act skyrocketed after your PSD team eliminated the Al-Rashidi brothers. Your path to reelection is all but assured right now."

Conrad's face turned sullen, and his eyes fell to the floor. "A lot of good that did the people in the audience at the Hoover Dam. Did they ever find that reporter that was still missing?"

"They found her three days ago in Lake Mohave. Her body washed eighteen miles downstream before they retrieved it."

Senator Conrad fell back onto his sofa and buried his face in his hands. A moment later, he rubbed his hands nervously across his pants and leaned back on the couch.

"That's everyone now, right?"

"Yes," Crenshaw replied.

"How many in total?"

Crenshaw tilted her head. "Don't do this to yourself. It wasn't your fault."

"It wasn't? You, Clay, and Jason were practically begging me to move the location, but I was so worried about the speech's optics. What was I thinking?"

"The American people don't blame you. They blame the people who chose to plant a bomb and blow up a diversion tunnel at the Hoover Dam. You could have also been swept up in the current. You did nothing wrong."

"You still didn't answer my question. How many?"

"Seventeen dead and eleven seriously wounded. Forty-three people made it out unscathed or with minor injuries. It could have been worse."

Senator Conrad nodded.

Crenshaw pecked at her phone until she broke the silence.

"Now that you're riding a wave of support, do you want to do anything different with your campaign?"

"Yeah, call it off."

"Senator?" Crenshaw replied—a look of horror cast over her face.

"I mean, let's pull back on the campaign stops. I put my PSD team through hell, and I can't keep doing that for another four and a half months."

Crenshaw sat next to Senator Conrad. "Can I be frank with you?"

Conrad's smooth forehead took on a half dozen wrinkles. "I always want you to be frank with me."

"Okay. The gesture is nice, but I know the PSD team, and the last thing they want is to throw in the towel on all campaigning, even if it means more work and danger for them. They believe in you and want you to keep fighting."

"Are you sure?"

Crenshaw nodded. "They're all like you—ex-military who fight to win. What would you do if you were in their shoes?"

"Point taken."

Crenshaw stood, strode to the door, and stopped before leaving.

"So, are we still good on all the proposed campaign stops on the calendar?"

Conrad pressed his index finger on his lips as he peered at Crenshaw. "Add some stops to visit victims from my speech and no cameras or reporters. I want to be sure they are okay and on the road to recovery."

"I love that, senator. I'll set that up."

"One more thing," Senator Conrad said with a wry smile. "Cancel everything out in the sticks. Focus on the population centers of Phoenix, Tucson, Flagstaff, and Prescott. I always love going to Prescott in late summer and early fall."

"Are you sure?"

"Yes," Conrad replied with a wink. "A wise person once told me that the bigger cities have more resources to keep my staff safe."

Chapter 51

<u>Washington, DC</u>

Jason stood on the sidewalk with his backpack over one shoulder as cars, trucks, and buses buzzed by and the roar of passenger jets echoed through the departures corridor at Reagon International Airport in Washington, DC. He leaned into the open passenger window.

"Thanks for inviting me to the party and dropping me off today," Jason said.

Clay leaned across the console toward Jason. "I can't have our star member of the PSD miss the celebration of the POLAR Act."

"I'm not the star member. It was a team effort."

Clay removed the straw from his mouth. "That's why I love you like a brother. Have a safe flight, Jason."

Three hours later, Jason landed, but he wasn't in the Valley of the Sun. He picked up a rental car and drove south through forested roads surrounded by pine, sweetgum, and maple trees. Jason crossed the Tennessee River and knew he was close to his destination. He turned onto a lane of single and two-story homes that all looked like they were built around the same time in the early 1980s. The GPS told Jason he was at the correct address, so he took a deep breath and marched to the front door. A moment later, he knocked and heard locks click open, and the large wood door swung open. A short African American woman in her mid-fifties gazed at Jason through the storm door.

"Gloria Woods?"

"In the flesh," she answered. Jason's lips curled up at the reply. *She's just like Archie.*

"You must be Mulder. Please come in."

Jason stood awkwardly inside the front door.

"Let's go into the kitchen," Gloria said. Jason couldn't wait to get to know the woman Archie spoke fondly of during their first three decades of marriage. He followed Gloria into the kitchen, where he saw Archie sitting at the kitchen table with a cup of coffee in front of him.

"I'd get up and say hi, but I don't feel like using that damn walker."

Jason beamed at the sight of his friend. It was like seeing a ghost, but Archie was real—badly injured but alive.

"Have a seat, Mulder," Gloria said. "I'll get you a coffee and let you two talk."

Gloria placed a coffee cup with a black-and-white image of the Huntsville skyline in front of Jason and left the kitchen.

Neither man spoke for several seconds until Archie broke the silence. "Stop smiling at me, Mulder. You're making me nervous."

Jason chuckled. "I'm just happy to see you. How are you feeling?"

"Better now that I'm home from the hospital. A broken collarbone, six broken ribs, and two broken legs below the knee are no walk in the park for someone my age. I think those physical therapy gals at the rehab were trying to kill me."

Jason's smile disappeared. "I didn't want to ask while you were still in the hospital, but what happened on the boat?"

Archie sipped his coffee. "Well, after you loaded the bomb on the stern, I drove it a mile or so away into a wide-open area of the lake. The bomb was too heavy for me to lift, so I went up front to grab an oar to help me push it overboard, and that may have saved my life because I was at the bow when the bomb went off. I was also lucky it was a shaped charge because the blast concentrated toward the rear of the boat. Mind you, it still blew the entire thing up and sent me tumbling through the air into the lake. Next thing I knew, I was in a fire department vessel with burns all over my back and these broken bones."

"I'm glad you made it. I thought we lost you back there until the next day."

Jason looked over his shoulder and leaned closer to Archie. "How did all this happen with Gloria?" Jason whispered. "Did you finally call her instead of just staring at her picture on your phone?"

"You saw that?"

"Yep."

The widest smile spread across Archie's face that Jason had ever seen. "I did. When I returned to Huntsville for rehab, I called her, and she visited me. Turns out she was hoping I'd call. We're still working on some things, but it's all good now."

"What about the boys?"

Archie adjusted himself in his chair. "Terrance has stopped by, but Thomas still hasn't shown up. I'm hopeful they'll both come around."

Archie and Jason talked for another ninety minutes until Jason looked at his watch and stood. He moved next to Archie and put his hand on his shoulder. "I have to get back to the airport to catch my flight home."

Archie put his hand over Jason's. "You get going so you can see your lovely bride and baby."

Jason nodded and started for the door until Archie called for him.

"Mulder, thanks for coming. I'm glad I got to see you again."

"Me too."

As the sun drifted below the trees in Jason's backyard in Whispering Pines, he closed the door behind him and pulled the cord to turn on the light in his shed. He shuffled to the workbench and picked up the wooden legacy box he'd built for JJ. Jason opened the lid and ran two fingers across the woodgrain of the pine on the empty bottom. He pulled expired tickets for the guided tour of the Hoover Dam from his back pocket and placed them inside the box. The tickets provided access to the internal workings of the dam, including the tunnels, inspection shafts, and hydropower generators. Jason stared at the tickets and spoke to the box.

"JJ, this is a tour I've always wanted to take but never got a chance. This is a reminder for us to do it together in the future. I like to think that I had something to do with the fact the dam is still intact, and we can still tour the Hoover Dam."

Jason closed the box and went inside.

In the family room, Shanna snuggled up next to Jason as JJ walked his toy blocks from one end of the coffee table to the other to build his fortress.

"I'm glad you got to see Archie and return to DC for the celebration. Did you hear if the senator or Clay plans to keep you after the election?" Shanna asked.

"No, we didn't discuss it. I was hired for the campaign, so the election may be the end of the road for me."

"Now that I'm not working, getting into something permanent would be nice."

JJ knocked his blocks over and immediately turned to his parents. They both smiled at their son, so he clapped and began reconstructing his castle.

"I hope they ask you to stay on full-time," Shanna said.

"You do?"

"I'd support you no matter what, but you must admit the pay is nice."

Jason nodded. "It is, but I'm not sure I'd take it."

Shanna moved to the edge of the couch and tilted her head so that her long black hair covered her right shoulder. "Why not?"

"I would be based in Washington, DC, so I'd be away for long periods. I'd rather find something closer to home to spend more time with you and JJ."

Shanna leaned over and kissed Jason. "That's why I love you, Jason Mulder. Do you have anything in mind?"

"Not really. I hate the idea of being 2,000 miles from you and JJ for so long."

"I do, too, but you may need to take the opportunity you have rather than the opportunity you want that isn't available."

"I know. I worry about you and JJ with me so far away."

"You'll fly back as often as possible to see us, right?"

"Of course."

"Then I'll take care of JJ and the house while you're away. I'm tougher than you think."

The response elicited a smile from Jason. "I know you are."

Jason moved a strand of Shanna's locks away from her face and kissed her. "I'll keep an open mind and consider it if Clay offers an extension. Does that work?"

"Works for me."

EPILOGUE

Jason stood watch as gilded chandeliers cast a warm glow over Senator Conrad's supporters, who mingled with nervous anticipation over the pending final vote tally. The PSD member from Arizona was positioned behind a row of tables draped in crisp white linens arranged around the perimeter of the ballroom, each adorned with mini flags in the senator's signature colors of red, white, and blue. Supporters, campaign workers, and senatorial staff circulated throughout the room while enjoying the plentiful hors d'oeuvres and champagne. Their laughter and chatter filled the ballroom.

Jason's post was near an empty platform erected at the end of the ballroom, flanked by American flags and campaign banners emblazoned with Senator Conrad's name and slogan. The platform sat empty and quiet like a fighter jet in a hangar until it took center stage with election results later in the evening. A large projection screen hung overhead, displaying a TV feed with live election results updates as they poured in across the country.

One hour after the polls closed on the West Coast, the crowd fell to a hush as Senator Conrad's chief of staff, Julia Crenshaw, stepped onto the platform and strode to the podium. Her vibrant smile tipped off Jason that she must have good news to share as she lowered the microphone to speak.

"Thank you all for coming here tonight and supporting the campaign during a tough year with your time and money. We had many ups and downs throughout the campaign and couldn't have done it without you. The good news is that all the effort we put into Senator Conrad's reelection campaign was worth it. The cable news networks have declared Senator Conrad the winner, and the Democrat and Republican candidates have conceded. We have six more years of Senator Conrad!"

Confetti rained down from the ceiling as the senator appeared on stage with his wife and two daughters by his side. Cheers filled the air, and the guests raised their champagne flutes to toast the senator once he reached the podium.

Senator Conrad stood at the center of the platform, his face breaking into a wide grin as he basked in the glow of victory. He shook hands with all his staff and waved to his supporters in the audience, whose sense of triumph permeated the air like electricity.

During the senator's victory speech, Jason continued to scan the room and noted Clay, Zee, and Central doing the same from their posts. The friendly crowd was a welcome change after the grueling campaign season stops in all corners of Arizona. Jason appreciated that he was invited to witness the victory and be part of the celebration, but he couldn't stop thinking about where he fit in the landslide win for the senator.

Is this my last event with the senator's PSD?

The victory celebration ended after midnight, and the ballroom staff arrived to clean up. Clay approached Central, Zee, and Jason, standing around a table full of empty champagne glasses. "Thanks for keeping it professional tonight even though everyone else was celebrating. I hope you got to enjoy the evening even while on duty."

"It was cool," Zee said. "I still had fun."

"Me too," Central echoed.

"Six more years, baby," Zee bellowed. He extended his hand and fist-bumped Central.

Clay stole a glance at Jason and sighed.

"That's a wrap for tonight, and it's getting late. Go home and enjoy the victory."

Jason left the ballroom and walked toward his hotel. He strolled several blocks with his hands in his pockets in the cool November air. Clay's silence about an extension spoke volumes, and now he had to find a new place to work to support his young family.

Jason approached an intersection where a long black limousine had stopped at a stop sign. He waited for it to continue through the intersection, but it remained still until he was only a few feet away. The windows in the back were tinted too dark for him to see inside, so he instinctively took his hands out of his pockets, readying himself for any potential danger.

The rear passenger door opened, and Jason's fingers inched closer to his concealed SIG Sauer P226.

"Get in," a familiar voice called out from inside the limo. Jason bent over and peered inside.

"It's cold out there. Get inside, Mulder," Senator Conrad commanded.

Jason climbed into the backward-facing seats next to Clay and Jasmine Mitchell, the deputy chief of staff, with Crenshaw and Senator Conrad sitting across from them.

The door shut, and the limo began moving again. Jason scanned the people in the dark limo for any clue about why they picked him up, but their stoic faces revealed nothing.

"What did you think of the campaign, Jason? Did you enjoy being part of the PSD team?" Conrad asked.

Jason nodded. "Yes, I did. You have a great team."

"I agree."

Senator Conrad scooted to the edge of his seat. His eyes were hidden in the shadows of the night, except when his intense gaze appeared as they passed under streetlights.

"Now that I'm starting another term, I'm wasting no time putting my team together. Julia and I have a list of staff we wish to retain, others that will be leaving our team, and a few new hires we plan to add."

He turned toward Crenshaw. "We learned from the events in Arizona during the campaign that having the best security team in this city on my staff is essential."

Jason nodded. He still wasn't sure where this surprise meeting was going.

"I'd like you to come to Washington and be part of my full-time security detail with Clay, Central, and Zee. I plan to keep pushing my common sense agenda that seems to piss some people off, so I need the best team possible."

Jason turned to Clay, and he opened his arms wide. "What do you say, Jason? Will you help us keep the Senator and his staff safe while he fights for Arizonans and the Country?"

Jason thought about Shanna and JJ. He hated being away from his young family but acknowledged his wife and son needed this income as much as he did.

"If I move here full-time, can I fly home to see my family?"

"Absolutely," Crenshaw chimed in. "You can fly home every other weekend and even stay for weeks at a time while the Senate is not in session or when Senator Conrad is back in Arizona."

"This last year was tough," Jason said, barely above a whisper.

Every head in the back of the limo bobbed up and down. "Yes, it was," Conrad said.

"Will you keep fighting like that all the time, senator?"

Jason saw Senator Conrad's cheeks rise in the dim light to support a smile. "Mulder, I'm a former Army Infantry Officer. You bet your ass I'll keep fighting."

Jason extended his hand. "In that case, I'm in."

Jason dropped his travel bag inside the back door of his Whispering Pines home. The sound of the door closing sent his one-year-old son, JJ, wobbling to the door to greet him.

"Dada," JJ said as he wrapped his arms around Jason's knees.

Jason picked up his son as Shanna arrived several steps behind him. He shifted JJ into his other arm and leaned forward to kiss his wife.

"How'd it go?"

"Great."

"Great? Did they offer you to be full-time?"

Jason nodded, and Shanna lunged forward and hugged her husband and son.

"No, mama. No." JJ scolded Shanna.

"I know you don't like working so far away, but that's great news, Hon. I was worried Santa's bag of gifts may be a little light for JJ's second Christmas. When do you owe them an answer?"

"That depends on you."

"How does it depend on me? I already said I'd support you working in Washington, DC."

"Let me show you."

Jason put JJ down, removed a hardshell case from his travel bag, and placed the case on the counter. He opened it to reveal a new Glock 19 pistol.

Shanna recoiled from the case like it contained a deadly animal.

"Why are you showing me this?

"It's your new gun."

"You know how I feel about guns, Jason. I don't need one."

"And you know how I feel about working two-thousand miles away from my family. I need to know you and JJ are safe even when I can't be here. We both must do things we may not like for this to work."

Shanna stared at Jason for several seconds before removing the Glock. At first, she held it loose like a baby chick, but then she gripped it firmly and bounced it up and down as if measuring its weight.

"It doesn't feel too bad," Shanna commented. She appeared to be warming up to the new weapon.

"We can go to the range together, and I'll teach you how to shoot and properly clean it."

Shanna quickly set it down in the case. "We have to store this somewhere to make sure JJ never accidentally gets to it. I know you want to teach him gun safety, but not until he's older."

"Absolutely. I already ordered a biometric gun safe, which will be here in a couple of days. JJ will never get into it without one of us around."

Shanna nodded and retrieved the Glock from the case. "I guess I would like to learn how to shoot," she said.

Jason kissed Shanna on her forehead. "Thank you."

"Don't get too excited, Jason. This is just an insurance policy for me when you're away. I hope I never have to use it."

"Me too, Shanna. I hope you never have to fire that weapon for anything other than practice."

***

If you're waiting for the next book in the Jason Mulder Thriller series, you can read a bonus chapter today. The bonus chapter for STRIKE BACK returns to that fateful day in Huntsville, Alabama when FBI Special Agent Archie Woods encounters the kidnapper at the bank that changes the trajectory of his life.

Visit **RobertGoluba.com/bonus3**

If you're ready to jump into Book 4 in the Jason Mulder Thriller Series, search for FINAL SHOWDOWN by Robert Goluba.

Final Showdown: A Crime Action Thriller

A man confronts an old enemy... only one will survive.

Jason Mulder's world shatters with a single phone call: his son is missing. Living two thousand miles away in Washington, DC, as part of Arizona Senator Conrad's security detail, Jason races home to confront a parent's worst nightmare. The chilling evidence points to an abduction, and his son is now beyond US borders.

The hunt for his child plunges Jason into the treacherous jungles of Central America, ruled by the cartel he dismantled in Arizona years ago. But the brutal drug lords haven't forgotten the former pararescueman who crushed their operation, and they have ruthless plans for his return.

The clock ticks relentlessly as Jason navigates the dangerous terrain, dodging cartel assassins and the unforgiving wilderness. Can he outmaneuver his blood-thirsty pursuers and find his son before it's too late?

Final Showdown is the heart-stopping fourth installment in the Jason Mulder crime action thriller series. If you crave white-knuckle vigilante justice, pulse-pounding jungle warfare, and a jaw-dropping conclusion that will leave you on the edge of your seat, then you'll love Robert Goluba's gripping tale of a family's unyielding determination to protect their loved ones.

AUTHOR'S NOTE

Strike Back is a work of fiction, but nearly all of the information on the dams, rivers, reservoirs, water use, a dead pool at Lake Mead, etc., are facts I gleaned from my research. As a Phoenix area resident living in the Sonoran Desert, I regularly hear stories on the news and see firsthand the impact of more people, structures, and agriculture on our water supply. A lot of smart people are working on the problem, but the issue is complicated and contentious. During my research, I also learned that potential solutions like hydroponics, vertical farms, aeroponics, etc., are showing promising results in their infancy and need more time and support to scale up. I believe solutions exist or will be developed in the near future, but they will cause some pain or at least disruption to everyone living, working, and farming in the Southwest. The status quo from the mid-twentieth century will no longer work in the twenty-first century. As an author of action thrillers, I don't claim to have the answers, but I firmly believe it will take bold politicians like Senator Conrad or Congresswoman Duarte to deliver the political and policy solutions we need. For the sake of my generation and future generations, I hope to see it happen in my lifetime.

ABOUT THE AUTHOR

Robert Goluba writes fast-paced action thrillers with grit, wit, and heart.

He was born and raised in Central Illinois, where he attended college, served in the Army National Guard, and met his wife. At age thirty, after a self-diagnosed allergy to snow, he moved to sunny Arizona, where he now lives with his wonderful wife, two kids, and canine companion.

He's published three books in the Jason Mulder Thriller Series, CARTEL HUNTER, REVERSE PURSUIT, and STRIKE BACK, with many more on the way.

Robert loves hiking, spending time outdoors, watching football, and reading thrillers and mysteries.

Learn more about the author at **RobertGoluba.com**